Happy Father's Day '95!

Love,
Andrea

BASEPATHS

JOHNS HOPKINS: POETRY AND FICTION
John T. Irwin, General Editor

BASEPATHS

JERRY KLINKOWITZ

THE JOHNS HOPKINS UNIVERSITY PRESS   BALTIMORE AND LONDON

This book has been brought to publication with the
generous assistance of the G. Harry Pouder Fund.
The author gratefully acknowledges fellowship support from the
Committee on Research of the University of Northern Iowa.

The Johns Hopkins University Press
2715 North Charles Street
Baltimore, Maryland 21218-4319
The Johns Hopkins Press Ltd., London

Library of Congress Cataloging-in-Publication Data
will be found at the end of this book.

A catalog record for this book is available from the British Library.

ISBN 0-8018-5092-4

These stories are works of fiction. Characters, names, places, incidents, and
organizations either are the product of the author's imagination or are used
fictitiously. Any resemblance to actual locales or events or persons, living ·
or dead, is completely coincidental.

CONTENTS

BASEPATHS

The foul lines are crooked, the outfield too shallow, and the infield's in crying need of repair. But it's a diamond nevertheless, with the same ninety feet along its basepaths that Kenny has seen big leaguers run all summer.

As bullpen coach for the Kansas City Royals, his view has been somewhat oblique, not really close to the action until a guy rounds second and makes the turn to third. If it's one of his, Kenny cheers. If it's an enemy runner, he listens for the bullpen phone to ring or the pitching coach holler "left" or "right" from the dugout.

Here in Massachusetts he's finishing up a quick visit to Salem State College, taking a last look at the school's diamond from above as he sits ten rows up with the painfully young athletic director.

"It sure would be nice to have you with us," the kid is saying. "Ken Boyenga of the Cincinnati Reds."

"I'm with Kansas City now," Kenny tries to remind him, but all he hears is blather about those Reds teams, the last of which he'd rather forget. Didn't he spend nearly all his career with the Redlegs, the AD's now asking; wasn't he their rookie of the year?

"No, no," Kenny demurs. "I was a slow starter, a late bloomer, like they say. And I came up with the Cubs, not the Reds."

"Really?" The young man brightens, then tries to excuse himself. "I guess that was before my time."

There's a silence the athletic director fills with some chatter about how Ken would like coaching here. "In a year we might have some staff for you," he's told. "A full-time groundskeeper in addition to the guys from physical plant, and maybe even a pitching coach."

"Oh, really?" Kenny asks, trying to sound interested.

"Most of those guys you caught in Cincy are novice coaches now," the kid is saying, "just starting in JuCo or even prep. I know you were pretty good friends with Don Kruse and Jeff Copeland, and Copeland even put in for the job you're looking at now."

"No lie?" Kenny wants to say, but stops short. Knowing Kruse and Copeland doesn't make for a good set of references. But this potential employer of his seems to know all about his days with the Reds, even if his first three years in Chicago are a dark mystery. For his day and a half on campus all those wild stories never came up—but now, an hour before he leaves for the airport, he's getting a this-is-your-life treatment from someone who must have been a teenager at the time.

"Ken Boyenga," the AD's saying again. "Only catcher who could handle the mound that staff writers said was the craziest in baseball. You could handle our student athletes here, no doubt!"

"No doubt," Ken repeats, looking for a way to say goodbye and ask where's his ride.

"Do you mind if I call you Kenny?" he's asked.

"Nope."

"Was that the only nickname you had in pro ball?"

"Yep."

"Wasn't there some problem when Kruse, or was it Copeland, tried to change his name? I mean his real name?"

This is just the conversation Kenny doesn't want to have, so he ignores the question and asks if they shouldn't be thinking about his flight. It's an indirect one, routed through Chicago rather than directly to Minneapolis, where the Royals are starting a weekend series, thanks to the airline he'd rather use being on strike. He really can't be late or risk getting bumped. But the kid is still full of questions. Isn't there time for just one? OK.

"Have you considered managing in the minors? I shouldn't really mention this, but as one old Redlegs fan to another, the others on our short list have done that."

Kenny's not a Reds fan and never has been, he wants to clarify, but decides to give an honest answer. "Haven't before," he says, thinking how his baseball career has come to this or nothing, as he's been told KC has someone else in mind for bullpen coach next year, an ex-Royal just released by the Yankees. "But to be honest with you, it's going to be that or this."

"I really do hope it's this," Kenny hears the kid saying, and is touched by his sincerity. Well, maybe he hopes so too, and takes a last look at this college diamond that despite all the work it needs still sparkles enough in the bright sunlight to make his eyes shed tears.

Back at the AD's office he retrieves his bag and is introduced to the school's driver who'll run him in to Logan. But today must be nostalgia day in old Salem, for the guy wastes most of an hour bringing Kenny into Boston the long way, past the river and through the academic area, where student traffic from three big universities slows them to a crawl. "There it is," the driver says excitedly and points to another field not unlike Salem State's. "What's that?" Kenny asks, forgetting why they've come this way, and is told that over there's the original diamond from old Braves Field. "Spahn, Sain, and pray for rain!" the driver waxes, and Kenny notes that the day is crystal clear.

Great flying weather, but he gets to the desk just ten minutes before flight time and learns he's too late, his seat's been taken. Worried she'll be cursed, the agent assures him he's already been booked on a later flight with almost the same routing. "Almost?" he asks skeptically, and is told he's still set for a nonstop to Chicago that connects to Minneapolis–St. Paul. "Just one stop," he's assured.

"For Christ's sake, where?" he asks, wondering what's between Chicago and the Twin Cities.

"Mason City. That's in Iowa."

"I know," he says, recognizing the name. "We have a farm team there," then immediately regrets the reference, fearing another interview about baseball.

"That *is* a good place for young salespeople to start," she agrees.

"Maybe some day they'll be selling out of Boston or Minneapolis like you!" She beams brightly, handing him his ticket and some coupons.

"What's all this?" he asks.

"Your flight doesn't leave 'til eight," she announces, and before he can complain adds that these are coupons for a dinner and complimentary drink at the airport VIP room.

"One crapping drink?" he blurts out and at once apologizes, but she's already smiling something more than her company-school smile and handing him a fistful of extra coupons.

"You didn't get them from me, did you," she advises with a wink, and Kenny says of course he didn't, he made them.

Feeling better than he should, he grabs a cabin tag for his bag and heads off toward where she's said he'll find the VIP club. But first a phone call to the Hyatt's desk in MSP, message for Marshall Adesman, Kansas City's traveling secretary saying he'll be late but ready to rejoin the team as promised. He's happy not to have missed a single game, easy as it seems they get along without him. What a way to end what should have been a dream career, he thinks: half a year on the Royals' bench, a boring winter back home in Cincinnati, and this spring and summer working as a bullpen coach, psyching out and warming up Kansas City's relievers. Now, as August ends, he's down to just two options: college coaching and minor league managing.

The one thing he won't do is coach in the minors. He's thought it over and there's nothing in Triple-A Tacoma or Double-A Chattanooga, let alone Single-A Sonoma, Mason City, or Charleston (not to mention the rookie clubs in Elmira and Bradenton) that could make him be anything less than captain of his destiny. Well, tonight he'll get his first look at one of the places he could be if Salem State doesn't pan out, at least as much as one can see from the airport.

In the swanky club he orders a surf 'n' turf, forks over a drink coupon, and counts the rest: over a dozen. Geez Louise, he mutters, and for the second time today thinks of Don Kruse and Jeff Copeland, for either of whom these would not have been enough. Well, maybe for Kruse, who swore he preferred to keep himself clean—for worse mayhem later. Damn that kid for bringing all this up. He heard about it when Kansas City picked him up and still must fend off requests for stories when the charter flights run late from the coast. Is it why they're not asking him back as bullpen coach? No, that makes no sense, since the minor league managing job they've teased him with is just as responsible, if not more.

Oh, what the hell, he muses, getting dizzy from the quandary. Fingering the coupons he knows he won't use, he nevertheless starts humming a line Jeff Copeland used to boom out on the charters from San Diego, Frisco, and LA after they'd been up for hours with many more yet to go: "It's all right, 'cause it's midnight, an' I got two more bottles of wine." Somebody must know the song, Kenny realizes with a start, for from behind him a voice is calling, "Cheers, fella!"

By the time they're in the air it's twilight, but Kenny doesn't mind. Always a nice view in the evening, the old city's population packed so tight that street lights cluster like a field of diamonds. The takeoff has sent them out across the bay; but now, as the jumbo jet swings back toward land, the urban map passes beneath as if it's moving and he's standing still. Dotting that map are reference points more focused than anything the natural landscape can offer: the gold-domed statehouse, the huge bridge over to Cambridge, and—nestled along the Back Bay and named for the marshlands drained for its construction so long ago—Fenway.

Although the plane is several miles away and already five thousand feet high, Fenway Park stands out as the brightest of Boston's lights. Such white luminescence compared to the city's amber, whiter still for being banked off the green he can discern even from here. Several minutes later the amber's turned to blue, a blue that's fuzzing away in the haze, but the striking glare of the Red Sox' stadium can still be distinguished. To Ken's amazement it remains a distinct point, so much brighter and whiter than everything else that half an hour later he can see it poking through the gloom. I'm five miles up, he thinks in amazement, and probably two hundred, maybe two hundred and fifty miles away: I don't be-

lieve this! Now he keeps his eye on it, compulsively, craning
around in his seat even as the lights of Buffalo and Toronto come
into view ahead. If he didn't know it was Boston back there, he
could never guess it, or even imagine that the one fine point sparkling in its dim smudge on the trailing horizon was Fenway Park.

Then, just as the last hint of it fades away, something else
catches Ken's attention. The pilot has said they're passing over
Toronto, and it is a rather nice looking carpet of light stretching
right up to the sudden darkness of the lake. But up ahead he sees
some dimmer clusters, probably London or Kitchener-Waterloo,
and beyond them another sparkling island: Detroit. And at the island's near edge he sees a point of light so much brighter than all
the rest. He makes a bet that it's Tiger Stadium, Briggs Stadium as
they called it in his youth and where, on a trip with his father, he
saw the visiting Red Sox and Ted Williams beat the Tigers with a
home run. For the next half-hour he keeps his eye trained on it,
until they're over Windsor. He can see the international bridge,
and follows the trailing lights of its off-ramp to the ballpark itself.

Thirty-two thousand feet, the captain says. That's over six miles
high, Kenny calculates, and marvels that, directly over the stadium
as they are, he can distinguish infield brown from outfield green.
Can't see the bases, couldn't bet he'd see the players, though he
tries. But from the shape of things, even so far away, he can visualize the basepaths. Maybe someone's rounding them right now,
sweeping past second and aiming, for a moment, at one of those
little cages down the lines they use as bullpen benches. God, how
he hates sitting out there, and here's where the team is coming after their weekend with the Twins. But how he loves this old park.

He hates to take his eyes away from it, but steals a moment to
open the *USA Today* that's been sitting on his lap unread the whole
flight. Toronto at Detroit, starting time 7:30. Nine o'clock now,
could be fourth or fifth inning. At takeoff the Red Sox must have
been just getting under way; right, New York at Boston, 7:30 start.
It amuses him to think that for twelve or thirteen games a year
he's almost face to face with the guys down there, playing before
the same crowds. He knows half the Detroit players and even some
of the regular fans, aficionados with season tickets in the first row

over the near-in bullpens. He looks down and Tiger Stadium's still
there, glowing green within and white without. See ya Tuesday, he
says with a nod, then figures he's been staring out the window
long enough and turns back to his paper. But there's the pitching
line for Minnesota at Chicago, and even as he's figuring where the
Twins will be in their rotation for his game tomorrow it dawns on
him that he just might see his third ballpark tonight.

What time? Seven o'clock start, and it's 9:15 now with well over
an hour to go. No way. But Carlton Fisk calls the slowest game in
baseball; the Sox are never out of there before ten. Who's pitching
for the Twins again? Kenny notes the knuckleballer, thinks
piteously of the catcher, and decides if the plane loops into O'Hare
from the south and approaches the city before 10:30 there's a
chance. Of course there is: he's gained an hour because of central
time.

Looking back, Tiger Stadium's a harder dot to focus on than Fenway, given that the greater part of metro Detroit stretches past it to
the west. But it's there, Kenny is sure. Then he wonders if he could
have picked up Municipal Stadium across the lake in Cleveland;
check the paper—no way, the Indians are out in Seattle. Maybe
the Browns were having a workout tonight, it's their exhibition
season. But who cares if it's football? And probably not, anyway, as
he recalls looking south from Toronto where the lights would have
been; if the ballpark were alight, right there on the southern shore,
he would have seen it, an easier shot than he has at Chicago now.

And Chicago's there, he can see it, a string of lights running per-
pendicular to his course: the western shore of Lake Michigan. He
traces the lights south and there, a little inland, is a spot so much
brighter than the rest he has no doubts that it's Comiskey.

Please, he prays, as his ears pop and he feels the plane slow a bit
and tilt forward: come in from the south. They're heading right for
the Loop, and at the north of it he can see the John Hancock sticking up above the rest like black tinkertoys. Again, all the other
lights are blue or amber, but Comiskey sparkles in pure whiteness.
It strikes him that these are the three oldest ballparks he's seen tonight, lit like freight yards with hundreds of incandescents boxed
atop metal towers. He's wondered how the new parks can be just

as bright with half the power, and now knows why: all that excess wattage at Fenway, Briggs, and Comiskey is going straight up and out. He thinks of the bullpens at Chicago, stuck out there beneath that tiny bleacher section beyond the center field fence, and remembers looking up to count the floodlights on each pole. An even hundred, ten across and ten down. How many poles? He'll count those when they end the season here in five—what is it—five and a half weeks.

Suddenly the plane makes a steep bank to the left, sending Ken's glance straight down into the blackness of Lake Michigan, and he realizes he's in luck, the pilot's going to cruise along the lakefront before turning inland a couple miles south. Make it three miles and he'll see the park. Another bank to the right and the shoreline passes beneath. Cars on the Outer Drive, there's a college campus—ITT, a tough one. Geez Louise, they're coming right down Wentworth Avenue at about five thousand feet. Less than a mile up, and he can see a person, at least a figure, at a mile, if he knows where to look. Holy cripes, Ken's thinking, breathing fast and as excited as a child on a first flight ever. Things are rushing past and he no sooner sees the Dan Ryan and its heavy traffic than the ancient stands loom up and his vision pours into the outfield. White on the grass. Who's behind the plate? Unless he's been lifted, and he wouldn't be unless hurt, it's Carlton Fisk, a thousand miles from the park that made him famous but one that Kenny was looking at just a couple hours ago.

At O'Hare Kenny sees he's got less than twenty minutes to make his connection, but he darts inside a terminal bar where he sees a TV set aglow. A commercial's showing, but the channel light reads 32, not 9, so it's the Sox. The game's back on with a scoreboard shot they're holding too long, something about it being knotted in the tenth. "Who's catching?" Kenny asks the bartender. "Catching?" the guy asks in return. "Who the hell do you think?" and that's answer enough for Ken.

"What's the deal, fella?" he's being asked by the salesman he pushes past, hurrying from the bar, and Kenny has to ask himself what is—after all, he was standing fifteen feet from Carlton Fisk three weeks ago in Kansas City, and can introduce himself right

here in Chicago on October first, second, or third. He could tell
Fisk about the answer to a trivia question: Which ex-Cub did the
White Sox trade to make room for free agent Carlton Fisk? For the
year and a half they've worked in the same ballparks Kenny's
never had the nerve to do that, but maybe he should, especially
now that he can say he's seen him from an airplane as well.

From an airplane? I've been in this game too long, he thinks, as
he lets the Mississippi Valley Airlines agent check his bag that's too
big for carry-on in these different dimensions of commuter flying.
Too long. It's what he's been thinking about all day, his day and a
half the Royals let him have off between series so he could look
into this college job. Professor Boyenga? What comes next, President of Yale? It really wasn't worth the effort. Nor does he find it
worth the effort to look from the window of this small, noisy plane
as it climbs westward from O'Hare and angles slightly to the north
for Minneapolis. Can't look into the Humpty Dome, he tells himself; and besides, it's dark, the Twins are here and so is he. "There,"
he corrects himself, and leans back to have a last look at Chicago.
But at this low altitude the city's out of sight.

He slips into a shallow sleep, then wakes with a start as the
stewardess eases his seat upright. Minneapolis already? No,
Mason City, and he realizes he'd forgotten the stop. This is
what he's supposed to be looking at—one-in-five chance, really
one-in-three he could be here next year if he tells Salem State to
take a walk. He tries to focus out the window but sees nothing. Because there *is* nothing, he soon realizes, and waits for the lightless
countryside to pass. Then some lights come into view, yard lights
from farms, corners where sections meet, a small town way off to
the right, and to the far left some lights that must be the interstate
he presumes they'll follow to the Twin Cities. Then the edge of
what might be considered suburban sprawl; they even have that
here. Then a river he guesses will lead to town. And suddenly
something so bright it actually hurts his eyes.

A ballpark. Jesus, four-for-four, Kenny thinks, realizing they're
about to pass over the minor league field where the Mason City
Royals, if that's what they're called up here, play. My God, it must

be near eleven, midnight Boston time. Then he remembers how late his own games in the minors could go, ineffective hitting rarely able to break out in a lead and sloppy fielding letting those leads slip away. Or it could be the second game of a doubleheader; bet they have to make up lots of wash outs and cold outs from April and early May, the poor suckers.

His interest aroused, Ken pushes his face against the window to look down. They're much lower, yet not as fast as over Comiskey, and he has time to see not only that white's in the field, visitors batting, but that the bleachers are stone cold empty while what he can see of the grandstand looks pretty sparse. Maybe their start was four or five hours ago too, who knows. Anyway, in a moment the ballpark's gone, there are some open fields, a factory (Closed? No lights, so at least no night shift), some tract houses, and right away a runway. Nothing more to see, not even a view of downtown. Ten minutes on the ground and they take off, banking right before they join the interstate and follow it at twelve thousand feet to the airport south of Minneapolis–St. Paul.

Kenny cabs it to the Hyatt, gives the bellman a five to take his bag upstairs, and heads right for the bar. No players here, he knows; players can't drink in the place they're staying—bad image. Not even encouraged for the coaching staff, and their manager has a favorite place across town where Billy Martin once had a famous fight and baseball folks can still cadge a drink. But Marshall Adesman's here, and he wants to be sure the traveling secretary knows he's back in time, before midnight, to merit meal money.

That's on Adesman's mind too, as his eyes leave Kenny's face and dart to his watch, missing because he's left it in his room, and to the bar's clock, which is such a mess of colored lights he can't read it. But the cagey secretary tries a guess nevertheless.

"12:01," he says as a greeting. "No fifty-five bucks."

"12:01 bartime, 11:46 real time," Kenny answers. "Cough up." Realizing he's been tricked with his own shamming, Marshall pulls an oversized wallet from his jacket pocket and counts out two twenties and three fives. "So I'm tipping fives all night, huh?" Kenny objects, and Adesman tells him to stow it, he'll pay for drinks and cover the tip as well. Kenny feigns surprise and the traveling secretary demurs, making an elaborate wave-off motion while muttering, "Unless you've got your buddies Kruse and Copeland along."

"Hell," Kenny laughs, "they're my coaching staff at Salem State, where we're all professors of intercollegiate athletics," and Marshall cracks up at the line, never guessing how true it could have been.

Nor will Kenny tell him, for at just this moment he's decided he'll forget about college and start talking seriously about managing in the minors, even if it's in that godforsaken park they just dive-bombed in Mason City. Mason City, he realizes, is in the same chain with Royals Stadium, which he hasn't seen since Tuesday night, and Fenway, Tiger Stadium, and Comiskey, where he tells Adesman he's seen games tonight. Salem State sure ain't, he reminds himself. Let Copeland and Kruse have it.

"So you really saw old Briggs Stadium from the plane?" Marshall accepts the stories about Fenway and Comiskey, taking off and landing, but tries to argue that you can't see anything that small from that altitude. "Small?" Kenny protests, remembering how big the park looked when he was fifteen. "Maybe you thought you saw it," the traveling secretary allows, but this makes Kenny even madder.

They switch topics to Mason City, and Adesman asks if Kenny saw a pitcher there named Freddie Guagliardo.

"Huh?" Kenny asks, and is told the kid will be joining them September first in Detroit.

"Small world," the two friends agree.

DRAFTINGS

It's the first day of winter, just a few before Christmas, and across America baseball is breaking out all over. Not on basepaths, which from the Ohio River northwards are snow covered, but on paper, where draftings for the new season take shape. In Huntington, West Virginia, former major league catcher and bullpen coach Ken Boyenga finds some quiet space at his in-laws' home to look over the contract that's about to make him a minor league manager. In Kansas City, the Royals' farm director Tom O'Reilly shuffles his next batch of contracts, these for the players who, after sorting out in Spring Training, will fill rosters at Charleston, Mason City, Sonoma, and upwards through Double- and Triple-A. And in Mason City, where a championship had been won the last day of August, a new general manager shivers in a poorly heated office and wonders how he'll ever make it to Opening Day.

Eleven weeks before, Ken Boyenga had said good-bye to the majors, coming out early and wandering past the batting cage at Comiskey Park, where the Royals closed their season. He was looking for Carlton Fisk but found just half a dozen extras, Triple-A players getting in last swings during their cup-of-coffee call-up. The gates had opened early and the stands were full, for this would be the old park's final day. But the regulars weren't hitting, so Kenny had to contend with an argument between two collectors leaning over the low box-seat wall. Did he or didn't he once play for the Sox? OK, he did. But why's there no card? Ken just shrugged, signed a blank page in their albums, and wandered back to the clubhouse.

That had been about the time Dave Hunt was flying from Louisville to Mason City, catching an inning of the Sox-Royals game on a souvenir shop TV when changing planes, and then glimpsing what looked like a minor league ballpark before touching down on the final leg of his flight. It had seemed a little shabby, but one of baseball's green cathedrals nevertheless. Now it's wintertime and he wonders if he can sell the sport. Well, he's sold Pepsi in Coca-Cola country, so why not? He's spent his first two months on the job selling fence signs and soliciting sponsors for big nights at the park. To his dismay, the Pepsi distributor turned him down, and so did Coke. So he's done something he once swore he'd never do: talk to someone from RC. RC Cola has taken the first Sunday afternoon home date, promising discount pop and offering to supply a thousand souvenir baseballs as a giveaway.

And so goes the baseball winter that will come up spring for the Mason City Royals. April begins with two meetings—one down south, the other up north.

In Florida, the Kansas City Royals farm director is starting off the last week of Spring Training with what he calls his A-ball powwow. He'd like to think he is sitting with a tableful of old cronies, but three of the guys are noticeably younger, trimmer, and more heavily tanned. They're the Single-A skippers: Tom Sloan and Jay Smaltz, holdovers from the high and low clubs in California and South Carolina, plus Kenny Boyenga, happily sitting in the middle and looking forward to his first team in Iowa. Though this corner of the 19th Hole-Inn-One is set up like a roundtable, the field men have clustered somewhat to themselves, while their boss—farm director Tom O'Reilly—shows his rank by sprawling across three places at the booth's end. This leaves hardly any room for the colleague whose expertise he needs most, Dan Yates, who as director of player personnel is the only one who can safely say he knows all the Class A players yet won't politically slant where they play. A former field man himself, he knows all three managers will want the best, while O'Reilly, infatuated with the big bucks he's told the vice-presidents and the general manager to spend, will be worrying chiefly how his fair-haired boys do, even if it means popping three dozen easy homers against soft tossers in the Sally League rather than playing for keeps at Sonoma with those chin music wizards and their late-breaking curves.

In Iowa the table is longer, with no less than a dozen of the club's local directors gathered along one of the VFW's banquet boards while the general manager tags along somewhat uncomfortably in the Judas seat. At such meetings the GM's role as the club's sole employee is ex officio anyway, but tonight the position is even more ambiguous, for he's a new guy, recruited last fall and selling all winter but only now getting down to business with each and every board member. Other than this, the scene is much like at the 19th Hole-Inn-One, the table awash with 50¢ draws for the happy hour and talk sounding more like a bull session than the serious business of getting a season under way with whatever O'Reilly and his boys send up from camp.

"Horsefeathers!" the KC farm director keeps barking to his captive audience assembled in Bradenton, Florida, every time Sloan, Smaltz, or Boyenga asks for a specific player. It's his new phrase, one he's pretending to fancy after being run out of the Sheraton last year and the Hilton's bar the year before for using too much vulgarity at such meetings. Now he relies on the old Marx Brothers term, less as a joke in itself than a comment on how these high-toned places stripped him of his profession's generative grammar. Once upon a time the classiest hotels let the baseball crowd talk as they pleased, but now poor old Tom O'Reilly has nowhere else to powwow except at this last-chance saloon sitting at the edge of a burned-out public golf course.

"For crying out loud!" Al Swenson is complaining to his board at the Mason City VFW, using his own favorite phrase to disclaim one of the vice-presidents' arguments that they go the first month or two without ushers. Al's been elected president after being the inevitable "no" vote on every issue for the past fifteen years. His original peeve had been the price of popcorn, and when he argued through a whole winter of meetings for getting it back down to 50¢ only to find on Opening Day that the GM had complied by stocking a smaller-size box, he'd become a traumatized radical, nitpicking at every flyspeck in the Mason City Royals' operation. And so, tired of his complaints, his friends have this year made him president, with nothing to moan about but himself.

Mason City's an egalitarian deal anyway, a civic-responsibility setup that has Al and eleven others volunteering their efforts to keep minor league baseball in town. Al's an electrician, in business for himself, his panel truck lettered "Swenson & Son Electric," even though so far he only has two daughters. The other board members include an administrative employee of the sheriff's department, an all-sports referee who fills the gaps between seasons selling annuities, a high school track coach working summer days at the city golf course, a short-order cook, an accountant, a couple of teachers, a grade school attendance clerk, a few people who run retail businesses, and a jack-of-all-trades named Mike Jacobs, who has just recently joined the group. This new member, like his counterpart Ken Boyenga down at Bradenton's Hole-Inn-One, is the one causing trouble—about ushers up in Mason City and shortstops in Florida.

"Sanmaarda hit .340 last year," Kenny's reminding his boss and rival managers. "You can't give me less than half that now!" Tom Sloan, who wants the almost-as-good shortstop they're fighting over, bolts in to say that Salomon Perez looks good enough for any A-ball team, so why not be happy with him at Mason City? Because O'Reilly has already insisted that second baseman Billy Harmon spend another year there learning how to hit, and two skinny little guys in the infield means one too many holes in the offense. "Nothing up the middle costs us ten games," Boyenga says, a calculation even the veteran field men can't deny.

In Mason City the calculations are more complex. "No ushers saves us thirty bucks a night when it's so damn cold we're making nothing because there won't be two hundred people in the stands," Rick Dillon, the versatile ref, has said in response to Al Swenson's automatic objection, and a few board members murmur that they agree. But Al responds that with no supervision in these early games the crowd will learn bad habits even twenty ushers in June and July won't be able to break. "You start letting the bums and little rug rats down into the boxes," he warns, "and you'll never get them out. All you'll get out are the paying customers they drive away!" He glances around in exasperation, looking for support, and finding none lets out one last hopeless cry: "For crying out loud!"

"Do we have a motion to drop our two ushers for April and May?" asks Newt Olsen, accountant and secretary, and is distracted by the new member, who is raising his hand for attention as if he has to go to the bathroom.

"Mike," Al Swenson asks, "are you going to make this goddam motion? And make me look like a moron for nominating you to this board?"

"No," Mike replies, the soul of innocence. "I just wanted to ask if we're going to have twenty ushers in June and July like you said, instead of just two like last year." He's hooted down and looks hurt as he's laughed at, taking especially hard the president's derisive "for crying out loud."

As the Mason City meeting begins to deteriorate, a few others spring up in and around the Kansas City Royals' Spring Training camp. At the apartments leased by the secure, relatively well-heeled Triple-A vets, couples are drifting out to seafood dinners, their kids left with sitters. At restaurants and bars several will cross paths, and while players talk shop and team politics their wives will share opinions about the better places to live in Tacoma. The Double-A guys eat out, too. Their $1500 a month is half what the older men get, but not as many of them are married, and so four or five will go together for a table of Chinese or pasta and get away for $70 unless there's a heavy drinker in the crowd. It's the A-ball kids who are hurting financially, and they're the ones who have actually tried to fill up on the dormitory-style dinner the organization has provided at the complex before their day ends. Good nutrition and sound eating habits are why the Royals spend dough on this, but to see their A players at 10 p.m. one wonders, for the evening's perfect balance of fruits, vegetables, salad, and a light chicken or fish dish is being thrown into dietary chaos by snarfings of deep-dish pizza washed down by a coolerful of beers, the empty twelve-pack cartons stacked up the kitchen wall like blocks of insulation from the hard world outside.

Outside is what the A-ball players have to worry about, and such worries are why they're hanging out tonight in the apartment complexes their employer has leased around town. At the Golden Falls a bunch of middle infielders are worrying over Mason City, with one of them, Billy Harmon, frightened near to sickness that his spring's not been good enough to get him back to where he was last year—it might get him demoted to Charleston or, even worse, released.

"You got nothing to worry about, man," insists Kelly Neff, a three-year veteran headed for a quick month at Sonoma before an assured promotion to Chattanooga. "The big beef here is over Perez."

"Perez?" Billy asks. "What about me?"

"The beef's over Perez *because* of you, *because* you're going there," Neff chides him, and Billy catches on just before it all has to be explained. Well, he thinks to himself, I did pretty good defensively with a Hispanic shortstop last year, so they want me back for this guy, too. Neff can read Billy's mind and just shakes his head in dismay.

At the Hole-Inn-One Tom O'Reilly is ordering more beers as his personnel chief wonders how much longer this can go on. Dan Yates has been trying to count the rounds but lost track with the eighth or ninth. His method of checking off the first as "pitcher," the second as "catcher," and so on around the infield and across the outfield having faltered when he forgot whether or not this drinking league used the designated hitter. It really doesn't matter that Tom is in his cups, since beyond the top draft picks he really doesn't know the players that well. But the field men, the guys who have spent the last weeks learning the organization top to bottom, even spying on the Triple-A camp, are running a course that veers from argumentative to combative to silly. And now, with the A-ball rosters nowhere near being set and notifications due at eight the next morning, Smaltz and Sloan are being led down a path to destruction.

"Let's run this like a draft," Ken Boyenga is proposing, and Yates takes great amusement in seeing how the novice manager sets up his hustle. It starts with the elaborate formality of calling for a

round of beers to start this "first round". For crying out loud, the
personnel director thinks, if they chase down a dozen more beers
to fill the rosters this table will be sailing. Not that O'Reilly would
notice, for he's loudly applauding the idea that will bring both order and more brew.

Everybody loves the idea, but only Yates can see what Boyenga
is doing: filling up the small talk as the waitress sets them up with
fresh Buds, chattering away about some of the finest prospects in
minor league baseball. Hence when Tom Sloan wins the toss and
drafts first, he goes for Alton Bonney, the number one pick who
won 16 games during his senior year in high school and struck out
185 batters in just 120 innings. That's a brilliant choice, an anchor
for Tommy's mound staff, except that starting next week Bonney
will be mowing down Sonoma hitters from the mound in Salinas,
given that he's property of the San Francisco Giants. Anyway,
when Jay Smaltz sees that Bonney's gone he proves himself a willing sucker by blowing his own choice on Tom Repensek, the burly
slugger from Ole Miss that Boyenga's been drooling over so obvi-
ously. Ignored in the process is Tom O'Reilly, who orders and pays
for another round—second time 'round the infield for sure, Dan
Yates guesses. But the focus remains on this improvised A-ball
draft, Kenny even making a show of disappointment over Repensek as he goes through the motions of picking up the pieces, loudly
resigning himself to taking Tom Remington, drafted later in the
first round but unique in that he happens to be under minor
league contract to the Royals.

Yates bides his time while Boyenga cadges all of Kansas City's
true prospects, Smaltz and Sloan pick mostly prospects from other
organizations, and O'Reilly shouts "Horsefeathers!" at the waitress
until the draft is over. Then it's time for an accounting. For Ken
Boyenga, flush with a roster of twenty-five ringers, the personnel
director doesn't have a word, other than a mumbled "go get 'em"
as he slaps Kenny on the butt and sends him off from the beer-
soaked table. O'Reilly is now weaving a bit even as he sits and so
welcomes Dan's invitation to head back to the suite they share and
draw lots for the shower. But for Smaltz and Sloan, Yates summons

forth some sternness and interrupts their laughter with a sharp ultimatum.

"Last call, guys," he announces. "You got ten minutes to fill these rosters, then we're out of here."

"Danny boy," Smaltz croons, "they're filled." He waves his gold scorecard ranked from one to twenty-five and in a moment Sloan is doing the same. Yates makes an effort to look them over, disguising the fact that he already knows they're pitifully short on both ends.

"Jay," he confides, "you're OK with a dozen of these guys, but you've mixed in the top picks of eight other farm systems. Nice fantasy team. But it won't work."

As Smaltz's face drops Yates turns to Sloan. "Tommy, you're in worse shape: even better looking team than Smaltzie's, but except for number eleven not one of them's signed with us." Sloan turns white and Yates wonders if some of those beers are coming back on the table.

But Sloan takes a deep gulp, Smaltz straightens up, and the two face their player personnel director with pleading looks.

"Here's who's left," he tells them, shoving three sheets of paper across the wet tabletop. "I suggest you take turns."

The two managers glance down the lists and come back with looks that are now of desperation.

"Don't look at *me*," Yates says, waving them away. He gets up to leave, guiding O'Reilly before him, but thinks of one more thing.

"Listen: an older and much wiser baseball man than either of you will ever be had just the words for this, and I suggest you think about them."

"Huh?" Smaltz and Sloan chorus, and Yates turns to Tom O'Reilly.

"Tom," he says, and the farm director cranes his head back in elaborately mimed attention. "Tell these guys what Paul Richards said down in Houston when he was putting that club together and saw what he could have from the expansion draft."

"Sure thing," O'Reilly mumbles, then clears his voice for the benefit of Smaltz and Sloan. " 'Gentlemen,' he said, 'we are fucked.' "

In Mason City the board meeting is winding down, their new member having said a few more stupid things, while Al Swenson's had his hands full fighting off the perennial penny pinching that, if implemented, would make the operation seem even cheaper than it is. Now, as the hour approaches ten, hazards of meeting at the VFW start to figure in. Not as bad as in the old days, when the board numbered over forty and was run by a bunch of beefy lineworkers from Case Equipment. Back then the circumstance of meeting in a bar could be dangerous, especially when having a few too-quick beers led to some nasty challenges. That was how Al Swenson first got his ornery reputation, "sitting there surrounded by beer cans," as his friends and a few detractors put it, disagreeing with everything on principle and being the single "no" vote on routine issues. But even in those days the steady flow of beer, in cans and as draws, would eventually douse all hostility, until by meeting's end the chair would be recognizing motions to the effect that "Newt Olsen is the best damn recording secretary this club's ever had!" and "Al Swenson isn't so bad, either; maybe someday we should vote him president just so he has to buy!" There would be cheers, a call for adjournment, and then some hasty last-minute business while half the group wandered out for fresh drinks. Tonight the meeting has gone more smoothly, even with Mike Jacobs and his astoundingly witless comments, so the only thing on anyone's mind is how soon Kansas City will send them a press release with the roster.

It's eleven when the last two board members say goodnight at the bar, matching the midnight Eastern Time farewells Tom Sloan and Jay Smaltz share at the Hole-Inn-One, nearly an hour after Yates and O'Reilly have left them. The two field men have cobbled together two reasonable teams, though there's no doubt they've been snookered for some of the best players, which leads one of them to make a suggestion.

"We could say we didn't mean it as a draft," Smaltz tries. "You know, we could say it was a game—just each of us picking his dream team."

"God damn it all!" Sloan roars. "You mean it wasn't? You mean you and Boyenga were taking all those guys for real?"

FIELDWORK

In Mason City, Iowa, the world welcomes baseball back for another spring and summer. Dave Hunt, whose first winter as a bona fide minor league general manager has been spent in outer offices around town waiting to sell fence signs, program ads, and special promotions to an endless corps of beer distributors, pop vendors, motelkeepers, and the like, is glad to say good-bye to breakfasts with the Optimists, lunch at the Rotary, and happy hour with the Chamber of Commerce. Now he can open up the ballpark every morning and stay there, eating some McDonald's biscuits on the way in and pausing for his own coffee any time he feels like it. Come Friday night and the opener, a kid named Rollo, just 20 years old but already a three-year veteran as ticket manager and chief intelligence of the stadium's operation, will be on hand, but for this past peaceful week of the off-season, Dave has the ballpark—his first ballpark—all to himself.

On sunny mornings he takes his coffee up into the grandstand, chooses a spot beneath the press box that's bathed in warming light, and enjoys one of the nicest places on earth.

Before him lies an ocean of green, fully colored in this early spring of dull greys and browns. Of course it's just fertilizer and the greenhouselike shelter of the brightly painted outfield fence. But the field is here for Dave to appreciate now, a perfect little square of neatly kept innocence, carved out of the Mason City sprawl and set adjacent to his crowded office where the real work lies.

At this hour even the stands are lovely. The worn boards beneath him, their pale blue paint worn microscopically thin by years of Royals fans, have been warmed by the morning sun, and the breeze feels refreshing rather than chill. All has been swept clean, first by the janitorial crew picking up the boxes, wrappers, cups, and peanut shells after that last of August game, and then by three seasons of wind and rain—the few dead leaves Dave himself cleared out when he opened the park April one. Now the rows of seats and neatly stepped aisles look like a rationalist's dream of nature ordered, a green cathedral with a touch of blue, built not just to worship play on the grass but to honor the notion that wooden stands can be built to such pleasing dimensions.

There's plenty of nature here, don't worry: swallows along the press-box roof and pigeons nesting in the rafters. Before the opener Dave will clean out what he can reach and use Rollo's pellet gun to kill off what birds insist on staying. But for now he can enjoy their rustlings and take note how a sudden gust of wind stirs them as if on command.

His last sips of coffee have cooled before he can drink them, and in rising he passes into the grandstand's shadows, feeling the chill himself. Time to move around, see how the outfield wall has weathered, as this is the first day he's found the shady corners totally free of snow.

Not glancing back as he walks the right field line or looking up until he gets to the power alley's well, Dave is stunned by how high the fence reaches and how far he's come from the plate. Imagine taking a liner on the carom way out here, then turning fast and getting enough on it for the throw to reach home. Even doing it on the bounce, as prescribed, would be a feat; but he's seen Dwight Evans and Andre Dawson hit their catchers on the fly, a low strike to the plate's left, just where the runner slides.

The wall dwarfs him as he walks the track along toward center, following its curve where after the light pole it arcs back to give the field some depth. Two years ago the fence was double-decked and moved back as far as possible, which even now means just a maximum of 385 feet, a bandbox by major league standards. With its grandstand of three sections just twenty-five rows high the place looks even more a toy, yet as Dave gazes up this wall to the scoreboard looming from behind and above, he finally gets some sense of awe, of how, for all its reduced dimensions, Mason City Municipal Stadium is indeed host to something bigger than life, certainly larger than anything else that might happen in this out-of-the-way town.

Strolling in along the left field line, Dave glances up at the press box, where for seventy dates the writers, scorekeeper, and P.A. announcer will keep track of every play and put it on the wire to Boston, where the news bureau compiles the night's record of over eighty such games and faxes them back to the clubs in question, their local newspapers, and—it just now dawns upon the general manager—to Cooperstown. Suppose on opening night a batter pulls the ball down this baseline, the fielder misjudges, and it bounces off the heel of his glove. "E5" the board will flash a moment after the scorer says so and marks it in his book. The local sportswriter will acknowledge the fact and make sure the scorekeeper marks it on the fax sheet destined for the Howe News Bureau, and even if the play's forgotten an inning later, the act is set to be enshrined in baseball records forever. Fifty years from now, if he lives so long, an old man named Dave Hunt will be able to visit the Hall of Fame, take down the volume of Mid-Continent League records for this year, and on the first page find next Friday's box score and the first Mason City error of the season. Right now he doesn't know who'll make it, doesn't even know who'll be playing third base. Or short, second, or first, as he walks the infield backwards, part of his windup of the long preseason.

Better check the mound, he thinks, but takes a few more steps to tag where the bag will be at first before walking to the diamond's center. Always tag up, Dave tells himself, hearing the voice of his Little League coach.

Dave's job, he knows even before the season, will be a lonely one, opening up the park each morning by himself and, as holder of the keys, closing it down each night. Who else would be here an hour after the game ends?

Well, maybe the manager. Dave has learned that the field chief will be a former Cubs–White Sox–Reds catcher named Ken Boyenga who's just finished his major league career coaching Kansas City's bullpen. Dave's not much of a beer drinker, but he'd welcome sharing a pitcher of brew at midnight in the manager's office, its door open to an empty trainer's room, probably even the screen door beyond the rub-down table standing open to the empty concourse and parking lot beyond. A warm August night. But it's April now and chilly, and the manager's office a musty mess, so he'd better attend to work.

At the Spring Training base in Bradenton, Florida, the basepaths are empty while everyone's watching the auxiliary mounds. That's where manager Ken Boyenga is headed now, together with coach Tim Anderson. T.A. knows the staff pretty well and stands just behind his manager so he can give a rundown of each thrower's repertory, strengths, and idiosyncracies, emphasizing the last, as that's what will count most when it comes to winning games.

"Remington, Gish, Kalmar, Day, and Hovet," T.A.'s checking off. "There's your rotation if you ask me," he tells his manager.

"Right-left-right-left-right?" Boyenga asks.

"You got it."

"Straight-curve-sinker-curve-junk?" Kenny confirms.

"Yessir-ree."

With these fundamentals of rotational strategy established, the two get down to intricate specifics.

"Remington's a powerful guy, but too damn smart for his own good," T.A. advises.

"A rocket scientist?" the manager asks, and learns that this brainy kid is prone to puzzling over velocities and degrees of rise on his fastball rather than bearing down on anything so humdrum as the .340 contact hitter digging in at the plate.

"Good face?" Boyenga should be ashamed, using such an outdated term from the unscientific days of scouting, but he's always liked that concept—that you can tell how well a player will perform in the long run by studying the look he has—and is anxious to see if T.A., just as new generation as he is if not more, accepts the measure.

"Not really," Anderson sighs, without rejecting the terminology. "I get the idea he was always the smartest kid in class, probably played ragtime piano and built an oscilloscope in third grade."

"All arms and legs; throws a baseball farther than any other kid."

"And still reads science fiction," T.A. says with disgust.

"Seven innings?"

"Every fifth day," the pitching coach assures him, "once we're under way," and it's on to the curveball artist, lefty Bob Gish.

"Part Cherokee," T.A. advises his manager, and Boyenga looks up. "A little ethnic, claims he learned to curve the ball in a ceremony his uncle conducted in Oklahoma."

"Does the ball curve?"

"Late and hard," Anderson assures him, and for now that's all that's needed.

"Good face?"

"Good face."

"Ernie Kalmar?"

"Nasty sinker," T.A. reports. "Comes at you like a flash, then drops straight down like a spider off the ceiling."

"Poison spider?"

"Deadly. Bites!" T.A. relishes the thought and anticipates Ken's next question. "Poison spider himself, nobody liked him at Charleston."

"Bad face?"

"Bad attitude. Plus a cheat. Had to take him out of short relief, 'cause if he came in with a lead he'd let the runners score to make his own ERA look better and get a save."

"But his fastball sinks."

"It sinks."

"Then fuck his face," and that's that. On to George Day.

"Everyone's best friend, even the batter's," Anderson laments. "Even his curveball's honest, you can call it before you're in the box."

"What's he got to go with it?"

"Fastball anywhere from the dirt up into the screen," T.A. laughs, and Kenny understands at once how that curve gets by gun-shy hitters.

"How about this junkyard artist?" Boyenga is all animation now. "I passed up Fred Pascoe to get him, got distracted with the brass."

"Hovet's better," Anderson insists. "Got a change-up so slow and easy he can release it looking like an axe-killer, then be leaning back like a possum eating candy by the time it drifts over the plate."

"Tie themselves in knots," Kenny says, thinking of the hitters.

"Send the ump around three times, looking for what's passed him."

"Throws the goddam kitchen sink," the manager marvels.

"Drying rack and all," the pitching coach agrees.

"Plates stacked in the cupboard and the towel hung out to dry," Kenny croons, "all before the ump can say 'strike three.'"

There's a pause as Ken Boyenga reviews his rotation.

"Got to make this Remington kid look like a demon," he decides.

"Already is a demon," T.A. warns. "Got to make him look like hellfire incarnate."

"Like The Doors' song."

"Absolutely."

And with that the coaching staff moves quickly through the bull-pen.

"Swope," the manager checks off.

"Straight. But it moves—90, maybe more."

"Good for an inning?"

"Max."

"A closer?"

"Once a series."

"Chuck Roberts?"

"Roundhouse curve. High school curve. Gets murdered with guys on, easy steal if it's not past the catcher for two. But OK for an inning after six or seven from your fastballer."

"Hiduke." Boyenga mispronounces it in three syllables, as if it's Japanese.

"HIGH-Duke," T.A. corrects him. "Mr. Erratic. Would rather be playing golf, but if he did it would be all over the fairway."

"Heavy handicap, huh?" Kenny guesses.

"But for the hitter, too. No telling what's coming. Pencil him in for mop-up; maybe he'll surprise us," T.A. counsels.

Which leaves Moreno. "Roberto Moreno," Kenny says, savoring the name and confident he's got it right. In fact, he can translate it—Bobby Brown. Sounds dull. Can he pitch better than that in Spanish?

"I like this kid," Anderson attests. "He's probably the smartest we have, smart for the tools he can work with. Four pitches, mixes them up—"

"Any of them good?" Boyenga interrupts.

"Not good enough to start," the pitching coach concedes. "But a bunch of tired batters won't have the minds to keep up with his selection. Never see the same thing 'less they work him past ball two. Plus he changes speeds."

"Middle man?" Kenny asks.

"Don't ask me about sadomasochism this early, OK?" T.A. begs, and Kenny lets him off. And that's the staff.

A NEW LINEUP

Believing that the board of directors needs new blood, president Al Swenson has spent the winter scouting out prospective members for Mason City Baseball, Inc. Unable to get any bankers or lawyers interested, he nevertheless found people well above the rank of common rum-dum such as the group has only recently attritioned out. Several years ago a restaurateur had insured his own continued presidency by packing the board with employees, down to dishwashers and floorscrubbers, most of whom stayed on well after the guy's move to Texas. But of the bright new candidates, only one has consented to join, and as luck would have it he's the one who's been causing most of the board's trouble since.

Mike Jacobs supposedly qualifies as the business leader Al has wanted to spiff things up. In a way, he overqualifies, since he runs four businesses and has noisy interests in half a dozen others. He owns a pet shop at the mall, a bottle redemption center near the county landfill, and the janitorial service contracted to three motels out on the interstate. He also owns half the downtown Dairy Queen, quarter shares in a hardware store, an ice cream parlor, and a used-appliance shop, plus minuscule interests in the new Hardee's and the even newer Days Inn. Most of his time, however, goes to garbage hauling, for he's schemed to get the contracts for several unincorporated areas of town, underbidding the older, more reliable firm (whose truck he now leases) by hiring kids to pick pop cans and bottles from each load of trash. This way he earns both the nickel deposit and the handling fee at his recycling center.

If there's something nickel-and-dime about Mike Jacobs' business profile, that's nothing compared to how he behaves with the board. From the start he's been concerned with things no other director has cared about, such as getting first dibs on handouts for promotions and other perks. There have always been special nights when gloves, balls, and various regalia are given away, and they're meant to be early-drawing affairs, advertised for just the first thousand fans through the gate. Apparently Mike had come late for most of these, and so now, as a member of the board, he proposes that such items be put back for directors and their families as a matter of courtesy. Though no one likes the idea of favoritism, nobody has the heart to vote against it either, given that Mike, with his trash rummagings and all, has paid $5,000 to join them. "That's one hundred thousand nickels," Newt Olsen has whispered behind the poor guy's back.

Now, as the season opener approaches, Mike has made another move. It surfaces as the general manager finalizes plans for the Friday night game at home against Cedar Rapids, followed by a Saturday game down at CR as the Giants' home opener. Given all this season-starting reciprocity, Dave Hunt isn't surprised to get a phone call from the Cedar Rapids GM, Rocky Halliday. But he is startled by the matter at hand, which Dave takes directly to his president.

"Rocky wants to know," he reports, "who the hell is our new owner and what's he got to do with scouting."

"New owner?" Al puzzles. "This team hasn't got an owner."

"I guess Mike Jacobs figures his five grand makes him an owner," Dave reflects. "Rocky says he called this morning requesting four courtesy box seats for their opener, so he, 'as owner of the Mason City Royals,' can 'scout their opposition.'"

"Scout?" Al Swenson starts laughing. "He's got it back asswards. We see CR here the night before."

"That's what got Rocky confused. Plus he wonders how to handle those four boxes." League policy is that one club's season ticket is good at all eight parks, but only for grandstand seating, and only one seat per ticket. And this guy wants four prime boxes on a sellout date.

Al agrees to speak with Mike about it and get back to Rocky, who has his own unique ego problems nobody up here wants to mess with.

◇ Pecking orders and egos are also proving a problem in the last days of the Royals' camp. Though Mason City has swept its opening twin bill against a largely disinterested Sonoma team, there's been some grousing about the batting order the manager has posted. Bill Grey and Billy Harmon haven't said a word about whether or not they like the number one and two spots, Harmon because he's too timid to speak about anything and Grey simply because guys like him don't care. But there's noise aplenty from Sal Nistico, hitting third.

"Where the hell are my RBIs?" he's asking as he kicks loose equipment around the clubhouse following the second game.

"You're 4 for 7, man," Jim Knowlton says, trying to shush him. "Be happy that you're hitting .500."

".571," says Bill Grey quietly—so quietly nobody takes notice.

".500 crap!" Sal says with a vengeance, his spikes flying against the opposite wall. "I got no runs scored and none batted in. Four goddam hits and all I did was move Billy here or Boris"—that's his instant nickname for the ghostly Bill Grey—"to third three times, for your highness," he sneers at Knowlton, "to drive 'em in twice with a goddam sac fly and stupid ground out!"

"So I got some ribbies," Knowlton offers. "I'm oh-for-five with a walk and a sac, that still means zip for a batting average."

"You put a run across in each game," Sal reminds him. "That's what Boyenga knows. Each of those guys could have made third on their own or somehow else, they didn't need me. I didn't do shit, man," Sal says, with some justifiable self-pity. "And as long as I'm hitting third, that's the way it's going to be."

"Go fry some eggs, cooky," Mark Wiggins mutters across the room, and in a flash Nistico's on him, flailing around his ears and butting him with his chest, as much for being the fifth-place hitter as for what he's compounded by making this reference to Sal's post-baseball plans.

The attack is intended as serious, but Wiggins laughs it off, saved

by Knowlton's and Arredondo's deft pinning back of Sal's windmilling arms. As the big DH laughs some more, Nistico spins away
from his teammates' clutches, but only to turn back to his locker.
"This lineup's a goddam crock!" he snarls, and is ready to whip out
at Mark Wiggins again when he hears the taunt "a crock of your
rotten pasta." But he stops short when he sees that it's coming
from the locker room doorway in the person of manager Ken
Boyenga.

"Actually I hear you're a pretty fine chef," Kenny's now saying
with a smile if not a laugh, and Sal responds to this line with all
the seriousness he can muster.

"My father and grandfather are grand chefs," he reports, "and
I've studied cooking at our ancestral home in Bari." Sal watches
Ken's face glaze over as if puzzled and adds "in Italy," but the manager's thoughts aren't on geography, just wondering where he's
heard this sentence, word for word, before. Then it comes back to
him—the media guide—and he starts laughing, remembering how
one of the other players handled the questionnaire. "Sir?" Sal asks,
confused himself, since the news that he's studied cooking abroad
has elicited many different reactions, yet never this.

But Kenny's stuck on the image of Pete O'Connor, the new third
baseman, who for the first week of camp was known as "Hawks"—
not because of anything to do with his looks or style of play but
because, when filling out the media survey mailed to him over the
winter, he'd dutifully filled in the line for "school" with "Whitnall
High, Milwaukee," "sports" with "baseball, basketball, track, and
band," and "nickname" with "Hawks"—not his own nickname,
which was being requested, but his high school's.

What the manager is laughing at is not just that O'Connor did
this, but that for days he couldn't figure out why everyone was
calling him that. It took a confidential session with George, the
trainer—"You've got to be honest, do these guys dislike me?"—
who told him of course not and then why the guys were using
"Hawks" instead of "Pete." Ken finds the episode hilarious, especially because Pete wasn't even hearing "Hawks" but rather
"Hocks" from those New Englanders Knowlton and Elliott, which
of course this chunky Milwaukee boy took as a reference to his

large-sized pants. Kenny still can't get the humor of it from his mind, despite all the seriousness and pathos in Nistico's doleful gaze.

"Focus," Kenny tells himself, but apparently he's said the word aloud, because the young left fielder, number three hitter in the order, is agreeing, saying "Yes, sir, I know I have to focus on my own game and not worry about the periphery."

"Periphery?" Boyenga asks himself, making sure to keep it silent but wondering if Nistico knows what the term means. Yet even if it is a rote sentence, like the line on cooking school in Bari, Italy, it should do the job if the kid follows through by doing what his coaches and counselors taught him to associate with the phrase. Sure enough, as the manager stands there, here comes the lesson he should be giving himself.

"I know I'm out of line to bitch and moan about the lineup," Sal begins, "as that's your prerogative." Another big word, a tip-off that the lesson is a product of conditioned memory. Ken feels, however, that his skepticism has been noted, for Nistico switches gears— volume, intonation, vocabulary and all—to speak more personally. "And I know I'm in Alpert's hair out there. In the field." Kenny hasn't heard a thing about this but pretends so as to keep Sal on track.

"Dave's too nice a guy to say anything," the left fielder explains so ardently that his manager is touched. "But I know I'm taking several steps off his range . . ." Sal stops for a moment, not so much to think as to get his monologue back on its roll, adjusted to the groove that will take "steps off his range" to its consequence. Kenny gives him time, and is rewarded with the kid's understand-ing: ". . . and that could cost us a hit or an extra base or even a run."

"A single run is going to win or lose plenty of games this year," Ken decides to venture, happy to join his player in the world of trite but true aphorisms. The line, however, has Nistico thinking. My God—the manager almost says it out loud as his stomach sinks—the kid's back to where he started, worrying about not get-ting RBIs. But no, it's something else, as a newly assertive Sal looks Kenny in the eye.

"You know, sir," he announces, "cooking school is pretty serious business, especially in Bari. In Italy."

"I can well imagine," Ken responds, trying to match the youngster's earnestness. "The language alone must be quite a challenge. Do you speak Italian pretty good?" he asks.

"No, sir."

"But you know enough to get by?"

"None, sir."

"Well, the dishes and ingredients and measures have the same names, at least."

"Not really, sir."

"Then how . . . ?" Kenny breaks it off, for he's getting no acknowledgment whatsoever that there's any problem or confusion.

"Sir?" Sal Nistico is asking as Kenny turns away. The manager pauses, thankful that this mix-up over the nature of apprentice work in Italy, for what it matters, will be cleared up. But all the kid has to say is "Thank you." Kenny smiles in what he hopes is a counterfeit of paternal satisfaction, but in leaving the room cannot help giving Mark Wiggins a look of quirky puzzlement, which Wiggins returns as a smirk.

Up North, Al Swenson is thinking about how much his job as president means acting like a field manager. Last year when he replaced Jack Hieber as organizational boss, Carl Peterson, the team's skipper, had been kind enough to give him some encouraging advice.

"Running a ball club is not just pushing the right or wrong buttons, like when to change pitchers or put the steal sign on," Carl had explained, "and in running this board of directors I bet you'll have to make your moves like a manager—and by that I mean taking into account the psychology of it all."

"You mean psyching them out?" Al asked, but Carl said no.

"You've got to remember that having the right answer or the right solution or even the right overall program isn't enough," Carl said, insisting that even with all the right buttons pressed things might still turn out wrong. "You've got to make the people working with you *feel* that the course is right, make them feel like it's *their* idea, not just yours."

"And how do I do that?" Al had wondered. "For crying out loud, am I supposed to be a witch doctor?"

"Well, yeah," Carl had mused. "But it's pretty easy. Just forget about telling your people something and figure out how to get *them* to tell *you* what you want."

"Just how do I do that?"

"By asking them a question, especially when you know there's only one answer: the one you want!"

Remembering this piece of wisdom from last year's manager, Al thinks of putting it to use with his ill-fitting new member. Though none of the Mason City Royals' directors are what you would call bar flies or even tavern hoppers, the last weeks before Opening Day usually have them dropping by the VFW late afternoons and early evenings—ostensibly for the more frequent meetings and ticket sale turn-ins, but really to get the ballpark ambience rolling before the stadium's fully open and the season's begun. Al can usually leave a job by 3:30 or 4:00—he's his own boss and also enjoys the freedom of not having anyone working for him just now, either; so when he's at a good stopping place on a commercial project or at the point where he can leave things for the home-owner, he'll lock the sliding door on his truck and park it downtown in front of the VFW, a clear advertisement that Mason City Royals business can be conducted inside.

Al's lucky, because Mike Jacobs is already in the bar. Not drinking, for the guy's a teetotaler, another thing that has the older board members bothered. But Mike does have alcohol on his mind, especially the empty cans and bottles drinking leaves behind. Seeing him talk to the bartender, Al pauses in the hallway to listen in on the conversation. Hearing it doesn't make him happy.

"Now Fred," Mike is saying, and continuing even as the guy protests that no, his name is Phil, "the Mason City Royals' board meets here, and I've noticed all the beer they put away."

The bartender laughs and admits the cooler underneath his bar usually gets depleted those nights.

"Which makes a pretty piece of change for you," Mike says, trying for a smile but coming across with a leer. Either way the bartender's backing off, turning away to change a tap barrel and grunting noncommittally.

"Well, I'm sure you deserve it," Mike says to the guy's laboring back. Then, struck with inspiration at this moment of need, he adds, "Running a bar is hard work."

Getting no response to this at all, Mike waits until the bartender has to straighten up to play his angle.

The time comes and Mike makes his shot. "Now since I've become the director," he begins—and Al nearly blurts out from the hallway, *"the* director?!!"—"I'm in a position to keep throwing you all the club's business here."

"And what business is that?" the bartender asks warily, unhappy at being drawn in.

"Why, what we've been talking about," Mike laughs, but winds up leering again, "our board meetings."

"Yeah, that's your business, not mine." He pauses to screw the tapline into this fresh keg, then looks Mike right in his leering face. "And I intend to keep it that way."

"But all that beer I buy"—Al once again wants to scream against these out-of-whack specifics—"is *your* business, and I'd like to intend that it stays that way, too."

To Al it's clear that some kind of shakedown is under way, and he bets it has something to do with getting the VFW's cartage or maybe handling its empties for the state refund, each of which is a Mike Jacobs business. So he leans back, pushes at the door to cause an audible swish, and pretends to make a hale and hearty entrance.

"Philly! Good to see you! Any fuses need changing?" Al's joke is more than a toss-away line, since from time to time he'll do minor patchwork at the bar for free, just in thanks for the VFW letting his board meet here without a function charge. Mike has shut up completely, trying to appear happy at the sight of the president but actually halfway between being furious at losing his chance for the kill and blushing in shame at being caught. Al won't say anything now, but he's added it to the list of things he'll need to discuss with this awkwardly behaving addition to the board. For now he'll try some of Carl Peterson's recommended psychology.

"Mike! For crying out loud, what are you doing in this dive?" Al chortles with false spontaneity. "Let me buy you a beer—I mean a Coke!"

Mike grins, an honest one this time, and says no thanks, he's brought one in of his own. Al can't believe he's done this, but looking from Mike to the can of Diet Coke sitting on the bar to Phil's weary face convinces him the line's for real and not a joke. That's it, he *has* to sit this guy down and get a few things straight.

"Mike, come on back here, we've got some business," and as Al hustles him through the archway to the larger room Mike Jacobs is all smugness and self-importance, fixing the worst of it on the bartender as they pass by. Al herds him into a booth along the side, out of sight and sound from the bar, and is ready to read the riot act when he remembers that questions would be more effective.

"Now Mike," Al is trying to begin, but can't, because of being interrupted at once by a bright, cheesy "Yes, sir!" as if this is the Army or something. So Al tries again.

"Answer me this question," he instructs, and pauses for Mike's overwilling assent—which as it happens fails to come. Now Al's really off his stride, and so he gives up Carl Peterson's method for a while and starts telling a story. Everyone loves a story, and even so hopeless a moron as this new member can be counted on to pay attention for at least part of it.

"When I was a kid," Al begins, "my Dad would always use this corny line when buying gas—"

"For the car," Mike interjects, and Al, surprised by the obvious reference, has to pause again.

"Yes, for the car," he states, and discovers that he's the one who's answering questions. "Anyway, each time he'd pull up to the pumps, anywhere, out on the road or at home, he'd say the same thing." Al waits to be sure Mike is following. "He'd tell the attendant, who'd maybe asked 'Fill her up?' or maybe was just standing there, he'd tell the guy 'Just give me a nickel's worth so I can make it down the street to the Skelly station.' That was his joke, you know?"

Al's laughing but Mike isn't. Mike also has another question.

"Was the gas cheaper at the Skelly station?"

"Mike, let me put it another way. You know my nephew? You know, the kid who works at the driving range?" It's clear Mike doesn't, but Al continues anyway. "Well, my wife and I like to take him out to dinner once in a while. And you know what he always says when the waiter brings the salad and asks if we want some fresh ground pepper?"

"No. Does he ask something?"

"Yeah. He asks, 'Is it extra?' You know, 'Does it cost extra on the bill?'" Al laughs automatically, but Mike's silent, so Al has to ask if he gets it.

"Yeah," Mike says proudly. "I get it. You really have to watch out for hidden charges. That's why me and my family never eat out. But do you guys eat out often?"

Questions! Al exclaims to himself, and, giving up, decides to plunge directly into the problem.

"Listen," he counsels, as gently as he can, given how bothered he was to start, how irritated Mike's monkey business at the bar made him feel, and how thoroughly aggravated he's been with the response to his stories. But if the guy's a conniving cheapskate, Al now realizes, there's no way he'll appreciate the humor of a cheapskate joke, let alone get the message. So saying it directly will be best, no matter what Carl Peterson tried to teach. Besides, the guy's so dim there's little risk of giving offense.

"Being on the board of directors is a responsibility, not a privilege," Al cautions his listener. "It doesn't mean that other people owe you something or have to serve you—it means you serve them."

"That's why I joined," Mike says proudly, and at once Al fears he'll be put back on the defensive, answering Mike's queries about how to serve best and giving him responses that suit Mike's purposes rather than his own. So Al resolves to seize the lead.

"Well, do you think you're serving the needs of baseball here with Phil? Today, when I was walking in?"

"As a matter of fact," Mike announces with some patience, "I was reminding the gentleman how Mason City Royals baseball serves him, with all the business we give him during meetings. Does that help him out or hurt him, I ask you?"

"Of course it helps, but he's helping us out by giving us a meeting room." Al feels that he's made a point but realizes it's been made with his own answer and not Mike's.

"So there's nothing wrong at all with one good service repaying another?" Mike wants to know.

"Nope. Not a bit. Nothing wrong at all." With this third answer it dawns upon Al that he's been trapped.

"So I was just suggesting how Fred—"

"Phil!" Al interjects. "For crying out loud!"

"—could benefit from us and us from him." Mike's pleased as punch and takes a long draw from his can of Diet Coke. Having drained his own glass Al stands up, moves to the bar for a refill, then turns back for Mike's empty can. But the new member snatches it away.

"Got to save it for the deposit," Mike beams, and Al gives up completely.

GETTING THERE FROM HERE

It's surely the last thing these soon-to-be Mason City Royals will do in style: taking a charter flight from Spring Training at Bradenton all the way up to Iowa. After this, they know, it will be bus after bus after bus, and so they have no trouble turning up at the airport by 6:45 a.m., where an overpainted 737 with "Florida Skyways" barely covering the legend "Midwest Express" waits at the general aviation gate.

Yet the guys still grumble about everything from stowing their own bags to who gets stuck in the back or with window seats. Then the flight begins as a bumpy one, steamy air rising from north Florida's flat pastures to bounce them around until they've passed twenty thousand feet.

It's eighteen hundred miles to Mason City, a long ways, but nothing like the hideous transcontinental haul Ken Boyenga remembers from trips out West with the Reds. Oh how he hates these boring flights, and how these kids of his will learn to hate them if they ever make it to the bigs. The things his friends did to make the all-nighters tolerable—tolerable for themselves, hell for the cabin crew. At least this one's daytime. As is his privilege, he takes a seat up front, motions his pitching coach to leave the middle open and settle down at the window, while he himself worms about for a comfortable position in which to rest.

Weather over Georgia slows them down, thunderheads to fifty thousand feet, which means the clapped out old Boeing must be flown like a Piper Cub, searching through valleys between these boiling clouds. Finally it clears, the sun glints off the Ohio River, and from twenty-eight thousand feet Kenny leans toward the window, searching the terrain for Cincinnati and Riverfront Stadium. But his seat companion, who had dozed off, objects to being wakened so with the next bank of clouds Ken gives up and wanders back to find an empty row.

There are plenty of seats back here, but some more clouds convince the manager he's better off looking over his team. His miniature draft has been supplemented with two utility players and some extra guys masquerading as a floating disabled list. Dan Yates, Kansas City's personnel chief, figured it would be easier to construct a DL if, when the first injuries came, these spare players were already on hand.

There are two outfielders among these "new guys," a term Kenny laughs at when he hears his players use it, for they themselves have been together only five days. As such, the additions are fringe players, for it's more likely a utility man will see service in the scrappy, bruised-up infield than out in the pasture, where he feels his starting lineup is set. To Ken's embarrassment, both outfielders are black. Sad that the numbers game makes them the least likely to get much playing time and have a chance to advance. Sadder too that even in their isolation they seem to be offering each other little support, since one's a country kid from northern Mississippi while the other's strictly urban, South Bronx written all over him as clearly as the slogans on his hat and shirt. Marius Webster and Derrick (spelled like the crane) Stevens. So far Marius, a quiet type anyway, has kept to himself, while Derrick's hit it off with Sal Nistico, boasting that his parents' generation ran Sal's people out of the Bronx—out of the state, in fact—and that now he wants to meet the neighbor he never had. From his back row seat Ken can also see Dave Alpert eyeing both new outfielders none too happily, perhaps figuring that if both Sal and Bill Grey go down, his job in center won't be any easier, as he'll still be flanked by a loudmouth on one side and silence on the other.

The last three roster slots are to Ken's mind rather empty ones, since with two deep at first and third and Perez and Harmon working well in the middle there won't be much use for Don Shaw, while Stan Sweet looks so strong behind the plate and Mark Wiggins at DH that the two extra catchers, Mike Blanchard and Matt

Zaharis, will probably spend every game except days after night doubleheaders out in the pen.

In a way, catcher Stan Sweet is already Kenny's favorite, and not just because they share the same position. Sweet's the first player on this club who's impressed the manager as being able to entertain himself while keeping a happy disposition open to all the others. There have been several examples of it already on the flight, starting with Sweet's choice of sitting back here away from the bustle in the middle and the rather violent shenanigans with the hapless stewardess going on up front. As the big guy sits there with neither book nor newspaper and is ignoring the musical programs on the headphones, Ken worries that Sweet might be looking for a conversation. But other than saying "good morning" across the aisle and handing Ken the unwanted sugar from his coffee service, the catcher leaves his manager alone.

Yet Stan is far from idle. An hour past Cincinnati Ken looks over to see that his starting receiver has fully disassembled his seatback table, unfastening the mounts and taking apart the swing-top mechanism without benefit of screwdriver or any other tool, and now he's exchanging parts cannibalized from the bulkhead's magazine rack and curtain rods to make the tray sit higher. After this, Sweet's never-idle mind turns to mischief, but of a playful rather than nasty variety, and Kenny's pleased to see a younger version of himself in the making. As a warmup, Stan jimmies the valve above the water spigot so that when Jim Knowlton ambles back for a drink he's given a splash in the face instead. Then Stan slips a quarter in the bathroom door's hinge, trapping Knowlton inside where he's gone to dry off. Only after letting the stewardess struggle with the situation for several minutes while Jim frantically pumps the call button does Sweet tug out the coin to let the door fall open and Knowlton tumble out.

Finally, the young catcher pulls his masterpiece, one Kenny has been admiring through each stage of careful preparation. While pretending to look out the window, Stan has worked the rubber life jacket loose from beneath his seat. Then for a minute or two he studies it, figuring out in which direction it inflates. Stage three, which Kenny loves for its patience and dexterity, involves slipping the flat jacket through to the seat ahead of him, where Julio Arredondo's sound asleep. With that accomplished, it's just a matter of waiting for some turbulence and then the motion of another player easing his way past to the john, making Arrendondo shift his position. At each squiggle Stan works the life jacket further beneath the slumbering third baseman, until Ken can see the leading edge poking out at the sleeper's knees.

Kenny guesses that Sweet's waiting for the announcement and brightening cabin lights that will commence the meal service, and in about ten minutes it comes. "Gentlemen, this is the captain," the P.A. system crackles and booms, and as the stewardess slaps down the first tray twenty rows ahead Arredondo snaps awake, reaches to pull up his seat, and is suddenly propelled half a foot into the air as beneath him the life vest inflates with a whoosh, Stan Sweet having pulled its CO_2 cartridge at just the right moment. There's some hysteria in Spanish followed by a chorus of laughter spreading from row to row through the plane.

After everything's died down Kenny leans over to share his first words all flight. "Nice job, well done," he says, and receives the catcher's salute—apparently this kid has heard some of the stories about Kenny's days with the Reds. Then the stewardess gets to their back row seats with her offer of Salisbury steak or chicken a la king, Sweet cons one of each plus four small bottles of wine, and the meals are eaten in relative silence. Kenny naps for a while, and after waking has forgotten about all the fun from across the aisle as he starts counting down the last hour to Mason City. But then, as the plane banks away from the corridor west of Chicago and slows for its long descent and approach, the manager notices some more activity from Stan Sweet's side.

The catcher has become a focal point for some quietly serious action: raising and lowering his folding tray, adjusting the level of the window shade, making minute changes in the seat angle, and taking a great deal of trouble in between all these duties to reach up and fiddle with the panel of air vents, reading lights, and call buttons. Soon there's a vocal accompaniment as Sweet starts muttering figures and call signs into his empty pop can, pausing for an air nozzle adjustment, and then dictating a new series of figures that echo back from the dregs of his 7-UP. He sees Kenny staring and gives a confident smile, saying he learned about it in a book about how ballplayers travel.

"Huh?" Ken asks, mystified.

"I always feel better," Stan explains, "when I help land 'em myself."

At the Mason City airport, half of the board's twelve directors are waiting to meet their new team, but the new member, Mike Jacobs, moves ahead of everyone else to direct the luggage carts toward a row of vans and panel trucks idling at the curb. There's one from each of the businesses with which he's involved, plus a few extra, and the last players out are headed into a sickly brown Maxi-van painted with the name and slogan of the local diaper service. As luck would have it these unfortunates are the hapless middle relievers, and for months afterwards they're known to their teammates as "the baby poop specialists."

There's some confusion when the caravan, which should be heading for the Ramada, where Dave Hunt has booked a wing of rooms at a discount in trade for some advertising, turns off instead at the Days Inn. Al Swenson, who has given Dave a ride in his Econoline, the truck that's supposed to be hauling the team's equipment but isn't, begins to mutter and swear.

"For crying out loud, doesn't Mike—"

"Yeah," Dave interrupts, "Jacobs owns a piece of it, I hear," and both of them sigh deeply.

"You'll get an invoice," Al says evenly. "Don't pay a cent more than two hundred dollars, no matter how many rooms he's got at what price. And no food bills."

Next day is a free one, the team's only time off for the next seven weeks, and it's in the schedule so they can find places in town to live. Since nobody has a car yet, it's a hassle, and so traditionally most of the board members and a few fans take the day off to drive the guys around. Both Al and Dave come early, each with his own vehicle, but not ahead of Mike Jacobs' convoy, which this morning includes a couple trucks from Miller

Development. One's a pick-up, and in the back of it sit Arredondo, Perez, and a forlorn looking Marius Webster, plus a broadly grinning Jim Knowlton, whom Al spots at once as an inveterate prankster. It's easy to shuffle the guys out into Al's own truck, but when another group starts climbing aboard the Miller van Al has to jump out and collar Mike Jacobs.

"It's a brand new complex, won't even be open until May first," Mike's protesting. "I can get the guys the rest of the month free!"

"Plus their utilities will be even cheaper," Al interjects, fuming, "because I know the electricians stringing that project—and other than utility lights, it's not even hooked up yet!"

"Come on, Al," Mike wants to argue, "you know they're out at the ballpark hours before dark."

"Sure, and can't keep their eyes open anyway when they get home at midnight. For crying out loud!"

Mike pauses to consider that as a further advantage, but Al is turning his riders away from the van and heading them over to his truck while directing the others toward Newt Olsen's station wagon.

"Oh, Al," the new member whines a bit, "be fair."

"Fair?" Al thunders. "I'll bet you've got an interest in Miller's new place!"

Mike's expression turns from one of self-pity to bursting pride. "Eight and a half percent!" be beams. "Plus all the janitorial and cartage!"

This debate has served one purpose, for by now nearly all the players have found rides around town with someone besides Mike, leaving just Ted Hovet, Pete O'Connor, and Derrick Stevens to ride with Al and nobody at all with Newt, as the curbside delay has prompted some of those in contention to slip off with Rick Dillon. That's a shame, because with the flip seat down Newt Olsen can haul eight, but at least everyone's been saved from the clutches of Mike Jacobs, whose trucks and vans would be idling empty except that even in the midst of the argument with his president the new member has signaled his drivers to switch off their ignitions and save some gas.

Then, just as Al thinks everything's OK, the doors of the Days

Inn fly open and Sal Nistico rushes out. "Hey, Wild Bill, wait for me!" Al shouts in good-natured mockery as Sal draws up with a confused look. "Who the hell's Wild Bill, sir?" he asks, and Al says it doesn't matter but that he should stay away from Mike. "Who's Mike?" is Sal's next question, and the man himself pushes ahead of Al with an introduction and offer to take him out for a look at the brand new Miller Villa apartments. Al shoves Newt between them, muttering that the secretary should grab this player and run, but Sal and Mike have begun a conversation and finished it before Newt can say a word about giving him a ride.

"Got a pool?" Sal shouts past Al and Newt, and Mike beams his most winning smile.

"Opening in August!"

"No thanks, man," and Sal's already turned away.

Mike's preparing another pitch and trying to step back into the departing player's path when Al blocks him and Newt grabs Sal as deftly as a halfback taking the handoff and scooting for a hole. "Are you Wild Bill?" Sal asks him, and Newt says, "Sure, just get in and let's get out of here."

"This is kind of fun," Sal admits as the clumsy station wagon spins past Mike, who's trying to jump in front of it. "I can see why they call you that. But is your name really Bill?"

"It's Newt. Newt Olsen."

Sal is taken with a look of grave seriousness. "Well," he admits, "I can see how 'Wild Newt' wouldn't quite make it." He reaches across the seat with a handshake. "Sal Nistico. Glad to meet you, sir."

They join up with the guys in Al Swenson's Econoline, and in less than twenty minutes the two vehicles are pulling into an alley off Seventh Avenue where board member Lefty Dunsmoor is waiting to show them an upper flat.

In all fairness, Lefty probably qualifies as an earlier generation's Mike Jacobs, at least as far as the varieties of businesses he's been involved with. But more than forty years separate Lefty from Mike, and with that gap comes a vast difference in attitude, values, and style. For one thing, Lefty's had a major line of work and thrived in it for nearly half a century, while using just his spare time to fiddle with a dozen other things. His main job has always been selling meat and other packaged butchers' products from the wholesalers in town to the area's markets. This was Lefty's calling after the war, and he's used it as a foundation for dabbling in real estate and even getting licensed to deal in commodities futures for a while. But the extras have never been schemes or hedges, and certainly not connivances. Instead, as with the real estate, they've come about simply by his being around town on a daily basis all these years.

Another major difference is that Lefty never hustles anything to the ball club. That's why, as a point of honor, he doesn't drive them around but waits until one of the club's officers asks if there's something cheap available for those guys who've come up from Spring Training broke. That had been GM Dave Hunt's big surprise when meeting this, his first team, at the airport and then checking them into the motel: almost to a man they were desperate for money, hoping to have postdated checks cashed by the club for amounts as small as for that night's dinner. When Dave told Al some guys had approached him for as little as two dollars each to go in on a pizza, Al knew at once that here were some tenants for Lefty—not because there was a profit to be made but because there probably wouldn't be any cash up front and no rent or deposit expected until the second or third paycheck at least.

So now Lefty Dunsmoor, past 70 and grey-haired yet still as bright and trim as the day he declined a minor league contract from the St. Louis Cardinals fifty-two years ago, is standing by the garage with "802 7th Ave" painted across its unhinged door and asking "How do you do, boys?" as they pile out of Al's truck and Newt's wagon.

"How do you do, sir," Sal is saying, jumping ahead of the guys from the truck. "Wild Bill here says you used to pitch in the major leagues!"

"No, no," Lefty laughs, wondering who this Wild Bill fellow is. "Some people think I could have, but I never went farther than a tryout camp."

"And how did you do, sir?" Sal sincerely wants to know, and Lefty tells how he was offered a chance at D-ball, a term that leaves Sal more confused than ever. "But let me show you what's available here," Lefty adds as he begins directing the four of them plus Newt and Al to the back stairs. "One at a time, though," he cautions. "I'm not sure about the lumber holding these things up."

Keeping a half-flight in between them, the gang files up to the landing and then into the overhanging hallway that's enclosed all along the building's rear wall.

"This is the apartment, sir?" Sal wonders, and Lefty laughs.

"Oh, no. This is what we call a sleeping porch. Welcome to Iowa, boys—you'll find the nights stay pretty hot by the end of summer, so folks have these for sleeping cool."

"No AC, man?" Derrick asks skeptically, and Lefty says sure, if you want to pay for it through the nose and probably burn the place down. "I don't know, man," Derrick shakes his head, but then Lefty throws the door open and the sight of what looks like a treetop heaven greets them.

"Oh man!" Derrick now revels as the others crowd past him to see. Lefty's gesturing them into a big, white-enameled kitchen, a huge room with windows on both sides opening into the blossoms of a flowering chesnut tree to the left and a deeply dark oak, its brown leaves having held through the winter, on the right. A big archway opens into another room—the dining room, Sal guesses—and then two carved columns frame what his memory, in the voice of his grandparents, calls the parlor. Opened doors along a facing wall promise bedrooms, but everything seems windows, fresh air, and sunlight.

"We'll take it!" The chorus comes from Ted Hovet and Pete O'Connor, the last guys through the door but already in love with the place. Derrick scoffs that they haven't even heard the rent, but he can't keep his own enthusiasm from showing, either. And so Sal takes the lead and asks Lefty, whom he's still calling Mr. Dunsmoor, the price.

"Doesn't have any price on it now, boys," Lefty counsels, adding that he was given it back on a broken contract sale and that he couldn't hope to sell it or even get it rented until June. "If you like," he suggests, "why don't you just move in, and come summer we'll talk about how much would be fair from then on."

Sal gets a surprised look on his face that becomes a welcome smile as he turns to Ted and Pete. Al and Newt are smiling too, but behind them there's a frown from a suddenly suspicious Derrick Stevens.

"Not to be nosey," he's saying, "but folks gotta know: what goes on downstairs?"

"Oh, downstairs," Lefty laughs. "You're wondering why you came in from the back. Well, it's an old meat shop—"

"A crib?" Derrick asks, startled and almost dumbfounded, for Lefty's used the current South Bronx slang for a very personal social club that's centered around prostitution.

"A what?" Lefty asks in return, then shakes his head. "A store where they sell meat—not butcher it, sell it already cut. But it's closed now, been closed for a year. I have a young couple who may reopen it when she finishes school, but it's all locked up 'til then."

"Not our worry, man," Sal tries to assure his friend, and Derrick relaxes a bit. The group now talk all at once, and there's a little embarrassment when Pete starts mentioning how there's room for six or seven in here and Al has to take him aside to say that Lefty wants to help the four of them out, not have his upper flat trashed by having a gang crowded in. But after a while the deal is struck— what deal there is—for Sal, Derrick, Ted, and Pete will be living rent free until further notice.

Across town, Jim Knowlton is leading Salomon Perez and Julio Arredondo through a rather deluxe suite of rooms at the Picadilly Trace Estate. He's picked the complex from a list Dave Hunt distributed that morning. Half the newer places had names redolent of old England, while many of the others spoke of the countryside and America's frontier, but this one struck Knowlton as a zany combination of the two. "What's their sign look like," he'd asked Dave—"a ten-point buck leaping through the fountain at Trafalgar Square?" Pulling into the complex, he's disappointed to see its logo is a simple Union Jack. "That's the cross of St. George," Knowlton points out to Perez and Arredondo, while a quiet Marius Webster takes serious note. "A good sign," Jim urges. Neither Perez nor Arredondo responds, so Jim says "Macho, macho! Dragon slayer! Muerte del gigante toro!" while the two players continue to ignore him.

Picadilly Trace actually looks better than its name, with new carpet, good-sized rooms, ample furnishings, plus the two ingredients Knowlton has demanded from the start: a pool and plenty of women. Everything's perfect, in fact, except the price, which is $800 per month plus utilities. At $200 base per player that's more than any of them can afford—especially Perez and Arredondo, who've pledged to send money home. But Knowlton has not only quizzed the manager about the male-to-female ratio but has slipped away to ring a few doorbells with likely names. Feigning a misaddressed delivery, he's got a good look at Karen Gold, Kathie Hinton, Judy Marshall, and Mary Burns, plus a few others he's rung blindly and will have to remember by apartment number.

He has to have this place, superfluities and all, Knowlton decides, but Marius Webster is holding back, dismayed at the price. So Jim turns to his Latin roommates, tells them the rent is "poco dinero," and confronts Marius with a three-to-one majority. Actually for Knowlton's plans the key factor is one out of four, because there's only one of them the girls are going to want to date.

WHEELS AND DEALS

Move into a minor league town for five months and there's two more things you need after an apartment: food and transportation. Last year's veterans have cued the new guys in to the ten-ounce burgers and open salad bar at the Golden Corral, and Newt Olsen from the team's board of directors is driving a bunch of the ballplayers from lot to lot, checking out the beaters. Catcher Stan Sweet has the engineering smarts, so he's done the talking. And from Earl's Autoville to Chuck's Classic Motors he's heard the same thing: "We wholesale all our value cars to Jim."

Jim? A call to directory assistance yields nothing but Jim's Easy Times Tap. Finally, as Newt Olsen's station wagon takes the half dozen of them out toward the interstate, a commercial jingle comes on the radio and Stan shouts that they've found their man.

"Crazy Jim, Crazy Jim," goes the ditty being sung purposely out of tune, "nobody honest deals with him. He has cars that will not run, deal with Jim and you'll really get stung!"

Unknown to Newt because it advertises only on the heavy metal rock station, Crazy Jim's turns out to be in Northwood, fifteen minutes up the road. That's where they head, and right there on Main Street Sal Nistico, sitting up front, spots Jim's catch of the day: a 1953 powder blue DeSoto convertible that Sal announces he has to have. Stan says shut up, let him do the talking, and they pull in.

Jim himself doesn't look a bit crazy. Avaricious, maybe, with swarthy features like a pirate, including curly hair and droopy mustache. His mechanic's overalls are a mess. Newt's about to introduce the guys as players for the Mason City Royals when Crazy

Jim gives him a quickly appraising glance, moves on to size up Stan Sweet and then Derrick Stevens, and finally, after pausing a split second before Mark Wiggins, Matt Zaharis, and Bob Gish with a pitch half formed, brightens at the prospect of Sal Nistico, who even though he's trying not to look at the DeSoto can't help feeling enthusiastic about the whole affair.

"That's a very special car we've got up there on the Ramp of Fame today," Crazy Jim opens, and before Sal can say a word goes on to explain that while he usually doesn't let walk-in customers drive such a beauty he can tell Sal knows a lot about cars and can be trusted not just to drive her but to appreciate what a special vehicle she is.

Sal is grinning, all set to climb up behind the wheel, back this dream job down the ramp, and see how good Northwood is for cruising. But Mark Wiggins steps forward to say they're ballplayers and need something with a deep back seat, since what they have in mind is picking up two big solid sedans, maybe three at the most, in which they can haul all the carless players around for the summer. "Nothing fancy, man," Mark warns with a cautionary wave, "just something dependable, like a station car."

"A station wagon?" Crazy Jim asks, and is told no, something like commuters leave at the train station all day while they're working in the city.

"Train stopped running through here thirty years ago," the car dealer says in wonder, and Stan Sweet, seeing an opening, steps forward to ask what he wants for the old Dodge Polara parked near the shop.

"Why don't you have a look at it," Jim offers, and Stan walks back with him. Meanwhile Sal has climbed the ramp, opened the DeSoto's door, and is settling in behind the wheel.

"Hey, guys!" he shouts to those below him. "This baby has a gearshift. On the steering column, of all places!" He seizes it, pushes down the clutch, and begins running through what he guesses are the gears when the car starts rolling backwards.

"Whaaa," Sal's tone changes and he reaches to pull the emergency brake, the handle of which comes off in his hand. Behind him Bob Gish and Matt Zaharis dive to either side, while across the lot Crazy Jim starts swearing and Stan Sweet yells to get his foot off the clutch. Sal hears him and complies, but the car's in neutral and continues to roll. "Hard left," Stan calls, and Sal turns the wheel that way, but because he's rolling backwards the car veers right, perilously close to the row of dusty old Fords and Chevies Crazy Jim has lined up as his second row of bargains. Seeing what's coming, Sal swerves the opposite way and spins back toward an open section of the lot, but not before his front fender clips the rear of a '61 Impala, giving it just a nick that causes its full rear deck, which includes a glittery spare-tire cover, to come crashing off.

Now Sal's about to roll downhill, down a perilously steep decline that leads to a fall-off anchored by some huge boulders and concrete rip-rap, when Sweet screams out one last set of instructions: "Get her in reverse, that's up and back, and pop the clutch. There's your power for the brakes!" Sal understands, goes for it, and as the engine grinds away feels the brake pedal and jams it to the floor. About twenty feet from the drop-off the DeSoto comes to rest, and the players, Newt, and Crazy Jim gather around.

"Jeez Louise!" the dealer says for openers. "Look at what you've done to my Impala!" He's about to go on, building to a monetary figure of some sort, and turns to the Chevy as if for support. But there's Stan Sweet, picking up part of the car's bumper and pulling off a mixture of soft epoxy and body putty from where it was joined to the frame. He gives Crazy Jim a level, knowing look, but the dealer doesn't miss a beat, going at once on the offensive.

"Not a bit of putty in the DeSoto," he crows, and Stan says he can see that, as none of the fenders have fallen off. "You should hear the engine," Jim now boasts, "a real sweet runner, a goddam honey of a motor," and Stan asks if the gas tank's been sugared.

At this the dealer goes into his spiel, praising Stan's understanding of how the nostalgia showroom down in Waterloo would throw on some paint, wax it to perfection, and put it under the lights for three thousand dollars. Stan lets him talk about how a restoration outfit would grab it up, do some minimal mechanics and touching up of the interior, and list it in a trade sheet for six or seven grand. Or perhaps a serious collector would take the car to pieces, clean each part in an acid bath, repaint everything from the frame up, and drive it to shows as a piece de concourse for a year or two before selling it for something well into five figures.

All those other folks, Stan replies, would be selling something else: an assurance that the buggy would run farther than the slope down from Crazy Jim's lot on West Main.

Jim starts to protest, but Stan says they don't want something for years, just months—a car that will make it to the end of summer.

"End of Summer!" Crazy Jim snorts. "Why, for this car, I'll guarantee it! Come on, let's take her for a spin!"

Stan Sweet says not just yet. What his friends need is a Dodge sedan half this age, twice this size, and built like an armored personnel carrier. Has he seen *The Blues Brothers,* Stan wants to know, for that's the car they're seeking.

Reluctantly Jim takes them back toward his shop to resume talking about the car Stan's described. Derrick, Mark, Matt, Bob, and even Sal, plus the ever-cautious Newt, all file behind the dealer, who begins to reel off prices as they pass by each car, starting with the big Polara. In a few minutes they've narrowed it down to that hulking black monster and another of some dark, indistinguishable color, but Sal's still yearning for the drop-top DeSoto. He turns back, sees that Stan has lingered behind to give it the once over, and hopes this wizard will see something redeeming in the powder blue dream car so they can buy it, $1500 and all. But Stan's just shaking his head.

"Five hundred's a good price for this baby," Crazy Jim's telling everyone, "but it's not half the car you'd get in that DeSoto. Think about it."

Sal's thinking about it a great deal when Stan Sweet finally joins them. This kid looks so pathetic, Stan realizes, such easy meat for a swindler like Crazy Jim—who is meanwhile telling Bob Gish, while Newt shakes his head in exasperation, that gas and a few quarts of oil will keep the old Polara running longer than they'll ever need, that they can surely sell it for a profit when the season ends.

Stan's been lingering as if he's not sure what he wants to do, but the moment he hears Jim assuring Matt that the Polara's a muscle car, something the girls will like, his mind's made up. Can they see

how the DeSoto runs, he asks—not in reverse, but forward; and
the crowd lights up with a round of expressions from Sal's delight
to Crazy Jim's undisguisable avarice and Newt Olsen's sorry, droop-
ing stare.

Now Sal's being hustled behind the wheel again and the dealer is
pulling the keys out from a pocket deep within his greasy coveralls.
With great assurance he hands them over to Sal, who wonders
where he's seen that look before, then remembers: on the face of
the board member who last night tried to sell him the motorbike,
that crummy little Honda scooter that looked like it had been
dragged in from the dump. But Sal's grinning, too, and the scene is
pretty as a picture, just about everyone proud as punch and totally
pleased with the situation. Say cheese, Stan mutters to himself,
and has to take a step backwards as his little buddy turns the key.

There's a roar and an almost blinding flash as the old DeSoto literally sparks to life, smoke and steam rushing out on all sides from
beneath its hood while the exhaust pipe belches flame reaching a
foot and a half. For a moment the group is hidden from sight, then
the picture clears as the last of the fire eats away at the smoke and
everyone's look of stark terror relaxes into a lesser style of fright
and then just confusion. Nobody wants to speak first, and thus the
scene is one of almost utter quiet. Then Sal realizes the soft hum
he hears is the motor actually running, but as he switches it off
there's another big pop and the tailpipe squirts out a spray of soot.
It's time for Stan to speak.

"Sweet little runner?" he asks Crazy Jim, and before the dealer
can formulate his response the big catcher has a challenge: "One
grand for the DeSoto and the Dodge."

"As is?" Jim asks, and Stan says fine. Sal can't believe it's happening, but the guys are throwing twenty dollar bills together and
their spokesman's stacking them up and asking about titles and
license. Newt tries to object that they haven't even driven the
Dodge, just rocked her springs and turned her motor over, and as
for this convertible . . . But Stan motions him that it's OK, so the
accountant holds his peace.

With a bit of paperwork the deal is done, Crazy Jim urging them
to send some more teammates up to Northwood and saying he'd

be proud to come down and see some games on their pass list. Then it's time to fire up the cars and convoy back to Mason City, the DeSoto first because nobody knows what it will do next and Newt's wagon last for obvious reasons. Sal takes the dream car's wheel, Stan sits beside him, and Derrick vaults into the cramped back seat—less for the joy ride than to hear Stan's tale of how he dropped some photoflash powder into the carb and jammed a paper towel soaked with charcoal lighter up the tailpipe. "Thought you smelled like a firebug on the way up here, man," Derrick says, and Sweet objects, saying pyrotechnics are a specialty but arson's not his line.

As the players return from Northwood, there's plenty of thought about travel going on at the ballpark. General manager Dave Hunt is laboring over the master list for the labels he'll use when parceling out each trip's meal money, which is $13 per player for each day on the road. The first game in Cedar Rapids is a commute, as will be Sunday's return down there. But after that his boys will take off for a six-day visit to Bettendorf and Dubuque, beyond the range of a same day back-and-forth, so that's where the money kicks in. It means he'll have to handle over $2100 in small bills, two fives and three singles ranked in six stacks in twenty-eight envelopes, one each for the active roster, coaches, and trainer. He'd assumed such planning would involve just a lump sum for each guy, but a memo from the farm director's office has reminded all the local GMs that some of the younger players would not be used to handling cash by the hundred; and so, as a help to learning how to use a budget, could they please be given smaller bills in a breakdown for each day out.

No problem, Dave has figured, since the cash flow from opening night's concessions will be awash in small bills. But counting them out might take too much time, and so he makes a note to hit the bank beforehand for 504 singles and 336 fives. Hopefully it will all work out OK. He's figured it out in his head three times rather than use a calculator and risk a silly mistake.

In the trainer's room, where there's room to spread out, Tim Anderson is balancing his pitching staff against the batch of variables these first weeks of the season will present: cold weather, slowly developing arms, an almost immediate six-day road trip, and the question of how to set up his middle relief, more of which will be needed as the starters ease up toward throwing 90 and 100 pitches a game. In time T.A. will have it down to a system he can operate from a corner of the couch in Kenny's office. But for now he appreciates the space of George's training table, countertop, and cabinets for laying out the schedule and his stacks of notes.

In the manager's office itself Ken Boyenga's on the phone, trying to get an answer at his wife's folks' in Huntington, West Virginia. This time after six rings there's an answer, and the "Scoggins residence" he hears raises his spirits. "Scott," he tells his elder son, "it's Dad. How's everything?" The boy says nothing much has happened but that he's eager to get out of the rural school that's been his nemesis since September. "These kids are weird, Dad," he complains, and Kenny says he knows. "Just hang in there a few more weeks," he offers in comfort, "and we'll spring you early so you can help me run the ballclub here."

In a moment Scott's mom is on the line listening to Ken's complaints about their strained communications of late. Lois tries to laugh and Kenny finds he misses her enough to drop it and talk about plans for her and the boys' driving to Iowa. He's known that if Scotty puts in 180 days of schoolwork he can leave early, and so the kid has endured Saturday mornings with the slow group and truants in order to have that number racked up before May. Marty's just turned five, so there's no problem with him. But Lois is uncertain about following her husband through the minor leagues. She was against selling their home in Cincinnati, and now wants them to buy another somewhere, anywhere: back in Cincy, near her folks in Huntington or even in Kansas City if Ken stays in their system. Once the kids were older she could join him in Spring Training, make his minor league managing assignment that year's summer vacation, and then have the whole family at home together from September through early March.

To her great disgust, Kenny can't see that far ahead. He has no long-term plan for them at all, except for everything taking care of itself when he manages in the majors. He hasn't given next year or even next fall a thought, and will only talk about the kind of place he wants to rent in May. It's been their theme song since he took the job after last season. As she listens to him for the first time from Mason City, she can hear him singing it now.

"Hon," he begins, "there's a guy on the club's board out here who can get us all set."

She needn't ask for what but asks anyway, just to let him know she's annoyed.

"Set with a house. A full house, not even a duplex. Seems the packing plant went bust here a while back and everybody left, so there's these homes out there nobody can sell or even rent for what they're worth on the mortgage."

"By a packing plant?" Lois questions, exasperation threatening to break into rage. "Ken! Are you out of your mind?"

Now Kenny himself is exasperated. "I said it closed. It's kaput! It's not there." Anticipating her objection, he quickly adds that of course the plant's still there but not operating and therefore can't be a problem.

"Aren't there all sorts of wastes around it?" Lois objects.

"Toxic waste?" Kenny has to laugh. "They just killed pigs and cows, there's nothing toxic about pigs and cows!"

"Oh yes there is," Lois counters. "And if there was a slaughter operation going on at that plant you can bet it stinks to high heaven every time it rains or gets hot."

"All right, all right," Kenny backs off. "But listen, this guy is really helpful. I think he played some ball for the Cards. And I think he can find something you'll like."

"I don't want anything near a toxic waste dump—"

"Lois!" Kenny has to exclaim, completely frustrated with the call.

"—so don't even bother calling me with things like this."

"But you're coming May first?" he asks, timidly for once.

"We haven't agreed on anything," she reminds him. "And you haven't even found us a place to live."

That much of what Lois says is true. Though everyone's had quarters for half a day, Kenny hasn't looked for anything for himself, nor does he intend to. He's arrived in town with housing plans that only take effect at the month's end; and now, seeing the old couch crammed into his office and realizing that the area's best facilities for keeping both himself and his clothes clean are right through the doorway, he's decided to live here at the ballpark until Lois and the boys arrive. He's run it past the club's president and the GM, and neither has an objection. They'll give Kenny a stadium key, and Rollo from the office says the manager's welcome to carry over the portable TV from the ticket window each night. It really won't be that long to bum it at the park, after all, for the team's on the road most of April, and after that he'll be in his rental home with wife and kids.

"I'll find us something you like, I guarantee it," Ken tries assuring Lois, and thinks how nice it would be to share this old sofa with her tonight.

OPENERS

Opening Day finds general manager Dave Hunt going nuts trying to get newly hired teenage help settled at their work stations and manager Ken Boyenga struggling with the sudden rush of media. The stretching session and most of BP have been disrupted by the *Courier* sports editor, who only today has shown up with a photographer for the season's head shots. "Just do Remington and Alpert and Nistico," Kenny tries to argue, saying they're the starting pitcher and the hitters likely to produce heroics. But the editor won't be dissuaded from getting his complete file tonight, so there's a wasted fifty minutes of calling guys in three at a time for wide-angle views that the photo room will cut up into mug shots. Then at six, just as Ken's trying to get infield practice under way, television arrives and asks for a live interview during the sports report at 6:25. That's right when Kenny wants to study the Giants' infield, to figure if his bunters should go left or right; but he gives it up for the dubious publicity of beaming a message out to fans who, if they cared at all, would be out here by now.

The park itself is filling up well, thanks to Dave Hunt's sale of the night to Mason City's Chamber of Commerce. For $700 the Chamber's bought out the stadium and given away free tickets through its member businesses, and so even though the night's a bit cool three thousand of the park's fifty-five hundred seats will be filled.

Normal opening night stuff takes away the minutes of free time running up to seven o'clock. The players are introduced one by one and line up along the basepaths, facing the fans but taking over-the-shoulder peeks at what the opposition has to offer.

From the Mason City Royals' point of view, the Giants are just that: virtual behemoths, a year or two older, several inches taller, and a good ten pounds heavier than their average counterparts. Kenny sees the disparity and knows why: this is not San Francisco's middle-A team but their best. It's been this way for years and has exacerbated the normal intercity rivalry, giving Cedar Rapids the chance to beat up on their opponents—literally beat them up, as bad feelings have made brawls an almost predictable part of the two teams' meetings. Ken has heard the stories and hopes there won't be one tonight.

Dave Hunt is thinking about brawls, too, since he's starting out with a larger than usual crowd, one that's in a party mood thanks to the festivities and free tickets. Plus his help is almost uniformly unexperienced and young. Thankfully the new security outfit has sent over two young men of college age, guys guaranteed to have experience handling crowds from the wrestling and hockey arenas this winter, so Dave figures a few minimal instructions will get them set and allow him to concentrate on the sixteen-year-olds who look so lost down in concessions.

"Up 'til about 6:45," he tells them, "try to keep the parking lot straight." He glances over his shoulder and sees that this will be impossible, as the players, pulling into the empty lot at four, have angled their cars every which way, making any hopes for orderly lines a lost cause. "Then come in and keep the people moving up the ramps." Once the game begins, their own training should provide all the answers, such as backing up the ushers, watching for any blatantly underage drinking, and breaking up fights. Should they use force? A good question, and Dave counsels only to keep the fighters apart. "Now don't y'all go decking anybody," he laughs, and both guards nod solemnly and pledge they'll just get in between the action rather than causing more.

Dave's done checking out his help just in time to find the mayor, escort him down to the field, past those two rows of players sneaking glances at each other across the diamond, and set him up on the mound for the national anthem and ceremonial first pitch. The fans are getting their first look at the team, scanning the starting lineup that begins right next to manager Ken Boyenga ("Remember him with the Reds?") with Bill Grey ("Who is this guy?"), Billy

Harmon (happy cheers of recognition), Sal Nistico (some laughs as he's run from the dugout at top speed and high-fived Billy so hard he's rocked the second baseman backwards), and so on down the basepath to the bag at third, where three unnamed guys in num- berless uniforms have trotted out after the last pitcher was an- nounced. They're the Mason City Royals' disabled list, signified on the more complete media sheet as "DL," something the *Courier* sports writer tells his TV colleague means "designated loser."

Finally the Marine color guard has about-faced and marched across right field to the equipment gate, leaving everything clear for the game. As Tom Remington takes his warmup throws, Ken Boyenga eyes the Giants' starter, finishing up his pregame routine down in the visitor's bullpen. T.A.'s now in the dugout, so Kenny asks what he knows about the guy.

"Not a thing," the pitching coach replies, but George the trainer chips in with two cents of knowledge.

"Ray Majors," he announces proudly, with a sense of definitive, vital information, and Kenny turns to him with a withering look, as if to say he's already seen that written on the lineup card. But the trainer has only paused for the mouthful he now delivers, a mélange of tidbits picked up from Harmon, Alpert, and Wiggins as they hung around the rubdown table before the game.

"Was their ace last year, won a dozen games—and in his first summer out of high school," George marvels. Ken's about to ask what he's doing back here when his trainer follows with the an- swer.

"Only lost four, but one of them was their championship game. Against us!" For a moment Kenny wonders who George means, then realizes it's last year's Mason City club, as the trainer now clarifies.

"Alpert told me all about it," young George says with a maturity he's not fully able to carry. "We not only won the game but no-hit them, and towards the end Majors was throwing at our guys."

"Poor loser, huh?" Ken mumbles as he ponders why the kid's still here in Single-A. Maybe a bad spring.

"Well," George muses, "Dave Alpert heard he had an attitude problem: refused Instructional League and quit Winter Ball after three weeks. He had a good spring, their trainer told me, but the organization feels he let them down—"

"Over the winter?" Kenny asks.

"In that last game," George clarifies, and Ken shakes his head in disbelief.

Will there be problems? Kenny's just about to tell himself no when Tom Remington's first pitch comes in a foot inside, catching the Giants' lead-off hitter squarely in the back as he tries to spin out of the way. "Oh Christ," Boyenga swears, "he thinks he's Rocket Man tonight," and T.A. turns to correct his manager with a more baleful appraisal: "No, more like Rocket Head." Kenny looks over and sees his number two and three pitchers sitting in the club's box, Bob Gish dutifully charting pitches and Ernie Kalmar six-shooting with the radar gun. "Put that gun away!" Ken yells, and his pitching coach walks over to a gap in the screen where Kalmar can hand it through.

"T.A.!" Kenny yells again, and motions toward the mound. "Go give him your location-not-velocity speech," then mutters to George "for the ninety-ninth time." Before the trainer can sympathize Kenny calls out one last instruction: "But don't use the word *velocity*."

Sending T.A. out to the mound is a mistake. Way too early, sure sign of a rookie manager, and not the right timing for the young rocket scientist out there, who with only one mistake will want to argue rather than learn. The real problem, though, is focusing attention on the mound—which plays into the Giants' hands, for the plunked runner starts yelling at T.A. about his lousy pitcher and their bench joins in.

What a God-damned way to start a season, Ken Boyenga curses, as T.A. gives the runner a dirty look before attending to his errant Einstein out on the mound. Remington does indeed try to argue— not the usual way a pitcher complains, with shakes of the head and violent protestations of how he's still got it, but by trying to involve his pitching coach in a seminar on speed and deflection. He's halfway into a dissertation on how the molecular imbalance of the cooler air up here in Iowa is deviating the projected plane of his rising heater when T.A. scowls and reaches for the ball.

Remington not only shuts up but seems struck dumb by the implication. Is he out of here after one pitch? Even when his needless glance to the bullpen confirms that nobody's warming up he still can't find any more words, *deflection* and *velocity* and *molecular density* being terms he now couldn't even stutter out in initial syllables. Which is just how T.A. wants him.

"You see this?" he asks the pitcher, and Remington's eyes shift back and forth from T.A.'s face to the ball he's holding in his hands.

"Just throw it to the catcher, OK? If the batter hits it, *then* we'll worry."

T.A. studies Remington's face and guesses that the kid is trying to work it out into an equation. Apparently he gets it, for with a smile and a cheerful "OK, Coach" the pitcher puts his glove out for the ball. T.A. plops it down, pivots, and trots back to the dugout where Kenny's waiting to ask if everything's all right.

Pitching coach and manager are just about to relax when they notice Remington's not setting up for the pitch. Rather than bearing down toward the plate, he's leaning toward first, broadcasting his intentions to the runner, who's standing squarely on the bag. The guy hasn't even lifted a foot before Remington flips a throw over to Jim Knowlton, who takes it nonchalantly and sends it back with the same motion.

"What a move! We give up!" The calls are coming from the Giants' bench, and now the runner, smirking at his own teammate's taunts, takes a step off the bag, an act that draws another half-hearted toss from the pitcher. This routine is repeated three more times, the runner taking successively bigger leads while the pitcher puts just a little bit more on his throw.

Now the crowd has joined the visitors' bench in heckling the pointless action. A winter away followed by all the pregame hype for this season opener has them ready for excitement, while soft tosses to first hardly make the grade. Kenny is starting to shuffle and curse, but T.A. stops him before he can stand up and yell at Remington to cut it out.

"Watch this next throw over," the pitching coach advises, and once alerted Ken can see it clear as day: Remington's moves are quickening as the runner's lead increases, but not as much. "He's deaking him," Kenny mutters in recognition, and T.A. says he thinks the payoff will come in just a moment.

"That last lead was a foolish one," Tim Anderson points out. "He wasn't even poised to run."

"Just took the steps by rote, one more because there's been one more throw he beat easy." Ken Boyenga is so charmed by it he has to laugh, pleased at seeing his pitcher getting tricky at such an early age.

"Plus the guy's rattled by his own bench," T.A. guesses. "It looks damn foolish, all these tosses, and he's part of it."

"So when does Rocket Head spring it?" Kenny asks and even as T.A. says "Right now!" the pitcher whirls to fire a strike at first base. The ball comes in at Remington's best velocity, and it's right on the money, screaming toward the low target Knowlton's glove presents. Problem is, the runner's been lured too far off for an easy return, and his frantic dive back brings his head into the zone just a split second before the ball.

There's a resounding crack as Tom Remington's lightning throw catches the runner's helmet just above the ear, splitting it in two pieces like an eggshell hitting the rim of a pan. But the space-age plastic does its job, for the ball goes sailing up like a towering pop fly. While everyone else looks at the fallen runner Billy Harmon angles over from second to haul it in. Seeing a body in the base-path, he shovels the ball to Knowlton as he would to catch a runner off. The player just lies there—Knowlton presumes he's unconscious—but as the big first baseman leans down to offer assistance, his glove drags across the downed man's back and the umpire signals "safe."

"What?" the perplexed fielder asks, and is shown how the run-ner's hand is wedged against the base, not that either could care.

The crowd has now quieted but the field's alive, both trainers rushing to the fallen baserunner, infielders walking over to see how badly he's hurt, and even the outfield drifting in toward this sudden concentration of arrested action. From his perch on the dugout's top step Kenny notes how the park's concerned silence lets him hear things normally lost in the ever-present buzz and murmur of a crowd. There's a chortle from a burly fan well down the line who's demonstrating to his buddy how the runner's helmet split in half, a sentiment soon corrected by a woman's gasp as the trainer lifts the kid's arm only to have it drop back in seeming lifelessness. A man Kenny recognizes as a local doctor—his picture was in yesterday's *Courier*, about the new hospital wing—sits just behind the on-deck circle, ignoring the chatter from his box-seat mates to stare intently at the scene down on first. For a moment there's some blather from the beer bar underneath, as a fan who's missed the play entirely tries ribbing the bartender with a dirty joke. But most disconcerting to Ken Boyenga are the words he hears drifting across from the Giants' dugout. No threats or curses and certainly no more taunts—just a low but steady muttering of deep offense and hostility that he knows will blossom into real trouble before this game is done.

He looks for the umpires but they're standing back, ignoring both the player on the ground and the current of nastiness flowing softly yet persistently from the visitors' bench. Ken's dismayed that he can see it all building, a threat to everyone while these two umps act like they're in another world. Well, nothing's happened yet, so there's nothing they can do, he guesses. But as he looks across once more into the bad guys' dugout Ken sees something take shape: Ray Majors, their chip-on-the-shoulder pitcher, has come in from his pregame in the pen, and one by one the Giants are walking down to his place on the bench, pausing to say a few words, then heading back with expressions running from quiet satisfaction to open glee.

"I don't like this," Kenny finally says to T.A., adding that fights are bad any time but even worse when it's early and cold with everyone tight and not yet fully conditioned—"plus those clowns have half a foot and fifteen pounds on the best of us!"

T.A. has to laugh, for as he scans their nine guys out there and the others on their bench he sees how right Boyenga is. Remington's tall but skinny as a pole, while his battery mate is big but not burly. There's some size on DH Mark Wiggins, but it's all baby fat and pudding—every time T.A. sees him he thinks of that Gerber label with the infant spitting up stewed peaches. "Aw, we got some tough guys," the pitching coach nevertheless tries to object, but as his manager asks "Where?" all T.A. can see is little Billy Harmon, Salomon Perez not much bigger, and an outfield that could succeed only as a tag team, with Sal Nistico as its muscle and weight.

"Don't worry, Skip," he laughs, looking one more time at Salomon and Billy. "If anything starts we'll send our Smurfs in there to bite their ankles!"

This makes Kenny laugh. "You're right," he pretends to agree, but knows his guys won't stand a chance.

By now the Giants' trainer, with George Karras assisting, has the stunned runner sitting up. He shakes his head and almost topples back, so dizzy has the beaning left him. Geez, that kid must have a headache, Kenny thinks, and recalls how back with the Reds Jeff Copeland had taken one in the ear one afternoon after a monumental Irish whiskey blowout and for days afterwards couldn't be sure if his lingering migraine was from the beanball or the quarts of Jameson's. This makes him laugh again, and T.A., thinking he's still amused with the Smurfs, slaps him on the back. Then, lost in their respective thoughts, the two grin like cats until each is startled by a clattering across the way. It's the Giants' dugout, where their manager has kicked down the bat rack and is giving their silly chucklings the most evil eye imaginable.

In a moment, however, there's the business of putting in a pinch runner and getting the game back in line. This early on, Kenny knows, it won't be a rabbit—probably someone who can take the fallen guy's position, but without the same speed. "Back," he yells, and waves his infield to double-play depth. Two pitches later it works: a ground ball to Perez at short, who with Billy's help and the runner's lack of quickness makes it an easy twin killing. For the third man up Tom Remington tries more scientific wizardry and runs the count to 3-0, but after a visit from catcher Stan Sweet goes to some off-speed stuff and gets an easy pop-up to third. Three up, three down, Kenny sees the box score reading, with fifteen minutes of unrecorded drama in between.

He's pledged himself to study each move the Cedar Rapids pitcher makes, but Ray Majors is already out there and halfway through his warmups before Kenny takes notice, so distracted is he by the subtext being written in this game. Dammit, he thinks, I've missed his fastball, as the next three pitches will be whatever else Majors has, curveball or slider. It's sliders, all three of them—this guy doesn't want to take a bit off anything. OK, for his last throw before the peg to second it should be the fastball again, with everything he's got on it, and sure enough it comes in with a whistle they can hear all the way over in the dugout. "Christ!" Kenny has to exclaim. Then he asks T.A. how the first four looked and the pitching coach tells him: as fast as that. Accurate? "On the black," Tim Anderson rues, "inside to a righty." And their lead-off hitter, ghostly Bill Grey, swings from the right.

Except there's not a thing to swing at. The first pitch whistles in about two inches under Bill's chin. The ump calls it a ball while the Giants' bench hoots and hollers, but the wraithlike right fielder hasn't reacted in any way, not even pulling back from this obvious bit of barbering. Jesus, Ken whispers, a thought for Bill Grey but also a plea that Bill's characteristic narcolepsy won't strike the pitcher as a show-up dare. But out there on the mound Ray Majors shows no reaction either, just looking in to take the sign and then set himself for another hard one, high inside.

There it is again, the same pitch, only an inch higher. Kenny can't believe that Bill Grey hasn't flinched—freshly shaven or not, he had to feel the heat from that one. If ball three follows this climb up the ladder it will be squarely at the batter's jaw, something Ken can't bear to let happen. As can't the pitcher, either, for he throws his third one in the classic manner meant to zap the hitter but not cause an injury, behind him so that in turning away the guy moves right into the ball and catches it in the meaty part of his back.

Except this is Bill Grey, who even on a good day is about as animated as a statue serving as pigeon roost. And so Majors' effort is almost a wild pitch as the catcher has to lunge behind the stationary hitter and grab the fastball that's screaming toward the screen.

In a flash Kenny's out of the dugout and charging at the ump. "For Christ's sake," he's yelling, "you want to get somebody killed out here?"

The ump plays dumb, forcing Ken to spell it out.

"How about a warning?" he urges. "You can see what's going on!"

"Going on?" the umpire asks. "Your guy lost his first pitch, then got it back in time for that accident with the runner. This guy's got better control—brilliant control, I'd say. He can put it in a tea cup."

"While my man's drinking?" Kenny now loses his temper and the conversation shifts from metaphor to discourse.

"Who's drinking?" the umpire chides.

"You stupid idiot, give a warning, dammit!"

"OK, you're warned. Now get outta here."

"*I'm* warned? *I'm* warned?" Kenny dances around with the rhythm of it. "What about the other guy? Come on, warn the pitcher, warn the manager!"

"What have they done?" The ump looks over to Bill Grey, who hasn't even left the batter's box, just standing there with bat on shoulder and gaze fixed somewhere out in center field. The implication, of course, is that Bill hasn't been touched.

"Oh yeah?" Kenny asks, now beginning to enjoy this argument because he thinks he can win it. "So where was that last one at?"

"Don't end a sentence with a preposition," the umpire cautions, which makes Kenny break out in a malicious grin.

"OK," he muses, bringing his jaw just inches from the umpire's. "Where was that last one at, you asshole?"

"You're out, you're outta this game!" the ump rages, not hearing any humor in Kenny's line. "Walk!" He gives an elaborate rendition of the ejection sign, as if he's pitching Ken over the far bleachers and out into the parking lot, but the manager just stands there.

"Sorry for the bad grammar," he laughs. "I can just imagine the fine." He turns to walk away, then pauses for what from afar looks like a sincere apology. "I'm really sorry, and I won't misuse prepositions again—you motherfucking asshole!"

Kenny's past the bench and heading into the tunnel when he hears T.A. call out the action for him: "Jesus Christ! Right at his head, but Grey ducked it!" Then he hears his pitching coach yell across the field to first base: "No lead! No lead!" OK, that should take care of it, Ken assumes, and sits down on some equipment boxes from where he hopes to monitor a finally decent game.

Except it won't be, he realizes at once. Billy Harmon's now up, the poor little squirt, and if Majors starts throwing at this little Bible reader it will hurt far more than taking a fastball in the ribs. He can see the painful look on Billy's face as he pulls back from the first one, tears forming as the brutal Giant cuts him to pieces with rockets at his head, arms, and legs. "I never hurt him or meant him harm," Ken can imagine Billy saying, "so why is he throwing at me?" He can see it now: Billy nailed with a pitch and sobbing at the unfairness of it, while Sal Nistico, that overcharged young puppy, sprints from the on-deck circle to lead a charge on the mound. And not even one official at-bat yet for his team in the whole damned season.

That's just how it happens, though from his position in the tunnel Ken can't see it. His mind's eye view will later be revised from Dave Hunt's perspective, since it will be Dave, hiding in the locker room from the umpire's ire, who'll rehash the whole affair for Ken's benefit.

For Dave himself, the brawl is an utter surprise. After squaring away his ushers, counseling the two security guards, and setting up the kids down in concessions, he's stood by the mayor, cheered the old man's ceremonial first pitch, then escorted him off the field. Remington's plunking takes place while Dave's been getting folks seated in the dignitaries' box, and by the time the Cedar Rapids runner is decked at first he's down in the beer bar passing draws to customers while trying to keep up with their jokes. Relieved from this duty by a call to the press box, Dave finishes with the scorekeeper just in time to see poor Billy Harmon drilled between the shoulders.

"Not a pretty picture," Kenny offers, pulling on a cigarette as he and Dave hunker down on the old broken box-seat chairs that serve the players in their locker room.

"Well, it was sort of pretty in a way," Dave drawls, not getting Ken's point. "Like a kaleidoscope."

"Sure," Ken forces with a bitter laugh, "a real collide-a-scope!"

Dave doesn't get the point or the sentiment, but continues as if in rapture over all he's seen. "I mean it was all colors, all the bright whites and pale blues on one side and a line of grey and orange and black on the other, all of them popping up and hovering there, then rushing together toward the center." He pauses to see if Kenny's gotten the point, then adds "like twisting the tube on one of those kid's kaleidoscopes!"

"I guess I have to think of the people," Ken says, not amused, but Dave's ready to join him on this point, too.

"Oh, you could see that there were people," he recalls. "There were these two dots of dark blue in each frame . . ." He pauses for Ken to get the picture, and seeing no reaction says, "The umpires!" This raises Ken's interest.

"Did they break it up?" he asks.

"Well," Dave drawls again, "you have to realize that this was like a kaleidoscope—it really was. There were these swirling masses of white and grey and blue and orange, and these two dark blue dots sort of got swept up and lost." Kenny smiles to think of the ump who tossed him being crushed at the bottom of the pile.

"And then these two brown dots popped up . . ."

Ken is startled, but can't think what to say.

". . . and came rushing toward the center!" Dave acts mystified himself by what he's said, and pauses for clarification. "Actually there'd be twelve brown dots if it really were a kaleidoscope, 'cause kaleidoscopes have six sections . . ."

"Two *what*?" Ken thunders, and Dave is taken aback.

"My two security guys. Beacon Security—brown uniforms. Out there between all those white and grey uni's." The more Dave says, the more ridiculous it sounds, until he begins laughing and Kenny has to join him.

"Don't tell me," the manager is chuckling. "You told them to break up any fights . . ."

"Yeah," Dave laughs, "and I didn't say where!" In their sudden camaraderie Ken lifts his pack and shakes out a cigarette for Dave, who takes it and accepts a light before remembering that he doesn't smoke. But as Dave looks for somewhere to put the cigarette down, Ken becomes halfway serious.

"So tell me what happened," he asks the GM, begging him to forget about the kaleidoscope.

"Well, my Beacon Security guys started pulling players apart and then hauling them off the pile—"

"Which couldn't have hurt anything," Ken interjects.

"—and finally they got down to the pitcher, Sal Nistico, and both umps at the bottom."

"Nistico charged the mound, huh?" Kenny asks, confirming his vision of what would happen.

"Like a blitzing safety," Dave says in awe. "But the pitcher side-stepped him and he ran into the ump, and that's how the pile began."

"So how'd your boys behave when they pulled it all apart?" Ken wants to know, wondering what ballpark security does after they've stepped between two brawlers.

"Well, they got in a heck of trouble," Dave complains, and proceeds to describe how puzzled the umpires looked, especially the one on the bottom.

"Puzzled?"

"Maybe groggy, disoriented. Hey, they were blitzed!" Dave tries for another laugh but Kenny is serious about getting to the end of this.

"Anybody hurt?" He's thinking of Billy, whose small, slender frame is the last one possible he'd want to take an aimed fastball.

"Yep," Dave says, and adds with a shrug that this is why he's in such trouble.

"*You're* in trouble?" Kenny asks in disbelief. "You mean you got out there, too?"

"No," Dave brushes away the thought, but then pauses to think that maybe he should have gotten involved. "If I'd been out there, I guess, the trouble wouldn't have happened."

"The fight? For Christ's sake, you're worse than your security!" Kenny's shaking his head but still can't relax. Dave notices that he's lighting new cigarettes before the last ones are half-smoked.

"Well"—and there's that middle Kentucky drawl Ken finds so different from his in-laws' West Virginia twang, reminding him that the other side of the mountain can be pretty different after

all—"having security out there with nobody to explain sort of pan-
icked the umpires, I think." Dave takes another cigarette, lets Ken
light it, then once more wonders what to do with it since he
doesn't smoke. "Anyway, when the umpire on the bases got up, he
saw the brown uniforms and got real huffy."

"Huffy?"

"You know, like the plate ump gets when you argue: chest out,
shoulders back, aggressive—you know, in your face."

"And so?" Kenny wonders, genuinely perplexed.

"And so my guy decked him."

"Oh Christ . . ." Kenny trails off, looking across his knees and,
noticing his cigarette pack, shakes another loose and lights it.

"Knocked him out," Dave adds. Seeing Ken at a loss holding two
lit cigarettes he says, "Here, give me that" and extinguishes the
half-burned one along with his own. "Of course, the ump was
pretty groggy to begin with."

"So how'd you get involved?"

"I didn't get involved," Dave says proudly, "that's the trick. When
I saw the plate umpire come looking for me, sending the batboy up
with an announcement, I cleared out of there and came down
here. Those umps won't risk it in the home lockers!"

At this moment there's some clattering of spikes in the tunnel
and a rasping sound as the interlopers turn to climb the two concrete steps into the locker room.

"Oh yeah?" Ken begins to ask, then sees it's not the umps but
rather three of his players: Jim Knowlton, Julio Arredondo, and a
dirty and disheveled Sal Nistico. Knowlton and Arredondo, his infield corners, look OK, but Nistico's sporting a shiner and nursing a
shoulder that looks like it might be dislocated. It is, Ken decides,
when he sees a worried-looking George Karras padding in close behind.

"We got run, Skipper," Knowlton says, and answers Ken's im-
plied question with a quick "Three of theirs, too."

"The pitcher?"

"He's history anyway," Knowlton laughs, somewhat like a ma-
niac. "Julio here knows kick boxing!" Kenny looks to his third
baseman, who gives him a sly high sign while Knowlton crows.

"I'll betcha he broke that guy's fuckin' *jaw,* man, with his fuckin' *foot!* And both guys standin' *up!*" Ken glances back to George, who confirms it with a wince.

"Who else?" Ken asks levelly. "Not hurt, just out."

"Their shortstop," Knowlton checks off, "for some goddam reason. And," he pauses to share what will be Kenny's obvious pleasure, "their manager, too."

Kenny is pleased, and leans back to light another cigarette, automatically handing the half-smoked one to Dave. Before Dave can grind it out, though, Knowlton has grabbed it and is taking long draws. Ken looks up, says "No smoking in the clubhouse," then lights a third and offers it to Dave. Dave shakes his head no, but Arredondo's already got his hand out, so Knowlton passes it along.

"T.A. got the game going? Who's at the corners and in left?" Knowlton says nothing's rolling yet because there's still some trouble with Billy Harmon.

"Huh?" Kenny asks with a start. He should have realized the kid would be hurt, and badly.

"Their trainer's with him," George offers. "I couldn't stay out there, not with Sal—he may have a dislocation and I've got to get him on the table. Plus I'm not a psychiatrist."

"Huh?" Now Ken's really worried; but George, embarrassed, points to Sal's shoulder and hustles past to his trainer's room.

Kenny looks to Knowlton, who just shrugs, then to Arredondo, who won't look up from his cigarette. He moves toward the steps into the tunnel, then remembers he can't go back to the dugout or the field. So he tosses Dave the half-empty pack and turns into the trainer's room, where Sal's already on his stomach and groaning while George works his shoulders back into line.

"OK," Kenny begins, "you're not a psychiatrist. But just what happened to Billy?"

George doesn't look up, and in fact concentrates harder on his work at hand. But he does give the manager an answer.

"I don't know, but it sure isn't physical," George says while Sal lets them know his own problem is physical indeed.

"He got hit, didn't he?" Kenny's question is presented as a challenge.

"Sure, but it wasn't that hard: he took it in the meat of his back and spun away with it. I'll be surprised if he has much of a bruise at all." Sal groans again and George asks him a few things about his shoulder.

"So what's the problem?" No challenge now but a fair amount of worry.

"You tell me," George replies with some exasperation, giving Sal's arm too rough a twist and getting back some curses along with the groans.

"You mean you left him lying there?" Ken's become indignant—of all the kids on the team for George not to care about!

"I tried to help him up, or at least roll him over, but he just stayed there all bunched up. And crying."

"Oh Christ—"

"Meanwhile Sal here"—another groan, reminding George not to use the shoulder for emphasis—"needed attention, and the plate ump wanted me to look at his partner. So I just left him be. Then the Giants' trainer came over for a look, and here we are."

"For Christ's sake," Ken explodes, "you mean he's still out there?"

George now turns to face his manager with a look of irritation and dismay. "I hardly think so," he scoffs, then moves past Kenny for some bandages to rig a sling.

Knowlton's coming out of the shower, smoking a cigarette he's somehow kept dry, when Ken Boyenga finds him. "Get dressed and take a look from the stands," the big first baseman is told. "Let me know where Billy's at. And get rid of that cigarette." Arredondo, meanwhile, is still sitting in his uniform, shoes off but nothing else, fishing out a cigarette from the pack Dave's handed him. "Hey," Kenny barks, "no smoking in the clubhouse," then takes the pack and lights one for himself, raising an eyebrow to Dave, who says "no thanks" but takes one anyway. For a moment the manager and third baseman sit there smoking while Dave fingers his. Then the screen door, which has slammed shut just a minute ago with Knowlton's exit, pops open again with a wet and worried looking first baseman waving for Ken's attention.

"He split," Knowlton announces, almost out of breath.

"Huh?" the seated group choruses.

"Gone. Disappeared. Vanished."

"Billy?" Ken now asks.

"Yeah. I ran into one of those guys from the board and he told me Harmon just lay there for a long time 'til everyone ignored him, then got up and walked out the gate where those soldiers went."

"And nobody went after him?" Kenny asks incredulously.

"Nobody goddam noticed it! The board guy only figured it out when he saw Billy in the parking lot. Thought he was just mixed up and looking for the clubhouse, says the one we'll see in Madison is out past the field like that."

"Oh Christ," Ken now fumes. "I better go get the kid—"

"He's not there!" Knowlton sputters, still not having caught his breath. "Board guy said he just kept walking, outta sight across those softball fields and past the trees."

"Oh Christ," Ken repeats, this time as a prayer.

LEFTY DUNSMOOR'S RED DESOTO

It's the top of the third as Ken Boyenga and Dave Hunt sit in the general manager's office, waiting for the police to call with any word about their lost infielder. They can hear the game going on around them—more properly, they can hear the crowd's reaction, loud enough to indicate there's been some scoring. Kenny has mentioned how ridiculous it is for both of them to be missing their first game, but their minds are elsewhere, on Billy. His fellow infielders, tossed from the game after the brawl, have gone in search of him. Arredondo's been sent out on foot in the kid's direction, while Knowlton has borrowed Dave's car and headed over to the apartment Billy shares with Bob Gish and a few others, not that there's been any answer to Ken's repeated phone calls.

But the game is going on out there, and soon the normal routine of small problems begins. A kid from concessions interrupts to say they need more ice, so Dave grabs a program, opens it to the page where the board of directors is pictured, and says to ask one of these folks to make a run. "But not this fellow," he cautions, pointing to Mike Jacobs.

Lefty Dunsmoor, sitting in the grandstand's first row just off the ramp and distinguished by his thick pompadour of silvery white hair, is the first board member recognized, and he tells the kid that sure, he'll fetch some ice. Handing his scorecard to a friend, he pulls himself up and starts shuffling down the aisle. But first he has some words for this teenager from concessions.

"They'll load her up for me over at the Pizza Pub," Lefty tells him, then cocks his head back the way he does to make his listener feel suspected (and rightly so). "But I'm going to need you to haul all these bags in." The kid nods, but Lefty keeps warning. "So you watch for me, OK? I've got a two-toned DeSoto."

"Sure, mister," the kid promises, wondering what a DeSoto is, and Lefty heads down the ramp, slides open the utility gate, and takes a shortcut to his car, which is indeed a beautiful old 1957 DeSoto, fins and all.

He's parked it way across the lot where the smarter ballplayers leave their cars, well out of foul ball range. But Lefty's chosen this particular spot, an even longer walk than necessary, because it's next to a cute little '53 DeSoto convertible. A smaller car, and no fins. My, my, Lefty thinks, looking at the two before he gets in: four years between these two models and it might as well be light years. And he bought his '57 with retirement in mind. No wonder people think he's old.

It's just a two-minute drive to the Pizza Pub, where they'll let him take all the ice he wants, a trade-off Dave arranged that costs the club just a small fence sign and a handful of free tickets. Lefty's in the door and searching through the barroom gloom when he's startled by a figure dressed head to toe in glowing, almost phosphorescent white. He cocks his head to squint at this apparition, and son of a gun if it doesn't have a big number 23 in the middle of its back. A softballer out this early in the spring? Well, maybe so, and Lefty begins to chuckle. "Hey, Ryne Sandberg," he laughs, slapping the player on the back, "you seen Freddy or Pat around here?"

Number 23 lifts his head and turns, making Lefty gasp. In the light of day he might recognize the face as Billy Harmon's, but there's little chance of that now, so twisted into grief are its features. In a second, though, Lefty's recovered, even though he hasn't had to face such an expression since the war.

"Hey, young fella," he begins, "you look like you just lost your last friend on earth." The kid tries to respond, but can't—yet he keeps looking into Lefty's eyes as if in need of something, of anything.

"So who's your team?" the old man asks, wondering where all the youngster's buddies are, and has to gasp again when Billy points to the lettering across his chest.

"Well I'll be darned," Lefty sighs, letting out a breath that's been caught in his chest and making his heart feel twice its size. How the kid got here and what he's doing in a bar dressed for the diamond are beyond question at the moment, so wretched does this number 23 look. Maybe he got lost looking for the stadium—but no, Lefty remembers penciling in that number in his scorebook. And then crossing it out. As the thought occurs, Lefty cocks his head back as if he's about to say it: so you're the kid who got hit with that pitch in the first inning.

What Lefty says instead comes from long experience. There's neither alarm nor judgment on it, just a casual note of happy coincidence derived from the destination spelled out across the frail young man's uniform top.

"Why, that's where I'm heading. And I need a hand with some ice. Maybe we could help each other out: a ride for a hand, how's that sound?"

Billy doesn't respond, other than turning back to the drink that Lefty now sees has been in front of him. It's a ten-ounce draw glass, but filled with what looks like bourbon or brandy, neat. What on earth is *that*, Lefty asks himself, as it's no drink Freddy or Pat would ever serve. "Is that what you've asked for?" Lefty inquires, and for the first time Billy gives him a spoken answer.

"Yes sir," he says, then chokes back a deep sob, "and I can't even drink it!" Another sob and his head drops halfway to the bar.

"Well who on earth would want to?" Lefty explains. "What is that, whiskey or brandy?"

"It's whiskey, sir," Billy struggles to say.

"Son, you take whiskey an ounce or so at a time, in a shot glass or over ice. You've got enough there to choke a horse. Don't tell me Freddy poured that for you!"

"I asked the gentleman here"—he indicates Pat, who's just coming in from the stockroom—"to give me the biggest glassful of whiskey he had. He said it would cost me ten dollars. He's holding my hat and batting gloves 'til I can bring some money back to pay . . ."

Pat's now in front of them, shrugging as Lefty cocks his head back to give him a suspicious eye.

". . . and I can't even drink it! I can't take one for the team and I can't play ball and I can't even drink a single glass of whiskey!" Now the sobs are uncontrollable, and Lefty realizes it's time for something to be done.

"Son," he asks, "what's your name?"

"William Harmon, sir," Billy repeats, the rote nature of it getting the better of his tears.

"Why of course: Billy! You were here last year! Sure—Billy!" Lefty now recalls putting "Harmon–2B" in his program, a Billy following a Bill, then a Sal. "Well, Billy, I have something I want you to see, and I guarantee it will be worth your while for carrying a bag of ice."

"Sir?" The mystery of it has Billy's mind off his troubles.

"You ever hear of a car called a DeSoto?" Lefty says the name proudly, and Billy brightens.

"Never did until this week, sir—then our left fielder bought one. A convertible!" Lefty thinks he catches the kid's eyes rolling a bit with that last word, as bleary and red as they are.

"Well, grab a bag of ice here, and I'll show you a DeSoto that will run circles around that old cabriolet!"

As Billy puzzles over the word Lefty walks down to the bar's end, where Pat is pretending to keep busy with a section of the Des Moines *Register*. He looks up, guesses what Lefty wants, and pulls out Billy's cap and batting gloves. He slides them across the bar, pushing back the ten dollar bill that's been offered.

"OK for a couple or three bags of ice?" Lefty asks.

Pat nods and Lefty shuffles back to Billy, shows him where to find the ice, takes a third bag himself, and heads for the door.

Outside the harsh glare from the parking lot's floodlight blinds him, and unbalanced by the ice he'd stumble were it not for the little second baseman, a full head shorter than himself, who's right there when he needs him. For the last ten paces Lefty's arm is on the youngster's shoulder, Billy guiding him to the car. "The red one?" Billy has asked and Lefty says yes, the two-tone, and the kid marvels aloud how distinct it looks.

"Yessiree, *distinct!*" Lefty's vision is back and now he's standing still just so Billy can take it all in. "See the breakthrough those designers made from 1953?" he asks. "This here 1957 was just about as far as automobiles could go. Take any model—Chevy, Ford, you name it—and that's the year everybody wants. But for DeSoto, this was their best, the real super deluxe. Come on, look at this."

Lefty puts down his bag of ice and reaches across the hood to pat something just ahead of the windshield.

"Just watch this," he says, "keep watching here." As Billy stares intently at a little chrome-trimmed rectangle, Lefty pulls open the door and reaches to the steering column's left. The kid hears something being pulled and presto, the rectangle pops up to become a louvered air vent.

As Billy smiles at the delicacy and detail in this design, Lefty's elbow hits the horn, and for a moment the youngster feels like he's jumped out of his skin.

"Sorry," Lefty calls from the driver's seat. "But as long as I hit it, listen to this," and he flicks a lever on the wheel's hub, taps it again, and gets a softer, higher tone. "Two horns!" he laughs. "One for the highway, one for town! Now come on in here." Billy holds up the bags of ice. "Just put them down for now."

Billy places both bags next to the fender and reaches for the door. Lefty waits a bit, let's him see it's locked, then touches a square on his driver's door and the passenger side pops up. "Central locking?" the young ballplayer asks. "Way back then?" Billy seems pleased with this marvel, and Lefty's happy to inform him that this was the only model, that you don't start seeing it on other cars until DeSoto went bust. But there's more.

"Look at this!" Lefty exclaims, starts the car, and to put her in reverse doesn't reach for a gear shift as they start to glide backwards. "The ice!" Billy yelps, but Lefty's concentrating on his trick, as again without any visible shifting he puts the car into drive again and they move back into the parking space.

"Sir?" Billy wonders, thinking that the car may be telepathic, and Lefty tips off his magician's trick.

"Where's my hand?" he asks his audience, and when Billy says, "On the wheel," Lefty laughs and asks again. "My left hand?" Now Billy looks over and sees it poised above the grid of push-buttons, not unlike a Touch Tone phone but only five of them, their legends

reading P, R, N, D, and L. It looks so cute Billy has to giggle, but
then remembers their errand.

"About that ice, sir," he ventures, and Lefty snaps to attention.
"Oh yeah," he says alertly, "you go put it in the trunk," and when
Billy asks for the key the old man just laughs, pushes a treadle on
the floor, and watches for the kid's expression as the lid pops open.
"Was that a first, too?" Billy asks, and Lefty says, "You bet."

Through all of this the youngster has seemed OK, but as Lefty
approaches Stadium Drive he notices Billy tensing up, and as he
signals a left turn—hoping the boy will notice how he's done it
with a tiny button recessed in the steering wheel rim itself—it's
apparent that the second baseman is beginning to shake and even
shudder. So Lefty flicks off the signal, continues straight on Fourth
Street, and wonders how to settle this poor soul down.

What can he tell the kid? As Lefty's eyes scan the cityscape heading down Fourth an answer pops up. "Hey, look at that," he indicates, and Billy, happy that Lefty's pointing in the opposite
direction from the ballpark, perks up to see. "That's an old meat
market I used to sell to."

"Where's that?" Billy asks.

"Right there, that empty building with all the construction in
front." Lefty tips his head back and reads through his black-framed
glasses. "Mennega Electric, huh? I'll have to call Gordy and ask
him what's the old Wendell Market going to be."

"You mean it used to be a butcher shop?" Billy seems genuinely
curious abut the building's past.

"No, a meat market, not a butcher shop." Lefty sees Billy ready
to ask what's the difference, so he tells him, glad to talk about his
old line of work. "A butcher shop cuts the meat they sell—they
'butcher it,' get it? Now a meat market, like Wendell had, buys
everything precut. That's what I used to do before I retired," he
says with a smile.

"You worked at this butcher's—I mean meat market?" Billy
wonders if he should tell this gentleman what the term means
today, a singles' pick-up bar. But, hating the words and the attitude
behind them, he doesn't.

"No, no," Lefty laughs. "I was a salesman—sold cuts of meat by the truckload to shops like this. Used to be one in every neighbor-hood." For a moment his grin fades as he thinks how nearly every one of them is now gone. In fact, even as they've talked the De-Soto has covered another seven or eight blocks down Fourth, an unobstructed arterial for the next couple miles. By the time they hit a set of lights, Lefty can gesture to another old business front with apartments overhead, a place brightly lit with a short counter, dispensing fried fish and chicken. "Used to be one over there: Komorowski's. 'Cept Romy used to do a little butchering, he'd ask me to get him quarters now and then, had customers who liked special cuts, Old Country things . . ." Even though Lefty can see Billy's listening, he trails off into silent memories.

When Lefty doesn't heed the green light, Billy interrupts his thoughts. "You have the light, sir," and Lefty snaps to it, sending the car off with a little squeal of tires. This makes Billy feel embarrassed, so he searches for intelligent questions to get his new friend back on track.

"So are all these shops, these markets, still there? I mean as different things?"

"You bet they are," Lefty tells him, then starts to chuckle. "You wouldn't believe what some of them are today!" Asking if Billy has a few minutes, Lefty pulls into the Apco station, swings around, and heads back on Fourth for a while before turning north. "Now if you've got ten minutes," he announces, "I can show you four or five markets you'd never know used to deal meats. In fact, I'll tell you when we're getting warm, and you can see if you can guess 'em."

Billy brightens up, the happiest he's been all day, and sits straight to peer out the DeSoto's windows. When Lefty asks him if he sees something in the next block he hits it with his first try: the dry cleaner's shop whose new smaller sign does not completely cover the lettering "PAT   EATS," which as he reads it makes Billy laugh. Why, this is urban archaeology, it strikes him, but he makes no mention, for fear of offending this very old man who's being so kind. A few blocks later there's another, almost as easy to spot: a market now reborn as a video rental shop. Then one Billy cannot guess, which Lefty indicates as a politician's neighborhood office.

"Once every two years, right before elections," Lefty says with a nod, and when Billy doesn't comprehend adds, "That's when the old blowhard shows up there."

The area's now turned shabby, full of ill-kept houses and corner bars where solitary drinkers stand in the doorways. "Never was a good part of town," Lefty remembers. "Mac and Susan always had it tough here. And will you look at what their market's become!" He points to a double front of broad glass windows that have been screened with what look like bedspreads, the sills strung with Christmas tree lights, and a bright strobe flashing on a block-lettered sign that reads "Lady Fingers Studio."

Lefty laughs, but stops when he sees Billy doesn't have a clue. Maybe a joke will work, he thinks.

"Of all the places in town, this one's still a meat market!" He laughs again, so Billy can get the humor.

"Sir?"

"So to speak . . ." Lefty's still chuckling when the door opens and someone glances out to see whose car is idling here at their curb. It's a tall woman wearing high heels, a string-bikini bottom, and nothing on top. Billy takes a shocked breath and then turns his head away—away from the half-naked woman and also away from Lefty, fixing his gaze on the DeSoto's floor as the old sales-man tells him, "*There's* your fresh meat!"

Wondering why the kid's not laughing with him, Lefty glances over and sees that Billy's starting to shake again, a quiver that be-gins with the breath he can't hold in his chest, that he can't seem to either let out or take in. My God, Lefty thinks, this boy is shut-ting down! He reaches over to take his shoulder, much as in the parking lot, only now to offer rather than take support. "Son," he asks, "does this kind of stuff bother you?" Billy's answer is just a half-controlled shudder. Thankfully he's still facing ahead and star-ing at the floor, for Lefty sees the woman in the doorway beckon-ing them in, giving her breasts a little jiggle that mimics Billy's quivering. The old man leans down a bit 'til she can see his full face, then smiles a "thanks but no thanks" before hitting the accel-erator and lurching off with another squeal of rubber and a rasp against the curb.

Thrown back in his seat and troubled by the noise, Billy is at least snapped out of his little fit and begins to look around. Lefty wonders if the topic of meat markets is now verboten, too, but decides to give it one more try. They've crossed Layton Avenue into a better part of town, and at the corner with Seventh he eases to a stop. "Up there," he motions to an upper flat, "is where some of your buddies live, as you may know already." Billy shakes his head no, but Lefty continues without noting. "And downstairs," he says proudly, "is an old meat market that next fall is going to be an honest to good one!" Billy doesn't indicate that the news has registered or means anything to him, but the old salesman goes on as if it has—as if indeed Billy has just exclaimed that this is the most wonderful thing possible. "Yessiree," Lefty exclaims, "the first new retail meat shop to open in Mason City since 1952!"

There follows a long story about the young couple Lefty's backing in this enterprise. Billy doesn't hear. He's just been staring out the window, letting the shops and houses and intersections pass while the gentleman drones on. Then he sees a church, followed by another, and finally a line of three that fills a whole block, for they're now at the edge of downtown. Then across the river to more shops and then some homes. When Billy sees another church he asks his new friend if they can stop for a bit.

Looking around, Lefty sees they're coming to the Open Bible Temple, and asks the boy if he wants to go in. "No sir," comes the answer, with a request that they just stop the car in front for a moment or two.

While Billy sits there, lost in contemplation, Lefty tries to settle back but can't get comfortable—he knows that while the neighborhood's not a bad one, nothing like the part of town that shook Billy up so badly, this is still foreign territory. The church belongs to a black congregation, and the homes surrounding it are part of Mason City's small but tight African-American community— "Negro" or "colored" as Lefty still thinks of it. Always been different here on this end of Fourth, he recalls, and wonders if he should tell Billy that the church he's parked in front of was, sixty years ago, the only synagogue in this whole part of the state. But the boy is quiet now, so Lefty leaves well enough alone. Besides, there's enough to worry about, including the stares they're getting from passing neighbors and the way they're being studied by a woman who's come to the big glass door. The minister's wife, he guesses, and hopes Billy doesn't see her, given how spooked he was by the lady at the massage parlor. "What am I thinking of?" Billy gives a start and Lefty realizes he's spoken his thoughts aloud. "The ice?" Billy asks politely, and suddenly Lefty's back in the real world.

With the same abruptness that he's used to hit the accelerator twice before, Lefty now swings his door open and lurches out. Billy's startled by this and by the motion he catches on his right: it's someone moving back quickly from the church's front door. But Lefty's calling to him—"Pop open the trunk, son"—and having to search for that release pedal gives him something to do. He no sooner pushes it than he hears Lefty make a little grunt, slam the lid shut again, and climb back into his seat. "Half melted," he says with a note of irritation and complaint. "But the ballpark's had to get some ice of their own by now." He pauses to think, then laughs. "Heck—we're both on the lamb!" He expects Billy to join him in this hilarity, but the kid's gone dead serious again, and starting to quiver like he's done before.

"Son"—he reaches for Billy's shoulder—"I was just kidding. Nobody's going to fault me for not bringing back the ice, and nobody's going to fault you for leaving the park. Heck," he stops to consider, "you were drilled pretty hard there. I'll bet everybody figured you were out of the game!"

"Sir?" At least Lefty has got his attention.

"Heck," he continues, "plenty of guys got run: two or three of ours, a bunch of theirs. And there was one boy whose shoulder looked bent up pretty bad. I'll bet you your manager just changed his lineup automatically."

"Our skipper was ejected already, sir." This throws Lefty for a momentary loss, but he's glad at least the boy's back on track.

"Yeah . . ." Lefty honestly can't recall what preceded the fight, but decides to make the best of it. "Well heck, with the manager gone you've got even less to worry about. Pitching coach take over?"

"Yes sir."

Lefty now cocks his head back, this time for a knowing look. "Son, I used to be a pitcher, and believe me, your coach will have so many things on his mind that who replaced who won't matter one bit."

Billy still looks worried—hasn't reacted much to anything Lefty's said, in fact—so the old man tries some straight advice.

"Here's what you do: don't say anything, and if tomorrow the manager asks, you say the trainer sent you home. And if the trainer asks where you went for your ice, you say the manager told you to go home and ice it. Heck," he now begins to laugh again, "that's exactly what we're doing, taking you home with some ice!"

It's clear Billy doesn't understand, so Lefty just turns the key, bringing his DeSoto to life, and pulls back into the traffic on Fourth. But they've only driven half a dozen blocks when the car's easing into the storage lane again, this time to turn off and enter a supermarket parking lot.

"Take your shoes off, son, before we get to the door," Lefty advises, and Billy dutifully follows him across the asphalt, pausing at the curb to pull off his spikes. It's fifteen minutes to closing and there are few shoppers to gawk at this silver-haired old man and young ballplayer in full uniform padding up the aisle to the meat counter. The counter itself is over half bare, but Lefty rings the service bell and an elderly gentleman looking much like him, except for a blood-stained apron, answers the call.

"Dunsmoor!" he says happily, wipes his hand on his trouser leg, and extends it for a long, warm handshake. Noticing Billy, he sees the kid look up, then begins to chuckle. "Hell, I know you own a ballclub, but you got players to carry your groceries now, too?"

"I need some steaks, Carl." Lefty's come right to the point, but has to pause for information. Turning to Billy, he asks how many fellows live in his apartment, and is told there are four plus himself—plus five others who share a two-bedroom right across the hall, making their top side of the four-plex one big household. "Good Lord," comes Lefty's reply, but when he faces Carl again his attitude is all business.

"I used to sell you rib-eye by the hundredweight," he recalls.

"Wednesday you'd sometimes take three orders. That what Sherman sells you now?" For this last line he's cocked his head back slightly, letting Carl know he's formulating a deal.

"Just a single order this early in April," Carl reminds him. "Folks aren't cooking out much yet—and you know beef's way down."

Lefty lowers his glance to the price tag sticking out from a heap of steaks and sees it reads $5.98. "Doesn't look down much to me," he laughs.

"You know I mean consumption," Carl warns him, but Lefty shoots right back with a question.

"Aren't we looking at about twenty pounds of tomorrow's hamburger at two bucks fifty a pound?"

"Oh, for my early shoppers I might keep a few whole and drop 'em to four dollars even."

"You'll get complaints . . ." Lefty's head goes way back with this caution, and while Carl shows no reaction, it's clear he's thinking.

"You want the whole lot?" Carl proposes. "There's more like twenty-five pounds there, if you ask me."

"Our player here has a dozen hungry guys to feed," Lefty announces, jacking up the number a bit to give his own side an edge, not that two pounds apiece is any less a pig-out than two and a half. "What do you say sixty dollars?"

Carl puts on a look of mock dismay. "Why, they'll be eating fresh rib-eye for less than ground chuck!"

"You bet they will," Lefty agrees. "And you don't even have to grind it, package it, and toss out what doesn't sell by Sunday." All that has been forthright, but now the head goes back a bit, and Carl gets the appraising eye as he's reminded how nobody's out grilling yet.

The old grocer's committed to the deal, both he and the retired salesman know. But Carl can't let the little act of larceny happen without getting his money's worth in pleasure at his friend's expense.

"Young man," he asks Billy, "are Dunsmoor and his cronies still paying you $630 a month?"

Billy blushes and is tongue-tied in his answer. "The Kansas City Royals organization pays us, sir," he stutters, "and this year it's—"

Lefty cuts him off. "Carl," he says more firmly than his words have been before, "I'm buying these steaks for the boys, and my social security runs $880 a month . . ."

"And so you spend it all on gas for that old showboat Chrysler of yours!" Carl looks to Billy for confirmation and encouraging him to laugh along.

"I believe it's a DeSoto, sir." Billy says in all seriousness, which now has Lefty laughing. But Carl is already reaching into the case and pulling out the steaks two handfuls at a time. Are these to be cooked tonight, he asks Billy, and Lefty butts in to say sure, save the freezer wrap.

While Billy takes the three heavy packages and tries to hold them along with his shoes, Carl and Lefty kibitz for a few minutes. Meanwhile a stock boy comes up with a cart, which Billy happily accepts. Then it's good-bye, and the two are off down the aisle. As Carl cranes his neck to see if there's a checkout still open he watches Lefty pause to toss in some items from the shelves. A lot of items, he notes, and realizes his old friend will be putting an order through the just closing register that will fatten the day's receipts by well over a hundred dollars.

To continue on Fourth to Billy's address will take them past the ballpark, but Lefty decides to chance it—the kid will have to face it sooner or later. As they skirt the stadium Billy seems to glance over at the light towers and hazy dust from the parking lot without emotion, so Lefty figures everything's finally all right. Yet the boy won't say a word until they're at the four-plex and icing down the steaks from what remains in the Pizza Pub's bag. And then it's a simple thank you—for everything—followed by a plaintive request to stay, meet the guys, and have some rib-eye with them, too.

When Dave Hunt
hears Ken Boyenga's phone
ring at 1 a.m., he realizes Opening Day's not done. It's probably
news about Billy Harmon, missing
since the first inning, so Dave wanders
over from his own general manager's office
to find his new friend bedding down. That's
right: the board of directors said their field manager could sleep at the park 'til he found quarters or got his wife
moved out here—fine enough. The two exchange data on the errant second baseman and say good night. But then Ken Boyenga
asks if there's any beer left and the GM gladly heads down to concessions and fills a pitcher from the vendors' tap. When he returns
Ken's cheered to see that Dave's brought two cups.

For a couple hours they talk about the route each followed to his
present job, marveling at their job tracks and how there have been
unnoticed intersections all the way. Dave recalls Ken's playing
days, especially in the National League, and even in the American
Association when the Iowa Cubs passed through Louisville. That
was the year Ken had Lois with him, in that huge apartment way
out on University Avenue so close to the Art Center, zoo, and
lovely homes that it almost seemed they were living a conventional life. To Dave, young and single with no present thoughts for
marriage, Ken's memories are not terribly pertinent but seem
pleasant nonetheless. And so the manager goes on, thankful that
he has a patient if not enthusiastic listener for his stories about all
this summer in Mason City could be.

There are his boys, aged five and seven, who've yet to spend
much of the warm months with their dad. Lois, with whom he'd
shared so much time as playmates but very little as parents or even

mature adults. There'd been a bit of family life for a time in Cincinnati, but then those wild men had taken over the team and the pattern of goofing off on road trips spilled over into the homestands at Riverfront. Some nights Kenny never even made it home, crashing in Copeland's room at the Hyatt rather than trying to make his way through the tangle of freeway interchanges leading out to his home in the suburbs. Bullpen coaching in Kansas City put an end to that, but at the cost of being away almost all the time from late February to the start of October. Taking the A-ball assignment was to be a move toward familial recovery—but now, as he explains it to the young GM, his wife is balking at having to spend the summer here.

"Why's that?" Dave's being polite, but if there's a bit of soap opera to it, that might make it interesting. Everyone loves a story.

" 'Cause all of us putting down with her folks got her excited about the hometown stuff again," Kenny explains.

"Where's that?" Dave asks, and when he's told recalls that Huntington was one of the places he'd visited as a regional man for Pepsi. "I liked the drive from Lexington," he recalls, "but that West Virginia stuff is really something else."

"You damn well bet it is!" Ken exclaims, then runs as if by rote through a list of the state's deficiencies, ranking 49th in this, 50th in that, until he comes to the pièce de résistance. "It's so backwards, it's like they're in a time warp there. Why, Lois's folks still got a picture of Robert Kennedy—Christ, two of them!—stuck up in their house."

What's so wrong with that, Dave wants to ask, then tries to imagine how he'd feel if somebody told him they had photos up of Richard Nixon—or of Lyndon Johnson, for that matter. Then he figures Ken is apolitical and is just referring to how dated everything down there seems. But those pictures, especially the ideas behind them, aren't. Dave's taken enough heat for his own politics, especially from folks at home, that he can't help standing up for one of his true heroes.

But Ken Boyenga's moved on to another part of the story, how this older board member, Lefty Dunsmoor, had a house all lined up that Lois nixed because it was near the old packing plant.

"Swift?" Dave asks. "Swift Hams? Heck, they've been dark for ten years, people tell me. Used to really support the ball club, but they're long gone."

"That's what I tried to tell Lois," Kenny sighs, not quite a whine but a deep lament nevertheless. "Your Dunsmoor fellow found something we could easily afford, cheaper even than sharing an apartment with T.A. and George, which for Lois was also out of the question, but even to the house she said no, she'd . . ." He trails off, too disappointed to continue, for he can't foresee a happy future.

"Heck," Dave drawls, taking some time for thought. "Lefty's got houses all over town—"

"Sure, in the slums—"

"Well, if you could pay a little more, I'll bet Lefty could pry something loose from one of his friends, a real realtor, you know, maybe a nice house in the good part of town that might not be selling real fast. You know, take it off the market for a while 'til prices go up, mortgages go down, something like that."

Kenny cuts him off. "Dammit, money's not a problem at all, she just won't listen. She just about hung up on me. What could I say?"

Dave brightens, because he has an answer. "Why don't you say nothing, just have Lefty Dunsmoor give her a call, tell her what he's got, and let *her* make the deal. Then she'll want to do it, because it'll be *her* thing."

Ken looks interested but waits for more.

"She be home tomorrow—I mean today? Later?"

"Saturday," Ken muses, then scowls. "Yeah, sure. Church Friday night, Sunday morning. Sunday night. Church night Wednesday. But no God-damned church on Saturday, people'd think they're Jews, I guess. Yeah, have Lefty call her." Kenny writes down the number, gives it to Dave, and the deal is done.

That morning at ten, about as early as he can get his eyes open, Dave calls Lefty's home but learns from his wife that the old gent's still sleeping. Had stayed out late doing a steak fry for the players. Wasn't that to happen three weeks from Sunday with the Booster Club? She sounds confused, and so is Dave. But Lefty will call him back when he wakes up.

At noon Dave's phone rings and the plan to call Lois Boyenga is made. Even before checking with his friends, Lefty's on the line to Huntington, but when he gets the answer "Scoggins residence" he has to say, "Sorry, wrong number," and call Dave back to learn it's the right number, that Lois Boyenga is staying with her folks. Then it's back to long distance, "Scoggins residence" again and Lefty's explanation to the polite young boy who's answered that it's Mr. Dunsmoor from the Mason City Royals. When the youngster brightens at this news Lefty's tempted to say they're looking for a batboy, but decides he'd better speak with the mother first. So he asks for her, makes a quick introduction, and states his business.

"You're right my husband's no good at finding homes," she agrees. "He'd have us living by some godawful rendering plant!" and Lefty laughs along with her diplomatically. Then he asks what she'd prefer, listens to a hopelessly ideal description of a home and location not even $200,000 could buy, then tells her he knows of two or three such properties for rent at the $300 per month she says she want to pay. She's pleased beyond belief.

There's some talk about how Kenny wants her to take their eldest boy out of school early and bring the family to join him May first. That would leave it to her husband to find the house, which all along she's felt is unsatisfactory. The team's road trip makes it impossible for her to see him much before that, and Scotty's critical 180th day of classes won't come until April 30th.

"Can't you come out here earlier, by yourself?" Lefty asks, and his directness surprises but pleases her. Unseen by Lois, Lefty's cocked his head back as he's asked this, and now he's smiling as she agrees, making him think that he's still a pretty good salesman. She'll fly out to Mason City Monday.

The team, meanwhile, has beat its path to Municipal Stadium in time to meet the charter taking them down to Cedar Rapids, where—hopefully without any more fights or disappearances—the Royals will help the Giants open their own home season. Yesterday's clear but crisp weather has soured, and a

cold, damp wind is stirring the low clouds and whipping dirty
leaves and scrap paper around the parking lot where the guys
are milling about, waiting 'til the last minute to get on the bus.
This is just a 150-minute commute, one they'll repeat Sunday;
but on Monday they'll board this bus again for the better part of
five hours all the way to Bettendorf, and Dave Alpert's already
warned the newcomers how endless are the rides to Peoria and
Green Bay.

Dave Hunt is there to see the guys off, promising he'll be back
after midnight to let them into the park for showers. "No showers
in CR?" a chorus of disbelieving players groans, and Mark Wiggins
says sure, two of them about the size of what you'd find in a summer cabin, and so the team resigns itself to a sticky, gritty ride back.
There are some serious complaints when the guys learn there's no
meal money—this is a commute, not a night over, the GM
explains—but there's so much grumbling and even vicious cursing
that he breaks a rule even before it's set and scurries back to the office for next week's pile of envelopes, the ones holding those me-
ticulous stacks of fives and singles for the trip to Bettendorf and
Dubuque.

This makes everyone happy except Billy Harmon, who remembers that on the dogleg from Veterans' Stadium to the interstate
those Cedar Rapids junk food dealers have thrown up one each of
every franchise imaginable, from Hardees and Mac's to some carry-
out Chinese places and a ridiculous little outlet that's gone through
three or four cuisines and affiliations while retaining a cobbled-up
sign from each, the place Freddie Guagliardo used to call "Arthur
Treacher's South-of-the-Border Deep Dish Backstage Deli with Fish
'n' Chips." Nobody's eaten yet, for at one in the afternoon it's not
quite yet the time they'd struggle over to the Golden Corral here in
town. As it is, they'll buy pop, chips, and hotdogs when they get to
the ballpark in Cedar Rapids, but by game's end the team will be
famished—at which point their bus will run the gauntlet of all
these outrages designed to knock the bottom out of next week's
meal fund. Knowing all this, Billy also admits he won't be able to
resist it himself.

In Huntington Lois keeps the news to herself, for if Kenny calls she doesn't want the boys telling their father she's coming out. Hopefully she can get to town, find a house, and be done with it by the time Ken's team returns, at which point he can face the double surprise of finding both a home and its mistress waiting for him. Then she'll fly back, pack what needs to be brought, and drive out with Scott and Marty at their leisure. With nothing to do until Monday, she decides to relax, but also get herself in the mood for rejoining Kenny's life. So she turns on the TV and looks for baseball.

Thanks to her folks' dish she at least has some choices, but the ones that are available present a quandary: the Cubs and Giants, a likely pick because she thinks Harry Caray's so funny, or the game where loyalty should be, the Royals at Minnesota. When she chooses the latter, though, it's not to watch her husband's employers but because she's curious about the weather so close to Monday's destination. But the first shot reminds her that the game's inside, so she tunes back to Harry and Steve for some easy laughs at how early the hapless Cubbies are looking to collapse.

In Cedar Rapids Ken Boyenga doesn't have a choice; he's getting a sample of both the Giants and the Royals, for the future of each major league team is right here before him. Even the uniforms are the same. Except there's an air of fraud about it: fifteen years in baseball and Kenny still can't accustom himself to the phoniness of such names as the Cedar Rapids Giants and the Mason City Royals, much less to the ludicrous spectacle of wispy little Billy Harmon in the same style uniform and playing the same position once graced by Frank White, or to seeing the CR center fielder—shame on him!—wearing Willie Mays' number, 24.

Turning from this bogus Say-Hey kid to the other players lining up along the basepaths for the hometown's opening ceremonies, Kenny has his fears for another on-field fight put to rest by the VIP who's coming out to greet them: league president Dr. Constantine Curris, in from Peoria's opener last night and Bettendorf's this afternoon. Ken would like to wonder if the guy even knows where he is, but needn't, since Dr. Curris's first words are spoken as he passes home plate where Ken and Roger Hampton stand just a strike zone apart at the head of their respective teams. "Let's have no shenanigans like last night, boys," the president tells them. "I've got a scorecard and all your numbers!" The game is played without a hitch.

A boring game, one that Kenny's pitching staff loses with walks in relief. Plus the drive out of Cedar Rapids is another no-win situation. Had the team pulled it out with a ninth inning rally, they'd have stuck around and glutted themselves on discounted food from the ballpark's unsold nachos, dogs, and brats. As it is, they leave the park as soon as possible to bury their sorrows in tacos and burgers and even a greasy bag of won-tons, cajoling the driver into making half a dozen stops along the boulevard that leads to I-380. T.A., who's heard all the good-nutrition lectures, still can laugh and call it a "feeder route," but Ken sits there grimly depressed, angled back to stare across the piles of styrofoam and tissue wrappers that clutter the aisle. His only words have been for the driver, a doleful "look at that!" as they pause for a light on Fourth Street before turning onto Stadium Drive. "Looks like a twenty-dollar clean-up charge," Kenny's told in return; and so as they pull into the parking lot he stands, takes the driver's mike, and says nobody gets past him 'til the bus is spotless.

As promised, Dave has opened the park and stoked up the water heaters, so everyone showers. Then the guys dress and drive home, while Kenny watches Dave lock up and then retires to the couch in his office.

There he's got the office manager's TV, but the local stations are off the air—without a cable hookup all he can get is snow. He recalls how Stan Sweet told him he could pull in the UHF channels from Minneapolis if he bent a coat hanger into a loop, stuck it on the roof, and ran two leads down the air vent. Son of a gun, Kenny chuckles as he sees the wires, his catcher's done it, for there's a note in Sweet's block lettering that warns DO NOT ATTACH IN STORM.

Hell, weather's clear as a bell now, and at 2 a.m. he lifts the screws that say "U" and fastens down the antenna. But a scan of the channels from 14 through 88 yields just one image: a fuzzy picture of the Stars and Stripes as a brass band plays the national anthem. Oh Christ, Kenny mutters, recalling how his professional day began with this same image so many hours before. But what the hell: he stands at attention, grabs his cap to place over his heart, then falls backwards to the couch and is fast asleep before the picture goes full white.

A LITTLE RIDE 'CROSS TOWN AND COUNTRY

The same Sunday that has the Mason City Royals doubling back to Cedar Rapids is a boring one for the manager's wife, stuck as she is half a country away. Yet as Ken travels, Lois packs—surreptitiously, as she still doesn't want the kids to learn what's up and tell their father if he calls that night. Apart since the start of Spring Training, the married couple deserves the spice of a pleasant surprise.

Monday morning comes with Ken and Lois Boyenga doing much the same things: he boarding the bus that will retrace yesterday's route and more as his team heads south for their series with Bettendorf, she climbing aboard in Huntington, West Virginia, for the drive to Charleston's airport, where she'll fly back over the same country on the flight to Chicago and then Mason City. The man named Lefty Dunsmoor has promised to meet her at the airport, and by nighttime, while her husband's running a ballteam 250 miles away, she assumes she'll be closing the deal for a lovely rental home.

Her day dawns brightly and, as Mr. Dunsmoor promised, things go well from the start, even before she's in his hands. The plane from Charleston gets into O'Hare early, a mixed blessing, as she fears it will only make her long layover more tedious. But when she checks in at ten for her midafternoon commuter flight, Lois is told that the morning plane, delayed by a mechanical problem—lack of passengers, she suspects—is just now ready to go. Begging half a minute to make a quick call, she rushes to a pay phone and dials the ballpark's number. Without time for the general manager's reply, she says she's coming in early—within the hour, in fact—and would he please have the board member meet her.

This is fine, except the "Mason City Royals, may I help you?" has not been GM Dave Hunt. Having given in to Mike Jacobs' badgering to cash in the pop cans hauled off the team's Saturday and Sunday charter, he has wearily punched the answering machine and headed out to the dumpsters, with Mike on his tail. But in passing the counter Mike has paused to retrieve a pair of 7-UP bottles he's spotted in the wastebasket, and when the phone rings he is just an arm's length away and so grabs it before the tape kicks in.

Meet the manager's wife at the airport? You bet! Loving all things official, Mike accepts the duty with cheer. Besides, he can charge this mileage to the club—which means he'd better not mention it to Dave now and be told no.

"I'll be back for the cans later," the new board member tells the GM, who pulls his head from the dumpster to give him a questioning look. "Got to run an errand," Mike calls, and is off.

He's at the airport in ten minutes and learns that the Chicago commuter's landing in about three-quarters of an hour. Handing the ticket agent a Mason City Royals schedule, he says he's the club's owner, and asks to be notified if Mrs. Kenneth Boyenga, the manager's wife, has inquiries on arrival. Then, as he starts to turn away, Mike spots a pop can sitting on the counter.

"Your RC?" he asks, and when told it's been left by a customer he picks it up. It's less than half empty, so his journey across the lobby to the video games is fueled with sips, a deep gulp, and a refreshing burp. As he leans over to check the coin return on a Mario Brothers machine Mike's stomach rumbles and he straightens up for a mighty belch, turning heads way back at the ticket counter. Jesus, he mutters, actually praying for relief, and quickly drains the can to douse the heartburn he's feeling. But a half-second later he's choking, swearing, and spitting out a cigarette butt on the floor. "Shriekin' Satan!" he yells, much louder than intended, but he's already attracted help.

"You OK, Mister?" It's the security guard come over from the gate, and Mike's pleased to see a CPR patch on the woman's shoulder. But he doesn't need her assistance, other than a sympathetic ear.

"The lack of consideration some people show!" he fumes, gesturing at the soggy butt resting in a pool of RC Cola at their feet.

"I'd say you should sue the factory," she advises, sharing his indignation.

"No, no," Mike waves her off. "Somebody left it that way on the counter." As the situation dawns upon her she's taken over by a sick look and turns away, ready to gag. But Mike draws her back with his real complaint: "You can't imagine how such thoughtless lack of hygiene makes my work so difficult!"

"Your work?" The guard is too put off to ask more.

"Refuse cartage and recycling," he says proudly, then reaches in his shirt pocket for another schedule. "And owner, Mason City Royals!"

By now she's pulled a tissue from her pocket, picked up the butt, and is ready to toss it in the garbage. But when she reaches for the can, Mike pulls it back. "Five-cent deposit!" he beams and shoves it in his pants pocket. Then he thanks her and walks away—looking for more cans, she guesses—with a large brown stain spreading across his backside, for he's shoved the can in upside down.

In fact, there are other things on Mike's mind: pay phones, pop machines, and newspaper vending racks, and in the half-hour yet to kill he nets thirty-five cents. With his can deposit that means a penny a minute, and he does some mental calculations to learn that if every spare moment of his day brought even this small return he'd be a millionaire by age one hundred and ninety.

He's wandering out along the curbside, seeing if anyone's dropped coins by the parking meters (no luck), when the announcement comes that MVA flight 9807 from Chicago is arriving at Gate 2. He can see the plane coming in on its final approach and laughs at its silly configuration, a folded up affair that looks like it was cut out from the back of a cereal box. There's a roar as it touches down and reverses its propellers, and by the time Mike reaches the gate the plane's stubby nose is pointing straight at him as it coasts to the terminal ramp. This is the part he likes best. Standing squarely in the tall window, Mike faces the plane and begins gesturing to the pilot, his arms held stiffly at right angles as he waves one way, then the other, finally rocking both together in a beckoning motion that concludes with a downward thrust and snappy salute. "Mister . . . ?" a little kid next to him asks in wonder, to whom Mike replies with a self-assured smile: "It's always better," he tells the child, "when I bring them in myself."

"Mister . . ." This voice is Mrs. Boyenga's, he's sure, for she's the only woman getting off the plane and he's the only man waiting at the gate. Before she can finish he's pumping her hand and exclaiming "It's Mike! Mike!" Well, Lois thinks, maybe "Lefty" is just his nickname at the park, so "Mike" it will be. While the half-dozen salesmen disembarking pass around them, Mike and Lois stop to chat about the flight and receive each other's thanks, the new board member saying how privileged they are to have the manager's wife make a visit and Lois enthusing over how wonderful it is that Mike has found her a rental home. To his credit Mike doesn't bat an eye, even as he mentally reviews what he knows is available around town, which isn't much.

While Lois excuses herself to freshen up, Mike agrees to wait for her baggage. There's a moment of temptation when he sees a stewardess come in from the plane with a garbage sack of cups and pop cans. He guesses from the clank and clatter that there's a good dozen nickel deposits in the bag, plus plastic cups he knows from experience are washable, but he doesn't want to be juggling a trash can liner plus Mrs. Boyenga's suitcases. So he lets the easy haul slip by with just a moment's pang of regret.

Mike's standing with the bags when Lois returns, and together they stride through the lobby and out the glass doors as another little tragedy unfolds: one of the deplaning salesmen has just hung up the pay phone without having gotten an answer, and is pushing through the doors ahead of them even as his change can be heard dropping into the coin return. Bing, bong, bing-bing-bing it goes, followed by a cascade sounding like a slot machine on pay-off. Jesus Christ, Mike almost swears, he must have been calling Brazil! He'd love to stop and retrieve it, but Mrs. Boyenga's chattering happily about what she calls her dream home and clattering forward so purposefully on her high heels that Mike can't dare pause or try to change their course. As they swish through the doorway he looks back longingly, his doleful eyes meeting those of the little kid who watched him dock that plane. *You little bastard*—Mike fixes him with a furious glare and sees the tiny hand freeze for just a moment before scooping out the cash.

Lois has crossed the sidewalk, stepped from the curb, and is crossing to the parking lot before Mike can catch her. "Over here!" he shouts, and she turns to see him gesturing with her tote bag toward the freight platform down past the terminal. Oh, she thinks, that must be his Taurus, a station wagon like realtors always have, but he steers past it and then past a window van until there's nothing left but a couple trucks. "My God," she says, "you didn't come out here in that semi?" "No, No," Mike laughs in comforting assurance, "this one's mine," and with no small pride he reaches up, pulls open the door, and hefts her bag up into the cab of a big blue garbage truck.

At this moment the Mason City Royals bus is rolling down I-380 in Cedar Rapids, right past where Kenny's team played last night. Utterly ridiculous, he thinks, and tries to ignore his feelings by staring out the windscreen, just as Lois in the garbage truck now tries to do. Except, unlike the team's bussie, her driver won't shut up. He's babbling about tonnage and efficiency, about how much sanitary waste he can haul as opposed to the other stuff—"I'd need a tanker for that," he says in a studious aside—but she can't bear to acknowledge it. Not that looking out the window helps, for in the past ten minutes they've come in from the countryside to pass some truly lovely homes, block after block of American dreams including one whose red brick and white-trimmed windows remind her of the home in suburban Cincinnati they sold last fall. Oh, how did I ever let myself get into this, she ponders in deep lament. A garbage truck!

As the houses start to change from sprawling ranches to smaller bungalows she decides to speak. "Can't we turn off here," she asks, "and go back to look at some of those nicer homes?" "No way," Mike informs her, "No trucks allowed on those streets, unless I'm collecting, picking up the route, you know, on put-out day," and she shudders to think of being involved in such work. Hey, maybe that's next? She remembers the expression, one of her husband's favorites from their younger days of shared adversity. Lois hears his voice and gives a little laugh. Mike notes this and laughs along, happy to believe he's finally hitting it off with the manager's wife. So at the next stoplight he turns right, chugs down a few blocks until he comes to a neighborhood that has its neatly lined up sacks of garbage ready for collection, and does a quick run through a cul-de-sac, showing off how from his cab he can swing out a levered basket that picks up each bag and flips it in the back. "This is Pink Lady's route," he laughs. "Moose and Toad—you'd love 'em— work it in the afternoon, and they're gonna wonder how all these folks forgot to put out. Betcha they bust a gut trying to figure what gives!" He laughs some more and waits for Lois to join him, but she's gone back to glaring out the windshield like there's some secret anger to be nursed. Well, ballplayers, he thinks—managers and their wives must be the same. It takes all kinds.

"What the fu . . . ?" Kenny can't finish the syllable because other expletives from the guys behind have drowned him out. They've reached Bettendorf and turned into the ballpark's lot and there sits the stadium, its outfield wall right against the water and curving with a bend in the Mississippi River. But their way is blocked by a fleet of garbage trucks, the first of them being heaped full by an endloader; and there's a man—a "suit," they'd call him, for that's what he's wearing—standing next to an official-looking sedan and waving them back. Not that anyone wants to proceed, as through the bussie's window and the door he's opened for instructions flows the most nauseating smell imaginable.

"Sorry, boys," the suit's explaining, "we have a little sanitation problem here," and is immediately smothered by the team's collective voice, a mighty chorus booming out a disbelieving "Naaaaaaahhh!" To hear and be heard Kenny rises from his seat and jumps down the steps, almost landing in the official's lap. It takes less than a minute to have it all explained: The lock just down river jammed last night and there's been a backwash. The outfield flooded for a few hours before dawn and then slowly drained this morning, leaving a harvest of carp, catfish, frogs, turtles, and God knows what else to ripen in the noonday sun. "We'll have it cleared by game time," the suit assures everyone, but says they'd be better off waiting at their motel.

"Oh sure," Mark Wiggins complains, and for credibility enlists Dave Alpert's and Billy Harmon's testimony that the hole they stay in down here smells pretty much like this all the time. "So you're used to it," Kenny tells them, and shares a story with the driver about how he'd once dated a girl whose family raised hogs. "She had this trick of getting me to handle the baby piglets," he recalls, "and once the smell was on me I wouldn't notice it on her all night!" So maybe they should just move into the sewer works, the bussie interrupts, and Ken joins him, saying, "Hey, maybe that's next."

As the team bus swings around to follow a heavily laden garbage truck out from the stadium, another big hauler grinds its load half a state away, a sound that's anything but music to the ears of Lois Boyenga as she tries to ignore Mike Jacobs' running commentary on the operation. He hates to pulverize it, Mike tells her; and even though she doesn't ask why, he explains that in the six sacks they've picked up there's an average of three dollars in returnable bottles and nickel-deposit cans. "Three bucks," he repeats, and makes some sloppy chewing sounds as the gears grind behind them. "Getcha quite a nice sandwich—uuummm!"

As the ballplayers skirt the city of Bettendorf, the Royals think the same thing: three dollars of their daily thirteen for meals is a fair share for lunch, after their late breakfast of burgers and tacos up in Cedar Rapids that cost them a ten-minute detour and left their bus a pigsty again, styrofoam clogging the aisle and pickle slices flying through the air just like on those two hauls back to Mason City. Three dollars is what they would have spent for a Coke and two dogs at the ballpark, milling around the locker room door in their cleats, pants, and undershirts while the batboy ran their order to concessions. Now they'll have to badger the bussie into stopping at a Mac's once more or it will cost them double in the motel coffee shop—Dave and Billy have warned that there's no junk within a mile of the place. But as the Golden Arches show up in the fumey haze of Bettendorf's commercial strip there's no argument, as with a whoosh of the air brakes their big sceni-cruiser slows down and swings into the little dip that precedes McDonald's driveway.

Everyone waits for their bus to make the corresponding lurch up as they enter the parking lot, but the familiar little porpoising motion the guys know so well fails to come. Instead, there's a screech of metal and sudden halt as the front bumper catches on the leading asphalt, the rear end scrapes behind them, and the bus stops, its big wheels useless to push or pull as the frame hangs wedged between the highway's slope and the driveway's steep incline.

The driver shares some words with Ken and the manager stands, disdaining the mike to shout, "Everybody out!" The guys file past obediently, and as they leave Ken can feel the vehicle lifting on its springs. Then he's off and the driver gives it a try, but only advances half a foot or so before they're hung up again. "OK," Kenny calls, "lift the frame—both sides," and the team separates for the task. Seeing just six or seven on each side, however, the manager looks around and angrily calls back a gaggle of pitchers who've wandered up to the order station and are shouting requests into the speaker. "I'm sorry, this window serves only vehicles," a tinny voice is replying, and as the others head back Jim Hiduke turns around and says, "We're working on that, ma'am."

There are still three or four malingerers trying to look invisible off to the side. Sal Nistico is excused with his dislocated shoulder, but Tom Remington gets chewed out when he tries to say his bonus contract stipulates no lifting. "They mean weights, Drago," Stan Sweet adds to Ken's vituperations, and, as if this clarifies things, Remington cheerfully puts his shoulder to the load.

Things are getting nowhere, however, when Sweet makes a suggestion to the manager. "All right," Kenny calls out, "start rocking this sucker. Up! Up!" He continues with the cadence until the bus is bouncing almost half the height of its wheel wells, the driver gunning the engine each time he feels the frame top out. With a thundering roar and awful belch of blue diesel smoke the bus comes forward and shoots up the incline, rocketing straight for the drive-through lane. The driver dares not brake, but even as he pulls his foot from the accelerator the massive sceni-cruiser sails past the window and sways perilously to the left as it's navigated at speed through the narrow lane around the restaurant. Inside, it's apparent that the window server hasn't even seen the bus, for she's only now responding to the call wire the rampaging vehicle has tripped. "Welcome to McDonald's," she says cheerfully, "may I have your order please?"

In Mason City the clock's approaching one—two o'clock for Lois, who left Huntington at seven without breakfast and has survived so far on just the cinnamon roll Delta gave her out of Charleston. She's actually not that hungry, but decides to use the lunch hour to her advantage, getting her off this miserable garbage truck and to a pay phone where she can call the ballpark, plead that their Mr. Dunsmoor isn't working out, and find a more conventional realtor. Like everything else that's happened since she stepped out of that airport terminal, however, this one blows up in her face, for she no sooner begins suggesting that Mike drop her off at one of these restaurants and leave the house hunting for another day than he wheels them into a Burger King and chivalrously asks her if she'd like a Whopper, Turkey Sandwich, or Fish Fillet.

"I'm sorry, sir," the order station is squawking, before Lois can reply, "our window can't serve a commercial vehicle of your size."

"What?" Mike asks, confused and put off while trying to impress the manager's wife with his offer of these sandwiches, all top of the menu.

He's told again, tries to argue that he'll swing aside to walk up for their food, and when refused flies into a rage. When his diatribe about how such junk food belongs in the back of his truck rather than in front gets spiced with some choice language, he's warned to stop. This elicits some truly foul vulgarities, and when he's told the police are being called, he mashes the truck's gears into reverse and makes an angry exit, fingering the restaurant as he pulls back onto Seerley Boulevard. Sure enough, three blocks later a police cruiser approaches from the opposite direction, swings across the lanes in a U-turn, and, lights flashing, pulls him over.

To the cop Mike is all sweetness, saying there's been a terrible

misunderstanding and that he's never heard such language in his
life as issued from that drive-up speaker. "Some people are so inconsiderate," he shakes his head at the skeptical officer. "I'm a
Christian," he adds in protest, "and of course the young lady
here . . ."

Pulling himself up on the running board, the cop is astonished to
see this well-dressed woman riding shotgun on a garbage rig. But
he says nothing, just cautions Mike to watch his behavior, is assured the truck's not returning to Burger King, and then leaves,
waving Mike back on his way.

Easing back into traffic, Mike allows himself a big grin, only to
have it fade away when he spots the police car following behind
him. "Oh crap," he says, Lois thinking that this sums him up pretty
well. "Now I'll have to do another route just to be legal!" For the
next few minutes there's a little procession as the big blue truck
picks up another dozen garbage bags while the cop cruiser follows
a few lengths behind before turning off at the next arterial.

Mike sets his grinder going, gets back in the traffic lane, and continues on to a Country Kitchen where there's room to park at the
curb. "Come on," he motions to Lois. "I know the guy who owns
this place. We can get a discount. Should have thought of that before! Plus I gotta make some phone calls." Trapped with this ma-
niac, Lois has little choice but to let him lead her inside and to a
booth, where Mike asks the waitress for two Diet Cokes—"cans,
please"—and then makes a beeline for the phone before his hos-
tage can plead that she'd like to use it, too.

Handily there's a newspaper on the counter and on his way
Mike flips through it to the classifieds. Homes for rent: hey, he's
wrong, there are plenty, and one has a familiar sounding number.

"Pink Lady Garbage Haulers," the woman answers, and Mike
identifies himself. "So who's got the house in West Cedar for rent?"
he asks and is told one of the drivers is handling it for a cousin
who pulled up and moved to Texas. "Moose or Toad?" Mike wonders, guesses the latter, and learns he's right. Can she get old Toad
on the radio and ask him to be over at the house in an hour? Of
course—Toad's desperate to unload it. There are some problems,
but all that can be explained when they meet.

◈ At the ballpark—Mason City's ballpark—Dave Hunt is
chewing the fat with Al Swenson and Rick Dillon, each of
whom would like to know why their chief employee is sitting there playing with three or four dozen empty pop cans. But as
Dave alternately groups them in circles and squares and then starts
building them up into a pyramid, both men are having too much
fun silently daring each other to ask what gives with all this trash.
They talk about the opening night crowd and query Dave about receipts for concessions, beer, and programs, Rick losing a beat and
almost cracking when Dave volunteers that pop sales set a record.
"Could have sold more," he says, eyes fixed on the Nesbitt's can
he's balancing at the pyramid's apex, "but we kept running short of
ice," and Rick forces himself to get serious by considering how the
premix setup they use is so dependent on bulking up the nomi-
nally twelve-ounce cup with ice chips. Settled down now, Rick
finds he can crack some jokes at Al's expense, and so, while running Dave through a rapid-fire series of puns, most of them along
the lines of being willing to pop for a bigger ice budget and how
Newt's son who served up sno-cones Friday night was really a chip
off the old block, he keeps giving Al the eye, winking at each metaphor. Yet Dave's the one to break, Rick's line about the club's "can-
do" attitude prompting a stifled laugh that shakes his hand as he
tries to steady the last of these seven containers in a superfluous
tower, bringing down the whole structure in a cacophonous clatter.

"For crying out loud!" Al Swenson blusters as more than half the
empty pop cans roll off the desk and into his lap. "What in the hell
are you doing with all this junk? We don't even sell pop in cans!"

Just then the door swings open and Lefty Dunsmoor enters,
head cocked back to survey this scene of chaos and disorder. Seeing the heap falling through Al's arms and legs to the floor, he gets
a knowing look. "Ah—so we've gone back to pop in cans, huh?"
Focusing on Dave, he says this will be a good idea, make faster service and be cost-effective if they can keep retrieving the cans. But
if they've switched, why did they send him for so much ice?

Dave's about to clarify that all the pop is still sold out of premix
tanks, and will be because it's so much cheaper, when Lefty moves
on to something else, so there's no need to tell how the cans came

off the bus and are being held for Mike Jacobs. But even as Lefty's talking about driving out to the airport to pick up Mrs. Boyenga, whose flight's due in an hour, Dave interrupts to ask if anyone's seen Mike, who at ten was so hot to have these cans immediately and then disappeared.

"Saw him up on the north side," Al ventures, "garbage picking up one of those little courts off Cedar Bend Drive."

"No way," Rick counters, happy to contradict the president just as Al himself loves to be contradictory at meetings. "He's working the residences over off Seerley today."

"Rick's right," Lefty says, "partly. He's on Seerley, all right, but not picking up, unless you count fancy women."

"Huh?" the others chorus.

"On my way here I saw him coming out of the Country Kitchen with some lady . . ."

"That's no lady, that's his wife," Al tries to joke and argue at the same time.

"No sirreee," Lefty croons. "No women in this town look like that. When's the last time you saw a redhead in tall heels and a leather skirt?"

"Well . . ." Rick pretends to muse.

"This time of day?" Lefty clarifies, "and coming out of a family restaurant?"

"Oh," Rick apologizes, "I was thinking of Mrs. Swenson's twin sister over at the massage parlor," and ducks as Al tosses an armful of cans in his direction. "But hey," Rick adds, "maybe that was one of his drivers working Seerley."

"Nope," Lefty says conclusively. "Mike himself had his truck right there at the restaurant."

"With the looker?" Rick sputters in surprise.

"You bet!" Lefty confirms.

"You see," Dave interjects, "it must have been a heavy date," and is buried in a hail of pop cans.

 At the motel outside Bettendorf Ken Boyenga is kicking through a mound of soft drink cups and hamburger wrappers the bussie has swept out, wondering if this clean-up will be billed to the club. Reading Ken's mind, the driver eyes him and says not to worry, that nobody saw the bus go through that drive-up lane so fast, either, and they both laugh the affair away. Then Kenny stares at the dreary landscape out beyond this gasoline alley strip and gets a little depressed again.

At this hour Ken's wife is looking at some similarly blighted countryside. Lots of empty fields, but none that have seen a crop, probably ever. And some dreary sheds that she can't believe, which Mike tells her have been vacant only a few years. She feels terrible, her Salisbury steak lunch—the only thing the restaurant manager would discount for her host, and then "as is"—churning in her stomach like the grinder working behind them all this time. Something's stuck, the board member has told her, then nearly brought her lunch up with the complaint that inconsiderate people sometimes break the rules and use their garbage to dispose of dead raccoons and even former household pets.

Finally they come to a tract of little crackerbox houses and there, parked in front of one of them is another garbage truck, this one bright pink. My God in heaven, she wants to say, I'm in the Twilight Zone, on the planet of the mad garbage men. They're going to make me their queen, she thinks, then ritualistically poison me. "Oh Kenny!" she sighs, just barely aloud, and is immediately corrected by her driver, who says "Mike—it's Mike!"

Now they're out of the truck and she's being introduced to a man named Toad—not that she needs to be told his name, for he's well under five feet tall, weighs surely more than 250 pounds, with a center of gravity in a belly that droops to his haunches and a greasy, unshaven face that actually has a pale green cast to it. Mike also waves an intro to Toad's partner, a man named Moose, who's remained up in their own truck's cab to work the grinder. "Goddam assholes" is his response, a reference to problems on their route just finished. "Fuckers putting goddam trash in their refuse," he adds for Lois's benefit, and Mike chips in that he's been stuck with a coon or small dog too. "Could be a fuckin' kid fell in," Moose says, and laughs viciously. Mike and Toad seem to be pondering the possibility while Lois looks away and pretends she's somewhere else—on the planet of the lost baseball wives—anywhere.

She's wondering where she is when there's a roar overhead and a funny looking airplane passes less than a hundred feet above them. Oh, take me away, she prays, then realizes it's the same kind of craft she flew in on this morning and that they're back out near the airport. That's it: it's time to get serious.

"Mr. Dunsmoor," she announces as Mike stands unresponsively and Toad screws his head up at his friend while Moose pumps the clutch on his grinder and curses about housewife sluts fucking up his garbage, "this is not acceptable!"

"Huh?" Mike and Toad chorus.

"I will not live next to a packing plant—"

"Been closed these years!" Mike objects.

"—that still stinks to high heaven—"

"The renderings are buried," Mike protests, wide-eyed with injury. "Sealed under a foot of slag!"

"—and at the end of an airport runway!" She nods her head for emphasis, and Mike can tell there will be no more words, not even his own. But at their side Toad is making sucking noises, working his mouth around as he organizes his thoughts, which come out amazingly clear.

"Air National Guard night bombers are just here two weekends a month, ma'am," he says politely, yet insistently sure of his information. "And we were a few days late on our route today," he adds, "so I think you may be smelling Moose's coon." He pauses to think. "Or whatever."

"Will you please take me to the ballpark?" As she makes this firm request, she thinks of Ken just arriving for his own game tonight. She's already had it, and his day's just about to start, or so she thinks.

Too itchy to wait out the delay at his motel, Ken Boyenga asks the bussie to run him out now. He's remembering how a groundskeeper in Helena, Montana, during his first year in pro ball, torched a field with gasoline to dry it, almost burning down the stands. A few years later in Des Moines, a squadron of National Guard helicopters hovered over the field, positioned like a hockey team, drying out an equally wet surface. When asked about the differences between the top and bottom of the minors, this has always been the one Ken cites, and it makes him wonder what they'll do in this full-season medium-A league that falls somewhere in the middle. Diamond-Dry, his instinct tells him, and he shakes his head at the thought of all that finely ground corn husk and powdered cob blanketing the infield.

Thankfully, he's wrong—the flood waters stopped well short of second base and the outfield drained well—well but too fast, for that's what trapped all the carp and bullheads that otherwise would have followed an easier current out. Jesus, he thinks, looking at big, ugly catfish the garbage picker missed: one minute you're in a nice big pool, next minute it's gone from under you and you're flopping away on a big sponge that's drying to a crust. Kenny finds a groundskeeper's rake, spears it, and looks for somewhere to give it a toss. Good question, and for a few moments he wanders across the outfield, rake slung across his shoulder. Then he hears someone whistling the "Andy of Mayberry" theme and calling out to him, "Hey Opie, over here," and it's a young man from the Dodgers' office motioning him over to a dumpster in line to be picked up.

Will the field be ready? No problem. In time for BP? No way. Maybe infield—make that definitely infield. Where can I find a phone? No problem, tell me when you want 'em here and I'll call your motel—the TraveLodge, right? 5:30? You're better off getting here at 6. OK. Their business done, the two acknowledge each other's identities and the GM says he has several of Kenny's baseball cards, adding that his one with the Sox must be pretty rare as it's never turned up in a show. There wasn't one, Ken tells him; that year the companies did a short series and never got to the third string. "You were always first string in my book," the GM says sincerely, and Kenny laughs but adds his thanks. Then he's off for a tour of this ballpark, the oldest in the Mid-Continent League.

By now Lois is getting her own first look at Mason City's Municipal Stadium and thinking it must be one of the oldest still used in baseball. But she doesn't share this with the dork she can now laugh off as her personal garbage man, as she's out of his clutches at last. Of course it's not the oldest: she knows from countless broadcasts that Boston, Detroit, and Chicago have the really ancient parks; and it strikes her that the only minor league stadium she's seen, Sec Taylor in Des Moines, can't be newer than these stands in Mason City. It's just that their small size and lack of top maintenance make them look a bit decrepit, like a chain smoker or heavy drinker old beyond his or her years. *His,* she thinks, for as Mike drives her underneath the grandstand's overhang (and right next to the dumpsters, she notes) it's apparent that the ballpark's roughness and blunt appearance make it a male rather than a womanly thing.

Ken Boyenga's first look at Bettendorf is producing a different story. What a nice park, he thinks, I really like the old girl. He's taken with the stadium's finer, even quainter touches: how there's a trim to the grandstand's roof that's repeated in the way the numerous steel pillars have been cast, a design touch he can't imagine any modern foundry wasting its time on. It's a diamond motif, making for a crosshatching around the roof's edge, an embossed effect on the pillars, and there it is again at the end of each row of seats, detailed so that you can distinguish square bases at the corners and top while a distinct little home plate anchors the bottom. It reminds him of how the grandstand rows were decorated at old Comiskey, and for a moment he's back there, looking over the park on the afternoon of his trade from the Cubs, killing time while the office books him a flight to join the club in Detroit. On that initial road trip he'd see all the old ballparks—Briggs, Fenway, Yankee Stadium, and that big white elephant in Cleveland—before coming back for his first game at Comiskey Park, older than them all, even as all of them had seemed so ancient compared to the equally aged but so much better kept Wrigley Field where he'd started in the majors.

"Your bussie says he'll have the team here at six sharp," the Bettendorf GM has come to tell Kenny, who gives a little start at being surprised. "Sorry," the young man says, "I get lost here lots myself." Kenny tells him how the seat-anchor design reminds him of Comiskey and is told he can sit in a real Comiskey Park chair if he wants to, and is motioned down to some loose seating behind home plate.

"Those came from Chicago in the early Eighties," the GM reports, "when we were a Sox affiliate and part of their upper tank went sky." Right, Ken thinks, when those skyboxes went in and Comiskey's capacity shrunk from fifty grand to less than forty thousand all those seats had to go somewhere. And here they are. The GM reads Ken's mind and speaks it.

"Folks watched you catch from those seats," and Kenny laughs.

"Yeah—all four games!"

There were more than that, of course. But just four starts in the parts of two seasons spent here, and he wishes there could have been more such regular games and not just pinch-hitting duties and late-inning defensive replacements. He and Lois liked Chicago, even more when his days were free and they could do more rewarding things than close bars on Rush Street while trying to forget about the Cubs' likely loss coming up the next afternoon. But from Comiskey he'd been sent to Cincinnati and one of the newer ballparks, everything about it the antithesis of both yards in Chicago. And once Kruse and Copeland joined the team, baseball turned into something else altogether.

As Ken moves over to the old box seats and sits a while in the past, Lois eyes the Mason City ballpark and wonders about her future. How much of it will be in broken down old stadiums like these, buried in the minors light years away from the big time life she'd enjoyed in Chicago and Cincinnati? As Mike Jacobs walks her through the cagelike gate and past the souvenir stand to the office, she thinks how lucky she'd felt to have missed all but the end of her husband's minor league years. And now they've started again! As a player he could chart his progress on the rise, but as a manager . . . They used to laugh at how ridiculous it was to be in an occupation that totaled just 650 jobs, some of them held for decades and many owned by unbudgeable superstars. Plus if you narrowed it down to Ken's specialty behind the plate there could be as few as 78 openings, even if each team carried three catchers. Not a lot of opportunities nationwide. But now he was looking to work where there were just 26 major league slots! Who's he going to buck, Lois asks herself: Tommy Lasorda? Sparky Anderson?

Mike ushers her through the door and there's Sparky Anderson himself. Well no, not Sparky, but a distinguished looking gentleman who has Sparky's head of dazzlingly white hair. But he combs it differently, in an old-fashioned pompadour; and for as long as Sparky's been around, a virtual fixture in her image of the game, Lois knows this pleasant-looking man is much older. He's the first to say hello and ask her what she'd like, in a voice that sounds familiar.

"Mr. Hunt?" she ventures. "I believe we've spoken on the phone. I'm—"

"No," Dave butts in. "I'm Dave Hunt. This here is Mr. Dunsmoor."

Lois turns to Mike, tries to smile but can't avoid a grimace, and says, "Yes, we've met."

"Mr. Jacobs," Dave tries to correct her, looking past to Mike, but she's now reaching forward to shake hands with Lefty Dunsmoor. "Mr. Jacobs," she smiles, happy to meet this nice gentleman and wishing he'd been at the airport instead of Dunsmoor the garbage man.

"Just a minute, now," Lefty is trying to caution her, and there's a flurry of reintroductions that leaves Lois even more confused. Finally a voice booms above the commotion, hollering "For crying out loud!" and bringing the room to silence.

"OK," Al Swenson says, having commanded their attention. He addresses himself more politely to the visitor but still can't keep the exasperation from what he has to say.

"Let's start with me and Rick before someone tells you I'm Donald Duck and he's Porky Pig."

"He's Porky Pig, not me," Rick interjects authoritatively, but Al cuts him off before there can be any laughs.

"I'm Al Swenson, the club president. The guy you think is Dave Hunt is Lefty Dunsmoor, one of our senior board members. Dave Hunt, our GM, is over here." Dave smiles and Lois nods to get it straight.

"Now the guy who's Lefty Dunsmoor is the one you thought was Mike Jacobs," Al continues, leaving Lois confused as both the men in question nod and wave. "And this here's another board member, Rick Dillon . . ."

"Pleased to meet ya!" Rick says in a Donald Duck voice, and finally everyone has time to laugh.

"And I'm pleased to meet you, Mr. Duck!" Lois replies, chuckling but in a way that leaves Rick with the thought he may just have acquired an unwanted nickname. "And whoever the rest of you are," she says, surveying the room. "I'm really pleased to be in Mason City." She wonders if she should stop now, but the memory of Moose and Toad and that miserable little house of theirs has scarred her deeply, and so she continues. "I'm afraid, though, that I won't be staying, because Fritz the Cat, or whoever this garbage man is, hasn't shown me a house to my liking." There's a murmur of confusion but she speaks right through it. "So would one of you nice characters *please* take me back to the airport?" She pauses, but thinks to add, gesturing at Mike, "not *him.*"

In an instant Dave and Lefty guess what has happened, and the GM struggles to get everything straight. By the time the real Mr. Dunsmoor stands up Lois is happy and relieved. Now the only questions left are ones the guys have for Mike, but in the meantime he has slipped away, leaving just a mileage receipt for them to curse about.

NO PLACE LIKE HOME

Lois just can't call the board member "Mr. Dunsmoor," and after hearing his wife refer to him as "Mr. D" she starts using the appellation as well. It fits their style of life, from the cozy neighborhood they live in to the style of cooking she's invited to share for dinner: an end cut of beef simmering in gravy that Mr. D describes as an Iowa specialty, Salisbury steak. Never one to shy away, she eats it bravely and listens as the kindly gentleman apprises her of a place that's available to rent. Unwilling to end the day homeless she implores him to let her see it after dinner, even though it's dark. So Lefty Dunsmoor takes this spunky manager's wife out to see a home his friend Jameson's been trying to sell from Texas, and after a phone call to Dallas says it's hers for $300 a month through August.

"He knows it won't sell 'til school starts," Lefty laughs, pleased at the deal he's got her, while Lois worries that Ken will find this too much, especially as the home's unfurnished.

"No problem," Mr. D tells her with a wink, and after dropping her off at the Motel 6 says to watch for a big truck saying "Bob's TV" outside her room at eight tomorrow.

"A television set is the least of my needs right now," she laughs uncertainly, but feels better when her new protector says that's the rig he always borrows to round up furniture on loan for the guys.

"We'll have you set with beds and tables and chairs and kitchen stuff if you need it," Mr. D assures her. "By the time your hubby gets back end of this week you'll have a fine piece of Salisbury right there on the stove."

Ken himself will be looking over a menu tonight down in Bettendorf, but Salisbury steak is something he'll pass by. Never trust a dish like that at Denny's or Country Kitchen or wherever—too much like mystery meat in a school cafeteria, he figures, too easy to hide red meat gone grey. As usual, he'll opt for New York strip—a whopping twenty-nine of them, treating himself and the team, plus trainer, coach, and bussie, to the best this all-night place has to offer. Not because they've won, though his Mason City Royals have, in a game against the Dodgers that's brought out their hitting and pitching best. It's because two more guys have gone down with dislocations: Julio Arrendondo diving for a ball, and Billy Harmon in a failed attempt to break up a double play. That's the spirit, he feels, so here's the heroes' reward.

Next morning Lois wakes at six, still on Eastern Time, and lolls through a leisurely breakfast before Mr. D shows up as promised and they start hauling furniture. Two training-school boys help them, the younger just a few years older than her older boy, and she feels a little homesick. Done before noon, she tries to pay them but they refuse. When Mr. D suggests the young men might appreciate having her husband's baseball card, she gladly pulls out her favorite, of Kenny's first full year with the Reds, and hands it over. But there are two boys, and so she removes the snapshot with it, of her own sons Scott and Marty, and gives it to the younger one, who feels he's gotten the better deal. Are these kids coming out this summer, he asks, and Mr. D jumps in to answer, "You bet!"

By the time Ken Boyenga wakes in Bettendorf his new home in Mason City has a TV, stereo, kitchen table, king-size mattress, and a set of bunk beds. But all that's still five road games away. For the immediate present it's a life of motel after motel, while he has no idea what's happening up north.

Having his own room on the road is a blessing. KC's contract with their minor league clubs provides for everyone doubling up, but with the trainer and pitching coach together he's the odd man out, and happily so. There was some talk of sharing with the bussie, but Dave Hunt checked the charter agreement and confirmed that the driver got a single to himself. So Ken wakes to quiet, just the distant sounds of vacuuming in the halls, something he's used to from half the days of summer spent on road trips for well over a decade. The room has all he needs—a coffeemaker, complimentary packaged rolls ("Breakfast Free!" the sign out front had claimed), and cable TV—so for the next hour or two he's set.

"Are baseball players oversexed?" the question comes, and Kenny looks up. "America wants to know!" It's *Geraldo,* a program he'd forgotten was coming up, and, as an ex-player he used to know and a panel of what look like bimbos pose for audience applause, the manager settles back to watch. But the phone rings just as someone knocks at the door. Fumbling with the receiver while reaching for the chain and latch, Ken finds himself getting identical messages from T.A. on the lobby phone and from George in the hall: does he want to come along as they take Julio Arrendondo back to the hospital for the checkup last night's doctor said would be in order? "Hell no," Ken answers, "I want to know if baseball players are oversexed," leaving both pitching coach and trainer perplexed.

"There's probably someone at the hospital who could answer that," George hears a voice from the receiver squawking, but he just shrugs and walks away. He's summoned back with a request to bring up a newspaper before they leave, and as George asks local or national a maid walks by, gives Kenny a long, hard look, then chides them both by saying, "this isn't the locker room, boys," and with a start Ken realizes he's naked.

"Sorry," he apologizes, and slips behind the door.

"All the teams stay here," she laughs. "No problem. I shouldn't have spoken, you never would have known. You boys . . ." she laughs again, even though she can't be any older than Kenny.

She's still standing there, vacuum cleaner in hand, so he tries a joke—less to tease her than poor George, who's turned crimson.

"Tell me," he asks, "do you think ballplayers are oversexed?" He gets a level look in return, punctuated by a sharp "No!" and she's off down the hall. Kenny shrugs at George and tells him to look for a Chicago paper, then closes his door.

Back on Geraldo's show the bimbos are gone and so's Jerry Rosen, his teammate from the Cubs so long ago. Now the host is welcoming a new group, not baseball groupies but wives. You could always tell the difference. Still can, and these wives are from his own generation, so all the signs are familiar. More jewelry than the average woman, but not too much—just some special things to show how much their husbands make. Lots of streaked, striped, and frosted hair, but no gaudy dye jobs or half-bleached looks the groupies favor, a look he could once appreciate for its forthrightly advertised trampiness. No, these are respectable wives, worst thing about them is that they might have to wear half their old man's Series bonus or MVP award. He knows the type, and one of them looks especially familiar.

"And welcome to Vicky Copeland, wife of former Cincinnati Reds star Jeff Copeland," Geraldo's saying, and as Vicky beams at the camera Ken blushes and grabs the phone book to cover himself.

Mrs. Copeland's well into her introductory monologue before Kenny can recover, but with his pants pulled on and shirt thrown around his shoulders he can pay attention to what she says. In a moment he's talking back to the screen.

"You see," Vicky is explaining, "I never had any of those behavior problems with my husband Jeffrey . . ."

"Behavior?" Ken mutters in disbelief. "I spent so much time and money covering for that clown's behavior . . ."

". . . that all this talk of sex addiction sounds completely foreign to me."

"Sure, foreign to you," Kenny scoffs, "foreign like what planet that yo-yo was on." He starts thinking of a typical prank and has to laugh. Turned the lights off on the charter, got the last four rows all naked, then had them pull the call buttons and start moaning so all three stews ran back there in a tizzy.

"But Mrs. Copeland," Geraldo is urging, "doesn't the fantasy of being married to a superstar ball player sometimes turn into a nightmare? After all, there are women galore who offer athletes like your husband everything they have, with no strings attached."

As the host leers at her, Vicky Copeland misunderstands, thinking he wants some sexy talk about private secrets. After all, that's what Geraldo's show is like day after day, and why she thought she'd been invited in the first place. Certainly, some of it was in that *Superwives* book the year Jeff won both those playoff games.

"No, no," Vicky smiles back. "All my fantasies stay just as that—except the ones," and here she gives the camera a wink, "that my husband Jeffrey turns into realities!"

"Oh gimme a break," Ken snorts, remembering the fantasies of Jeff's that made his life and Don Kruse's a darkly comic show of horrors. Calling the hotel desk at 3 a.m., one time even dialing 911 and shrieking in a high-pitched voice about being only thirteen years old, here on a Girl Scout trip, and these awful baseball players have dragged her to their room—then hiding in the bath while Ken and Don are terrorized by the squad of cops and hotel security arriving there like gangbusters. Or threatening to bring up some willing thirteen-year-olds he claimed he'd met at a card show. Never happened, but Kenny always worried that was coming next.

"So what was your best fantasy?" Geraldo asks, almost drooling. "I mean your best *reality?* After all, when your husband grew that red beard and called himself Erik, he really looked formidable in that Cincinnati uniform."

"Oh, the beard and name were his own fantasy," Vicky laughs. "And I never liked him in his Reds outfit. It was more fun when he was a Mariner. You see, I always wanted him to be a pirate."

"With the Pittsburgh Pirates?" Geraldo asks, wondering why.

"No, no," Vicky shakes her head emphatically, "as a sailing pirate, a real pirate!"

"Oh?" Geraldo asks, feeling that they're getting warm and sensing the show's ratings rise.

"You see," she explains, "Jeffrey and I both believe that in a previous life, long, long ago, he was a pirate."

"And you were the booty he carried off!" waxes Geraldo.

"What a crock," Kenny guffaws, remembering that Copeland can't even swim—for laughs, and to get even, he and Kruse would get him on a rubber raft, then keep pushing it out to the deep end of the pool where he'd whimper like a lost puppy.

"Oh yes," Vicky croons, and proceeds to tell how one night before Halloween Jeff came home in a pirate costume he'd bought downtown.

"Boots and all?" Geraldo asks, then rolls his eyes at the camera as Vicky answers, "Boots and all, then nothing *but* boots," while the audience shrieks and applauds.

"And I put on my clothes for this?" Ken grumbles, throwing his shirt across the room. He'd like to turn the show off, but now Vicky's talking more seriously, so he listens.

"Well, Mr. Rivera," she's saying, "in the not too distant future you and your viewers will be able to share Jeffrey's fantasies. And some of my realities," she adds saucily.

"Oh, really?" Geraldo asks, all ears.

"Yes," Vicky says, now prim and proper. "My husband Jeffrey is writing a novel, a romance novel I think you would call it . . ."

"A sex novel?" Geraldo prompts and the audience squeals again.

"You might call it that," Vicky replies with a little smile. "But it's really much more. You see, part of it's been published in a magazine already, which I understand I can't mention here, and it's about a CPA—"

"A *what?*" Geraldo interrupts, and Ken listens more closely.

"Yes, a CPA, for that's what my husband Jeffrey is studying to be at the same college where he's baseball coach, which I understand I can't mention, and this CPA has flashes where he goes back in time to be a handsome pirate plundering and ravishing over the bounding main!"

"And does your husband's book have a title we can look for?"

"Oh yes," Vicky Copeland responds. "It's called *Buccaneer Accountant!*"

In Mason City, Lois Boyenga thinks she's had a fantasy, then shakes it off: that couldn't have been Vicky Copeland's face on TV as Mr. D ran the scanner through the channels. Vicky's husband Jeff has been out of major league baseball even longer than Kenny. God knows what he's doing now; Kenny never mentions him at all. And they'd been such friends, the two families liking each other and also pitching in to care for that hopeless bachelor, Don Kruse, who was always in trouble and grossing out both the wives. Oh well, the set's showing a string of blank pictures now as the indicator flashes those ridiculous channel numbers 86, 87, 88 and then settles back on 2 where a fuzzy picture

shows a weather map and what seems to be the Minneapolis fore-
cast. "Look at this," Mr. D is telling her and pointing for his young
helpers, "you're pulling in a signal from over a hundred miles
away. Looks like Bob's lending you something with a pretty good
antenna." She agrees and turns back to her pizza.

For the next three hours Lois works, while in Bettendorf Kenny
lazes; then at midafternoon their roles reverse. She clears a path
between the boxes of borrowed kitchen utensils, plates, and bedding, then settles down on the couch those training-school boys
have lent her from their own lounge. Meanwhile Ken is out at the
Bettendorf ballpark, walking the basepaths while George leads the
players in stretching exercises down the line in left field. They're
an hour early today, Ken having asked the Dodgers' GM for extra
field time to make up for the session lost yesterday. But Lois is running an hour behind, spending her afternoon's quiet period later
than she'd like, later than she usually can since now's the time
Marty is fetched from day care and Scott should be coming home
from school.

West Virginia. Mountain Mama. She thinks of her first year back
home—half-year, really—since marrying Ken, and misses it already. Not just her folks, though them a lot, but also things like the
curvy roads and the music in everyone's voice. Everything's so flat
out here in Mason City. Flat, straight roads, all those miles in the
garbage truck and she hasn't seen a curve yet—just hard left, hard
right, hard left again at corners where the only thing that's different is the number on the street sign. The dull, flat way the people
talk, like that garbage man, who spoke in monosyllables except
when he was trying to pull something on her. Lord, how he talked,
kept putting periods in everywhere they didn't belong, hard to get
more than three words in a row out of him. At least Mr. D has
some color to his speech. And Dave Hunt at the ballpark, but no
way is he from around here. Sounds Kentucky, but the other side
of the mountains, plus she bets he's worked down south, has spent
time talking with Georgia people, hilly Carolinas. Mountain
Mama—that's what Kenny called her years ago, but didn't once all
this fall and winter, right there in West Virginia. In fact, he seemed
to hate everything about it.

There's music on the PA for Kenny's guys as they drift in for batting practice, but it's a John Denver tape that prompts them to
make gagging motions up at the booth. So the Bettendorf GM pulls
it and tries a selection of punk stuff more pleasing to nineteen-
year-olds. Yuck, Ken thinks, but yuck for John Denver, too. Whatever happened to the Beatles and Stones stuff they played during
his own minor league BP?

Extra hitting and a rigorous infield session leave him and the
team hungry, and so, as the Dodgers take their own drills, he sends
George and the batboy to concessions for three dozen hotdogs, two
dozen soft drinks, and however many nachos and pizza slices they
can carry. It takes three trips even with a kid from the park helping, but the players never stop marveling: "Two feeds in two days;
the Skip musta robbed a bank!" As he sends George back with the
$140 check, Ken tells himself he'll have to stop this, for if Lois is
writing drafts back in Huntington they'll be overdrawn before his
paycheck and their dividends are deposited. But it's fun to see the
guys eat so happily and so well.

"Are ballplayers overfed?" he shouts to the noisy locker room as
faces stained with mustard and nacho cheese look up.

"Who the fuck wants to know?" asks Jim Knowlton, spunky as
ever.

"America wants to know," Ken calls to them in the same mega-
phone voice. The team recognizes it and responds.

"Ask Phil Donahue," somebody yells.

"Or Oprah," calls another.

"Or Geraldo," Knowlton says. "He'll fucking know."

In her new home, which still looks like a warehouse, Lois
has switched on the television while she unpacks and ar-
ranges, but turns it off when the local stations start doing
those banal human interest stories that pass for early local news.
She's pleased with how much Mr. D has found for her. There'll be
no need to pull a U-Haul from Huntington, as their summer
clothes will fit in the trunk and everything else they'd need is right
here. No towels yet, but those have been promised for tonight—in
plenty of time for her bath, Mr. D has teased her. He's off returning

the borrowed truck now, but has said he'll be back at 5:30 to take her out for groceries.

Her kitchen's all set up, minimal but serviceable, when Lefty pulls into the drive and gives a two-toned honk, actually a honk and a beep that reminds her of overflying geese. Well look, she notices when pushing open the door, there are some geese heading north, and a few have dived down to circle as Mr. D presses his car's horn to attract them. He laughs and points while she marvels at the great birds' size. Then Lefty stops and motions her to listen, and she hears the whistle of their wings as they make one last circle before flying off. "Twice a year I do this," he tells her, "and every time they're fooled just like the first."

At the store, where her host seems to know everybody, Lois is cheered by the display of such plenty and gets the idea to invite Mr. and Mrs. D for dinner. Lefty says fine, it sure beats reheated Salisbury steak, but thinks he'd better call home to be sure. No phone at her place yet, Lois reminds him, and so while she checks out Lefty rings his wife from the manager's office (where he seems to have the run of the place). They pick up Mrs. D on the way over, she helps with the sauce, and soon the three are enjoying big plates of spaghetti. Only one thing has Lois worried: stopping at the store's cash machine after the grocery bill nearly cleaned her out, the automatic teller has refused her request for $500. Maybe it's because she's out-of-state, she reasons, but it says no to $400 and even $300. Finally the machine yields $200, but shocks her with the printed admonition that her checking balance is now just $58.52. How did this happen, she wonders, but figures two hundred will last her 'til she gets back.

That night Kenny's hitters come up broke, shut out for the game and actually no-hit through seven innings. Then in the eighth Salomon Perez, of all people, leads off with a triple. But there he sits as Marius Webster (subbing for Sal Nistico), Spook Elliott (platooning with Jim Knowlton), and big Mark Wiggins embarrass themselves and their team with a wrong-side ground out, shallow pop fly, and strikeout looking. The ninth inning goes one-two-three, and Ted Hovet's fine outing, allowing just a single run followed by scoreless relieving from Roberts and Hiduke, goes for naught.

One advantage is that they're out by 9:45, but there's no talk on the bus and not even a murmur as they pass the brightly lit Denny's. Ken sees a Wendy's up ahead, though, and motions the driver toward it. "Betcha you can fit through *this* drive-in," Knowlton shouts from the rear, "if ya get a rolling start," and finally everyone is laughing.

The bus parks and the players file in, leaving their manager and his lack of appetite behind. In five minutes they're back, loaded down with food for themselves plus a big warm bag for Kenny.

"Eat this, Skip," Knowlton's telling him, "you'll feel better."

"OK," Ken mutters, and reaches for his wallet. "What do I owe you?"

"On me," Knowlton says, and is immediately poked from behind. "Well, on us," and poked again by Caspar Elliott. "Well, actually on Harmon over there, but he said not to tell you," and Ken sees his second baseman trying to look away.

"Billy!" Ken snorts, then regrets calling out his name. But he finishes the thought anyway: "Christ—Webster and Spook and Wiggins should be paying for this, each of 'em twice!"

LET'S HAVE A CARD SHOW

Next morning brings new ideas all around, Ken Boyenga shaking up his roster by adding some speed and guile (Barry Gifford and Ray Mungo, respectively) and Lois turning her own travel plans upside down. Trainer George Karras tries to argue that the dislocations will reset themselves sooner, but Ken still puts Harmon and Nistico on the DL, so he can activate this pair who drove the New York–Penn League nuts last summer stealing signs, driving pitchers crazy, and keeping their own bench alive. Lois too sees the need to reverse things: why fly back to Huntington and turn right around? Her mom can drive the boys out in their car, visit a few days, then fly back on the unused ticket. When the phone's installed this afternoon she'll call; won't even wait 'til five.

The truly dangerous thoughts, however, are coming from a different part of Mason City. Mike Jacobs, finding no action or loose cans at the VFW, has dropped by the Country Kitchen, where he suspects Moose and Toad will be catting out between loads to the landfill. He should apologize for Monday and also find out how little Toad will let that house go for, because he knows some kids from a crossroads out in the county who are looking for a party pad in town. He doesn't approve of their drinking but guesses he could clear twenty bucks a week collecting their empties—dirtballs like that just trash 'em. But Toad won't talk about the house. Maybe he's still offended, Mike guesses, knowing that both he and Moose can be really sensitive types.

What Toad does want to talk about is a card show. His cousin—not the one that owns the house but another, on his aunt's side—is a baseball card dealer and has a shop on the other side of town.

"Over by that Lady Fingers place," Moose grins, and reaches across the table to nudge Mike.

"A cousin, you say?" Mike asks to get away from Moose.

"Yeah, that I set up in the card business," Toad replies proudly.

"You put up money?" Mike asks, not quite believing.

"Nope," Toad says, "didn't have to. Was pitching stuff at the dump, found a shoebox full of baseball cards. Got Moose here to give a yip if he came across any other shoeboxes, and guess what?"

"You found more cards?"

"You bet. And a brand new pair of Reeboks!" Toad points to the floor and Moose sticks out a foot laced into an expensive tennis shoe that a couple years back could have been new.

"And that's what kept him in business?" Mike wonders again.

"Hell no," Toad snorts. "But every week I find at least a box more. Hell, every mother in town—"

The waitress, just coming by with coffee, blanches at the word, but Moose assures her his friend is talking about real-life mothers—housewives, "not mother fuckers, ma'am"—and she turns away without serving them.

"The mothers . . . ?" Mike prompts Toad, but knows the answer, wanting just to shut Moose up.

"Yeah, they're throwing out their kids' cards every week. And then the dads come out and buy 'em, 'cause their own mothers threw out theirs."

"The dumb shits!" Moose laughs, and Mike decides it's time to leave. But Toad is motioning him to stay.

"He's having trouble with his card show, though," the little gar-bageman confesses. "Rented the big room out at the stock pavilion, advertised it and all, counted on getting a couple dozen tables leased out."

"And?" Mike asks.

"Show's Sunday and only three are leased. It's a disaster!"

"So what should I do?" Mike wonders, anxious that he's going to be touched for something.

"Well, you're in with that baseball team, aren't you?"

Mike allows a brief smile and lowers his eyes in mock humility. "Yes," he says quietly, but not so quiet that the booth behind them can't hear, "I'm owner of the Mason City Royals. Why do you ask?"

"Well," Toad is saying, "I figure the card show's not leasing up 'cause Dolf—that's my cousin—hasn't got a draw, you know, a famous ballplayer signing autographs and getting his picture taken and all that."

"You're right," Mike says, but Toad keeps talking.

"Like Pete Rose. Boy, he'd sure draw some folks. Or that guy I saw on TV with the sex addiction, used to be with the Cubs . . ."

"You mean, oh, what's his name . . ."

"Yeah, you saw that too? But I guess the little kids wouldn't care for him."

"But their mothers sure would, the mother fucker!" Moose is chortling. "Wish we had an addiction like that, why I'd—"

"Well, can you get us somebody?" Toad asks. "Some major leaguer from this team you own?"

"It's a minor league team, Toad," Mike demurs, trying again to leave.

"Yeah, but don't some of those guys go up and down? They're always saying on TV that so-and-so's been sent back to the minors and so-and-so's being called up."

"Not to this level, Toad. We're for new players. Back and forth with the big leagues is Triple-A. We're Single-A. They gotta go to Double-A first, get it?"

"Oh . . ." Toad deflates visibly, and Mike almost feels sorry for him. But not enough to make him stay, especially as he can see the waitress starting to figure their bill. Yet Moose interrupts again.

"You got coaches, no? Aren't they in the major leagues?"

"Not now. Used to, some of them. Our guy used to be with Cincinnati."

"There you go!" Toad says brightly, reinflated and happy as ever.

"Why would he want to do it?" Mike asks.

"Dolf would pay, or give him a percentage, that's why. A good show with all the tables leased and a share for the organizer brings in thousands."

At the word *percentage* Mike has sat back down and even takes the check the waitress is trying to hand Toad. He covers it with a

five, waves away the change, and leans toward his friends.
"Maybe we can work a deal here . . ."

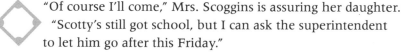 "Kenny Boyenga: yes, very interesting!" Cousin Dolf has lis-
tened closely and now starts pacing back and forth behind
his card displays. He works in the names Jeff Copeland and
Don Kruse and soon has himself in a lather. Mike and his garbage-
men pals have to ask why, and are told all the stories of their Cincinnati cut-ups.

The time they entertained the fans during a rain delay doing
belly flops on the tarp. Doesn't everybody do that, Mike wonders.
Dolf explains: this time it got out of hand, half the crowd ran down
there with them, and security had to call the police in to restore order. Then Copeland changing his name to "Erik" and going nuts
when writers called him Jeff. Kruse being tricked into pitching a
World Series game wearing mismatched shoes, something that had
been one of Copeland's weird fetishes. Story after story, all guaranteed to draw exhibitors and buyers alike, not to mention the casual
browsers who can be sold memorabilia. Plus food—folks at these
card shows will eat anything.

But how can Kruse and Copeland be obtained?

"I know an agent for these things," Dolf mutters. "He has ways."

"And what about Boyenga," Mike wonders. "He won't even get
back from the road trip 'til pretty late. What if he doesn't want to
do it?"

"Simple," Dolf says with pursed lips to indicate closure on this
topic. "You are the owner of this club. You will order him."

"Of course I'll come," Mrs. Scoggins is assuring her daughter.
"Scotty's still got school, but I can ask the superintendent
to let him go after this Friday."

"Then you can leave Saturday morning?" Lois asks.

"Yes, dear. We'll stay overnight somewhere before Chicago and
be with you in time for Sunday dinner. Won't that be nice?"

"Yes, Mama," Lois agrees. Now not just her week but all her
months of summer are secure. This is home now, she feels, and
turns back to the task of making things comfy.

At Bettendorf her husband's comfortable with his new lineup, a winning strategy that lets him call Dave Hunt to boast. With some embarrassment Dave gives him news of the card show being advertised around town.

"Of course Al's mad at Mike Jacobs," Dave admits. "But first we knew of it was from the paper, and everyone figures that to cancel now would look bad. Plus Mike says the promoter could claim damages, as he's booked some former stars."

"Stars?" Ken sputters. "For Chrissake, who?"

"I didn't get the names, just Mike ranting that this would be better than Pete Rose and Shoeless Joe together."

"Oh, that's just great," Kenny sighs, thinking of the hopeless wretches he knows who make a living peddling themselves at such affairs. And he's sworn he'd never do it himself, that he'd starve first. But now all he can do is give a weary assent and just figure on one hell of a day come Sunday.

Friday evening everything's in transit, or just about. Kenny and his team bus up to Dubuque, where Billy Harmon's charmed to find his old home team reaffiliated and dressed in bright orange Houston Astros' uniforms, since childhood his favorite colors and logo in the bigs. At Dubuque the Royals split, losing the first in a well-played game and winning the Saturday contest, a welcome turn, since it sends them back toward Mason City in a happy mood. In Huntington, Scott Boyenga has said good-bye to the two or three decent friends he's had at school and started packing for the trip to Iowa, though Saturday morning he's still remembering things here and there around his grandparents' house and is rushing to throw them into the overcrowded back seat. Finally, when his grandmother says they have to leave, no one can find his little brother Marty, who turns up under a pile of dirty clothes in the car, sound asleep.

Lois's Friday is spent with Mr. D again in the "Bob's TV" truck, picking up some living room chairs and then a washer and dryer Newt Olsen has been trying to sell since buying his wife new ones at Christmas. That surprises Lois and makes her want to ask what Mrs. Olsen bought for her husband, who she's told is an accountant: a new adding machine? But she lets it drop and accepts the appliances on loan gladly. She knows she'll need them; as generous as her folks have been all fall, winter, and spring, her mother balked at doing so much extra laundry. That had been her daughter's job, and she knows quite well Mama will not have done the boys' clothes this week while she's been gone but can be counted on to heap their dirty clothes in the trunk to be washed in Mason City. At least on Saturday she can neat things up.

Mike Jacobs, Dolf, and Toad also have a busy weekend. Mike's involved even beyond his baseball connections, since he's taken over half-interest in the show, giving Dolf $500 up front (rolled, in nickels) and the promise of another $500 for 85 percent of the memorabilia profits. On Friday they start hauling the tables Mike's borrowed from the VFW "for a ball club function" that the bartender assumes is a booster club picnic, and by Saturday they're ready to bring in the boxes of cards, videotapes, and assorted other collectibles from Dolf's stock. The rabid little dealer is quite agitated for a while, until Mike explains that since his truck's been hosed out and the compactor disconnected there's no risk whatsoever in carrying this stuff in the big blue garbage hauler's scoop.

They cart Dolf's boxes all day Saturday, and by 10 p.m. the show's set up, just as Kenny cheers his team through a four-run ninth inning to put the game safely out of reach in Dubuque, and elsewhere in Mason City Lois falls asleep early, exhausted by the top to bottom housecleaning of the home that nobody's living in but herself. In Hammond, Indiana, Lydia Scoggins finds a Howard Johnson's, her favorite on the road, and takes a room for herself and her grandsons—early enough for the boys to enjoy a butterfly shrimp dinner, let it settle, and swim in the indoor pool 'til they're tired enough for bed—almost as tired as the funny-looking bunch who've set up the biggest card show ever to hit Mason City, Iowa.

SURPRISE!

At 10 p.m. on Saturday not quite everything is quiet. O'Hare Field, for example, still has a few flights arriving, including a Delta from Atlanta with Jeff Copeland on board and a TWA DC-9 from St. Louis bearing Don Kruse. Neither has seen the other for a year and a half, and with different agents their paths would not likely cross at card shows and fantasy camps. But each of their representatives has received a call from some booker in Milwaukee saying it was imperative that both ex-players drop everything and accept prepaid tickets and a $500 advance on a card show appearance in Mason City.

"No fucking way," each man assured his agent in the same identical voice. "With the local manager, a guy named Ken Boyenga," both were told, and their tunes changed in perfect harmony: "I'm there!"

But now, just after ten, they're staring at each other's faces in front of the Mississippi Valley Airlines counter and swearing blue streaks. For a moment Kruse had been surprised and happy to find his old friend Copeland unexpectedly here at this desolate commuter gate, making a connection to a place each considered two steps past the end of the earth. But on reading the schedule board Don's face had dropped—"10:45 FLIGHT 1086 TO MASON CITY AND MINNEAPOLIS, CANCELED"—and so even before saying hello to Jeff he's cursing out everyone in earshot. Which isn't much, as at this hour it's only Copeland, the MVA agent, and a kid vacuuming the carpet.

"Canceled!" Copeland himself is raging. "What about all the people who've got to get to, ah, Mason City, and what's this, Minnesota tonight?" Jeff's somewhat blitzed from the free drinks on his flight from the South and can't read the board that clearly, plus because of the Twins he always calls the town by its baseball name.

"There's just you, sir," the agent says patiently, then sees Kruse waving his ticket. "And this gentleman. Sorry, sir," she says to the fuming ex-pitcher, "we can't take you tonight either."

"Can't take me?" Kruse erupts. "You got a 300-seat widebody out there. Whaddya mean, you don't have room."

"It's not a matter of room for you, sir," she explains. "And that's a 30 passenger Shorts 200 on the ramp, sir, our regular equipment to Mason City and Minneapolis–St. Paul. I'm afraid we've had a mechanical difficulty tonight and cannot fly."

"Mechanical my ass," Copeland interrupts. "Your problem is that you can't afford to fly that shirts or whatever you call it 'cause you got only me and this doofus here to pay!"

He gestures to Kruse, who blusters, "Who you calling a doofus, you doofus, you," and the two collapse on each other in a wrestling hold. The agent watches them give way to laughter, then waits for them to separate. When they do, she offers them coupons for an overnight stay, dinner, and complimentary drink, plus confirmed seats on the flight tomorrow morning.

"Tomorrow morning!" Kruse roars, but is overpowered by Copeland's bellowing.

"One drink! Lady, you gotta be kidding."

"It would be two drinks, gentlemen, one for each of you. But if I may say so, with your well-being in mind, it might seem you've already—"

Copeland draws up, wounded and affronted. "Listen, I'm sober as a fucking nun."

"He's right, lady," Kruse adds. "A few too many and he's barfing like a pig on expectorants!"

"A what?" the agent has to ask, laughing despite herself.

"You'll have to excuse him, miss," Copeland interjects, now the soul of politeness. "He's a country boy from Missouri." Turning to his friend he shakes him, asking, "You raised on a hog farm, Kruser?"

"Hell no!" Kruse objects. "I'm from downtown Hermann."

"Same difference," Copeland confides to the agent, then asks where's the car rental.

"Terminal 2, lower level, at the baggage claim," she says.

"Kruser, we're outta here," Copeland tells his buddy. "Miss, these tickets are prepaid, just send 'em back. But gimme an extra drink coupon."

As the Mason City Royals hold off Dubuque and the Boyenga children fall asleep to the sound of their grandmother scanning previews of movies on pay TV, Don Kruse and Jeff Copeland hit the Seven Continents Restaurant at O'Hare. They've wisely rented their Ford from Hertz first, knowing the clerk would never let a car go later, hammered as they're likely to be.

"One lousy drink?" Copeland has challenged, but then sees what the Kruser is doing to both their drink coupons and the extra Jeff conned. As the Hertz agent completes their rental agreement, Don is diddling the "One complimentary beverage" legend to read "ten," not with any attempt at deception but by boldly crossing out and initialing "JBK/MVA, ORD."

"Who the hell is Ord?" Jeff asks, and Don tells him it's not a *who* but a *where*.

"So where?" he asks again and is told right here, it's the airlines' abbreviation for Chicago.

"Huh?" he asks a third time.

"You should know that," Kruse reminds him. "Remember when we'd fly to the coast and play the Dodgers? Your baggage tag would read LAX."

"So Chicago's CHI."

"No, doofus, There's two airports here and this one's O'Hare."

"So OHA, or ORE," Copeland says firmly. "Not your ORF."

"ORD," Kruse repeats. "For it's old name, Orchard Field."

"Used to be an orchard here, huh?"

"Oh Christ, yes," Kruse says to shut him up.

By now they're almost to the Seven Continents, jumping steps on the escalator and stumbling off into the maitre d's lap.

"Gentlemen?" he asks, checking closely to see if they're inebriated beyond the room's admission standards and finding to his surprise that they're not.

"The bar, chief?" they chime together.

Sorry, drinks are served at table only. Can they just grab a table and have a tray of Margaritas? Sorry, tables are reserved for diners, who may of course order drinks with their meals.

"Then give us a table and the best food these will buy," Kruse says, pulling the meal vouchers from his pocket.

"Yes, sir," the maitre d' says, and sweeps his arm forward.

"Where the hell did you get those?" Copeland whispers. "I thought you just took the drinks," and Kruse replies he guessed they might sell them at the bar—"You know, trade 'em for a bottle we could take with us, a homer."

At the table they're given menus and told Maine lobster is the best meal their vouchers will provide, so even though they're not hungry they decide to let the waiter bring them two, along with that tray of Mexican tomato juice. And how many Margaritas would that be, Kruse is asked. He points to the ten on his first coupon and the waiter leaves.

When the huge red lobsters come neither ex-player knows what to do. For a while they ignore the intimidating beasts, then Kruse alarms the next table and frightens Copeland half to death by swatting his with the wine list.

"Jesus Christ!" Jeff shrieks, pushing himself back. "What in the hell was that?"

"He moved his feeler at me," Don informs his buddy. "You want me to lose a finger or something? Look, they don't have his claws clamped or anything, that mother could be vicious!"

"It's dead, Kruser," Copeland explains patiently, but alarms his friend nevertheless.

"Dead?" Don jumps back as if being shocked with killer voltage. "For Chrissake, get the damn thing away from me!" he yelps, and throws his knees up from the chair. They hit the table, send the plate flying, and propel the lobster past Jeff's ear, over the railing beside him, and down into the lounge twenty feet below. As Kruse gets ahold of himself and Copeland takes a deep breath after his close call with the careening crustacean, they hear a cry from down beneath, followed by some breaking glasses and alarmed shouts.

"Outta here," they say at once, throw the meal coupons on the table with a twenty for the waiter—"He's going to catch hell for serving us those Margaritas," Kruse calls to Copeland—and beat a path for the door.

"Here, chief," Kruse shouts to the maitre d', tossing him the second crumpled but unused drink coupon. "Open it up," he calls as they jump on the escalator, "it's good for ten stiff ones."

"You'll need 'em," Copeland adds, and hurries behind his friend.

Don Kruse is several steps down the moving stairway when Jeff sees him stop and start coming back. "Whaaa?" he struggles, and feels his own feet being taken from beneath him. Christ, this escalator's moving *up*, he realizes, then remembers it's the one they rode to the restaurant's balcony. Where's the down one? Not here, and as Copeland turns around he sees both the maitre d' and the waiter striding toward him.

"Move it!" he shouts to Kruse, and shoves him forward. With feet and legs windmilling the two of them race against the escalator's momentum until they come out on the floor, exhausted but happy to be away.

"Don't stop now," Copeland warns, and Kruse keeps wandering even on solid ground, his shoes still slippery from the lemon juice and melted butter that had pooled around their table. Above them the maitre d' is hurrying around the balcony to the down staircase just as Jeff sees a group of Japanese businessmen looking past the menu display as if they're ready to dine.

"Migi-no-kaidan-o ue-ni agatte, kudasai," the big ex-pitcher stops to say politely in the best direction-giving Japanese he learned while playing over there. The businessmen nod politely and turn to walk up the stairway. Hopelessly blocked and overwhelmed by requests for the soup of the day, the tuxedoed maitre d' is hung up halfway down the stairs while his two nemeses clatter from the rotunda and are quickly out of sight.

On the Hertz bus Kruse is cursing again. "No damn second tray of joy juice," he swears. "No damn homer. Jesus, how far is Mason City?"

"Mason City, Iowa," the driver responds, thinking the question's for him. "Bout 380 miles, take you seven hours or so at the federally mandated speed limit."

"Oh, we always observe mandates," Copeland leans forward to assure him. "Especially those federal ones." He gives the driver a solemn nod and then throws his arm around Kruse, muttering "five hours, easy."

After some confusion at the lot's exit the two former big leaguers are on the road again, tearing up the Northwest Tollway in an overpowered Ford Taurus at ten minutes to midnight—just about the time the Mason City Royals, showered and cologned and flushed with victory, are climbing into their bus outside the Pizza Hut on Dubuque's west side, stuffed with a deep dish each and burping from endless pitchers of pop.

As for making their destination, the Royals have a three-hour lead on manager Kenny Boyenga's old friends just now peeling out from Chicago. But their bussie will observe the speed limit, while Kruse and Copeland have something else in mind.

But not at the risk of being caught. Approaching the first toll plaza, Kruse eases his Ford in ahead of a nifty little Toyota MR-2 that's neatly packaging a pair of cute young women. "Stews," Jeff says as Don points them out, "little Iowa chicklets coming home to their mommies for Easter."

"Watch this," Kruse tells him, then rolls down his window to advise the tollway guard he's paying for his car plus the sports job behind. As they pull away Jeff cranes back to see the girls taking out a dollar and having it waved off, the booth attendant motioning toward the car ahead.

Next toll booth Kruse does the same, and by the third the stewardesses in their little car can be seen grinning and laughing as they're told once more that the way's been paid. This late, both cars move fast, but on the empty road stay within easy sight of one another, and as the fourth tollgate looms ahead Kruse announces that now they'll really make some time.

"And risk a ticket?" Copeland asks, making a dare, to which Kruse says no, just clear the road of cops.

"How?" Jeff asks again, and his old partner in crime shows him.

Pulling into the toll lane just ahead of the Toyota, Don hands the attendant a five and takes all the change without saying a thing. Jeff's about to object when he gets the point and swivels around to watch the fun.

And what fun it is. Coasting through, the young women don't even roll down their window, for the evening's chill, but just smile and wave at the guard, then gun it to catch up with their mentors. Copeland starts whooping as bells ring, lights flash, and tollway personnel can be seen darting out of their office. In a moment a pair of red and blue flashers can be seen miles ahead as a state trooper hears the alert. With the patrol car screaming past them in the opposite lanes, Kruse jams down the accelerator, Copeland lets himself be thrown back, and their Hertz rental starts testing out the top limits of its speedometer. As still other sets of flashing lights whiz past them on the other side the two guys cover fifty miles in less than thirty minutes, knowing every law enforcement vehicle on what remains of the Northwest Tollway has something other than them in mind.

As a result, the ex-pitchers are well past Dubuque and into Buchanan County by two. At this time the Royals' bus should be past Waterloo and angling up Highway 218 for Mason City, but as it happens they're sitting on the Buchanan-Delaware county line, the driver underneath, struggling to get the loosened drive shaft back in line.

At 2:30 the bussie thinks he has it, but standing out here in the cold has put the team on edge. Dave Alpert tells them, with Harmon and Wiggins agreeing, that they're still not halfway home. They've started taking the logical precautionary step when a soft whisper down the highway turns into a whistling roar and a big Ford Taurus shoots past them at what must be ninety or even one hundred miles an hour.

"What the hell?" Cap Elliott exclaims and spins around, drawing curses from Knowlton, Pete O'Connor, and Sal Nistico, who has troubles enough, struggling along out here with one arm in a sling.

"What in the hell was *that?*" Don Kruse wonders aloud as he's had to swerve a bit to avoid clipping the huge silver hulk.

"Fuckin' bus," Jeff Copeland says, laughing at what he's seen.

"What was it," Don wants to know, "an overnighter to the coast? A church group? What in the hell's so funny?"

"No fuckin' church group," Copeland laughs harder. "Fuckin' ballplayers, if you ask me."

"Why ballplayers?"

"Didn't you see it?" Copeland chides him. "All those dicks hanging out there? Musta been the whole fucking team."

◇   At 4 a.m. the rented Ford pulls up to the Mason City airport where their flight was supposed to arrive at 11:30. Except for a security light the place is dark, but taped to the door is a sheet of paper reading "KRUSE + COPELAND COME TO BALLPARK" with a rough map for the guys to follow. It brings them not just to Municipal Stadium but to a pair of interesting sights: a big blue garbage truck and a neat looking red and white DeSoto, each of them idling near the gate where some other notable cars are parked, including an even older DeSoto and a beat-up Dodge Polara straight from *The Blues Brothers*. "What in the hell is this," Copeland asks, "the Chrysler Corporation Twilight Zone?" and Kruse responds by telling him to check the head of hair on the old guy sitting in the sedan.

"So where do we go?" Copeland asks, and Kruse makes it sound like a fairy tale question or game show trick.

"That geeze in the car looks spooky, man. And he's nodded off in there."

"You're right," Copeland agrees. "Could be dead. Imagine what the exhaust system's like on those ancient wheels."

"Yeah," Kruse notices. "Look at the fins."

"A real dinosaur."

"Dinosaurs don't have fins, doofus!"

"You calling me a doofus, you doofus, you?" Copeland roars and tries to slide across the seat and sit on his friend. But Kruse is out the door and rapping on the window of the garbage truck, where Mike Jacobs snaps awake.

"Gentlemen," he says, "welcome to Mason City. I'm Mike Jacobs . . ."

"You're the guy that owns this team, huh?" Kruse asks, and is given a smug "yes." Then as Copeland struggles to get free from the center console and gearshift where he's hung himself up, Kruse and Jacobs discuss what's happened and what to do.

"I left a note when I learned your flight was canceled," Mike explains. "Figured I could meet you here."

"Yeah, sure," Kruse says, wondering about the garbage truck but giving it no mention. "So what's with the dude in that finned dinosaur over there?"

"Oh," Mike replies, "that's one of our board members, probably here to meet the players, maybe he's their ride home."

"The team?" Don asks.

"Yeah, we had a game in Dubuque tonight, but they're way late. Bet they got lost or had a breakdown."

At this Kruse lights up and calls to his friend, who's now stuck between the steering wheel and the pulled-forward driver's seat.

"Hey, doofus, those dicks you saw *were* Kenny's ballclub," he shouts, and Mike Jacobs wonders how he can speak of the team with such vulgar disrespect. But as Copeland tries to acknowledge this news they're all distracted by the commotion as he hits the dash and sets off the car's alarm system, flooding the quiet parking lot with high-pitched wails, staccato honks from the horn, and four-way flashers stroboscoping like mad.

As Kruse dives in to turn it off Mike notices that Lefty Dunsmoor's wakened in a panic, so he rushes over to assure the old man everything's OK. That accomplished, he asks him what he's doing out here, learns about the house, and hears about how Lefty's come to surprise Ken Boyenga with the good news he won't have to sleep in the office tonight or ever again.

"Where exactly is the house?" Mike asks and Lefty tells him, then says it's getting chilly and can he please roll up the window. But before doing that he asks what's going on in the big Ford and is told nothing, just some drunks who got lost.

"We're riding in the goddam garbage truck?" Copeland is protesting, plenty loud for Mike Jacobs to hear, but Kruse coaxes him out of the car. Boss's orders: the Taurus stays here, he doesn't want them on their own and getting into more trouble tonight. The big guy's quiet 'til Mike tells him to put his things in back; at this he growls "no" and pulls his bag to his chest like a grizzly bear staking claim to a salmon. Halfway across town he's still clutching it and fuming as Mike tries to initiate a conversation.

"Not much time for shut-eye," he begins, reminding them the show opens at ten. "But I've arranged a very comfortable place for you to stay."

"Days Inn," Don says, recalling the contract. "Single rooms. Tab at the bar for doofus here."

"Oh, you'll have two rooms, all right," Mike agrees, smiling at the $100 he's going to save. "And I'm sure Mrs. Boyenga can provide all you need in the way of food and beverage . . ."

"Lois Boyenga?" Copeland thunders to attention. "She runs a motel and bar out here?"

"No, no," Mike tries to sooth him. "She and her husband have rented a nice big house with plenty of room for guests. I'm sure they'll be delighted to have you—I understand you're such good friends."

"But fucking Boyenga's not even here!" Copeland roars. "Christ, he's back there a hundred miles somewhere, pissing off a bus!"

Kruse, for once more level headed, now speaks up. "You see," he tries explaining to Mike Jacobs, "Ken Boyenga is a real good friend of ours—"

"Fucking good friend!" Copeland growls, squeezing his bag all the harder.

"—but his old lady never quite hit it off with me." At this Copeland starts laughing and tells a story of how one night when old Kruser lost his keys and had to stay at the Boyengas' overnight he showed up at the breakfast table buck naked except for every piece of Lois's fine jewelry he could find, having ransacked her vanity table while she was down in the kitchen struggling with eggs benedict. "In front of their kids, too!" Copeland roars in delight.

"Hey, Marty was just a baby, he couldn't see anything," Kruse objects. "Besides, I had that heavy charm bracelet on with all his logos and uniform numbers and crap on it covering my nuts. Hell, I was decent . . ."

"Not that I heard, man," Copeland laughs, and Mike starts wondering what might happen when he shows up on her doorstep with these guys. If either of them starts pulling off his clothes, Mike decides, he'll . . . Well, it's pretty cold, so that won't happen.

◇ If anyone's worried about being naked, it's not Lois Boyenga. When Lefty said he'd wait for the bus and bring Kenny home to this great surprise, she thought a bit and then asked Mr. D if he'd mind just letting her husband off at the curb. For a moment he felt disappointed at not being able to see Ken's reaction to the new home, but then had to smile at his naïveté when he finally noticed the twinkle in her eye. Lefty must have twinkled, too, for before he knew it Lois was reaching up to give his cheek a little peck and send him back down the walk flushing as red as the fenders, trim, and roof on his 1957 DeSoto.

◇ On the Mason City Royals' bus there's one person quite worried about indecent exposure. While Billy Harmon reddens with shame and Knowlton and Elliott struggle to keep straight faces, manager Ken Boyenga stands in the aisle of the swaying bus and, driver's mike in hand, lectures his team on public urination. "What does it say in big letters on both sides and on the front of our bus?" he asks them, and only Billy mumbles an answer. "And what do you suppose those people thought when they saw you guys, the Mason City Royals, standing there hosing down the highway?" Stan Sweet raises his hand and says anyone who noticed probably realized their manager had them guzzling pop, a diuretic, rather than beer or wine, which dehydrate, but Ken ignores him. Then Jim Knowlton feels he must speak up to defend his teammates.

"Come on, Skipper," he pleads. "You're talking like it was Fifth Avenue during the fucking Christmas parade or something. For Chrissake, it was two in the morning on an empty road."

"You saw that car, Knowlton," Kenny scowls.

"Yeah, at a zillion miles an hour. You think they were counting pricks?"

"They'd never see yours, that's for sure," Cap Elliott shouts from behind, and everyone laughs.

"They sure saw Harmon's," Knowlton shoots back. "Four times

the size of yours," and Billy blushes even deeper. "Christ, you never know who's going to get a huge one," and even Kenny has to laugh.

Back in his seat with the busload of players restored to its usual level of happy chatter, Ken feels like chatting himself. And so he slides over to the aisle to share some time with his captive travel partner, the bussie.

"I should have realized," he begins, while the driver settles in for a half-hour monologue, "that whatever happened when I was playing would come around again when I managed—you know, right in my face."

"Yep," the bussie says.

"Not that we ever pissed off a bus, or next to a bus, or whatever."

"Nope," comes the automatic agreement.

"Worse, in a way. Knew some guys who'd get undressed on charters, call the stewardesses back, you know."

"Oh?" the driver asks.

"Yeah, 'cept they'd be up, not down. Isn't that disgusting?"

"Sure is." He flashes his brights at an oncoming car. "Ever do it yourself?"

"Yep," Kenny says, then launches into one of his more vile Kruse and Copeland stories. It fills the rest of the half-hour and even runs a bit longer, because the bussie can't resist asking a few questions. Finally, Ken concludes and yawns as if he'll try to catch a quick nap before they reach Mason City and the ballpark. But there's one last query from the driver.

"Ever see those guys anymore?" he wonders.

"No way!" Ken emphasizes. "Only in my worst nightmares."

There are no nightmares for Lois, who's napped peacefully after dinner and has no problem waking to the borrowed clock radio set at two, the hour Mr. D said she could begin expecting her husband. She's been wearing one of Ken's old jerseys that makes a good nightie, and for a moment considers keeping it on. But no, since their wilder years back in Chicago and even through parenthood and early middle age they've played the fantasy game where after a road trip, especially if the team had won, she'd meet him at the door nude except for one small item: a favorite bracelet, necklace, or other piece of jewelry. It was actually quite a moral idea, Kenny's testament to her that on the road he'd stayed clear of the groupies and girl friends that forced some of the other husbands to come off the plane pretending to be horny. This time their innocent little routine is even more appropriate, for she knows he's been living like a monk in that tiny cell of an office. So it's off with the jersey, on with what she knows is Kenny's favorite piece of jewelry, and into the bathroom to fix her makeup and hair.

Mike Jacobs' trepidation as they approach the neighborhood is eased a bit when Copeland starts growling "Food! Food!" and Kruse advises that it's probably best to feed him. And so half an hour is spent at the town's only twenty-four-hour Hardees while a skeleton staff order-fries a stack of burgers for the three of them. Belching his way back to the truck, Copeland seems subdued by the mushrooms, onions, and cheese, not to mention the four pounds of hamburger Mike estimates he's eaten. But as the Boyengas' street looms up ahead the garbageman/club owner panics.

"My truck will wake the neighborhood," he stammers lamely, "and I'm not legal on that street except for put out days—"

"So Ken's old lady ain't puttin' out today?" Copeland guffaws and Kruse hits him with an elbow and says to shut up.

"Can I drop you gentlemen here?" Mike asks at the corner. He calculates some numbers mastered from driving garbage routes and says it's the seventh house up. "Number 642," he says, and lets them out. "Just a minute," he calls to Kruse, then hits the lever to open the truck's big chute. "OK, there's your bag," and with a whine of gears and hydraulics it flips out onto the pavement.

"Surprise!" Lefty Dunsmoor is saying at this very minute to a bleary-eyed Ken Boyenga who's looking for Dave Hunt to open the stadium and his office. "Climb in here—you can't stay at the park, you've got to come with me." Too tired to argue or even ask, Kenny throws his bag in the back seat and collapses in front. The big DeSoto's smooth ride lulls him back to sleep as Lefty starts the quick trip across town, a fifteen-minute ride that with no lights or traffic takes hardly more than five this time of night.

"Surprise, honey!" Lois is singing sweetly as she answers the front door. She's kept the yard and porch lights off while switching on everything inside so she'll look the image of the showgirls Kenny's always passed up for her. "All for you!"

Lois throws her arms open but there's no one there, just heavy footsteps hurrying away down the walk. At the same time she hears a car door slam, followed by a mighty thud, some yelling, cries of pain, and two shouted names she hasn't heard in years. Then before she can grab her jersey or even turn away, it's Jeff Copeland and Don Kruse being pushed into the house by her husband Kenny.

"Howdy-do, Mrs. Boyenga," Kruse is saying. "Evening, Lois," Copeland offers, and "Honey! What the . . . ?" from a thunderstruck Ken Boyenga as he stands before her, wondering who to be more amazed at, her or these guys at his side. Kruse decides he'll say something, but as he's wondering what his eyes are drawn from Lois's lovely breasts to the way she's struggling to cover herself between her legs. "Can't see much, ma'am," Don finally offers, as for a moment he's been hypnotized by the elaborate charm bracelet that's almost keeping her decent.

FREEBIES

Across Mason City the players struggle home to their apartments and hit the sack, while lights burn late at 642 Magnolia Drive. Lois is back in Ken's old jersey plus a pair of her jeans and has quickly pulled on shoes and socks in a determined effort to look modest. Nobody's said a word about how she answered the door, and she's left Kenny's blurted question unanswered. She's managed just a hurried jump into the living room where she'd left most of her clothes while Don Kruse, ultimately the one to use his head, yelled "Beer call!" and asked Kenny where was the kitchen. "How the hell should I know?" was his response, perplexing Kruse even more, but Copeland, yet to be surprised by anything tonight, simply said it had to be around here somewhere and started hulking down the hallway toward the back.

Sure enough, there it was, a kitchen with a nice big copper-toned refrigerator built in. "May we?" Kruse has asked, to which Ken responds with a hospitable "Go right ahead," followed by an invitation to find a chair, something he's meant quite literally as he has no idea if this kitchen comes with chairs, counter stools, a breakfast nook, or what.

But now the guys have settled into captain's chairs around the big oak table that fills the room's dinette and are sipping their brew, happy as any group of ex-jocks in a Miller Lite commercial. When Lois comes in, both Kruse and Copeland act as if they're seeing her for the first time, while Ken behaves like he's been home for a week. That he hasn't seen her since leaving for Florida on March 5th doesn't seem a factor, any more than does the layout of this strange new house, of which he's only seen the hallway and kitchen so far. But at least Copeland and the Kruser aren't saying a word about all *they've* seen tonight, for which Ken's grateful. It's the least he can do to look like he belongs here, though the forced politeness of this strange affair strikes him as a 180° turn from his usual times with these guys.

Lois has brought them a bag of chips, which she pours into a bowl, and glasses for their beers when Kruse decides to talk a little business.

"Thanks for the gig, man," he ventures, and is joined with a "Yeah, thanks" from Copeland.

"The card show," Ken says. He should have figured, though having these characters crash into him in the dark didn't leave much time for deductions.

"First I knew doofus here was on the bill was when I saw him at the goddam airport," Kruse states, and Copeland adds, "Me too!" So how, both guys wonder, did Kenny know where to find them.

"I didn't know," he states, then adds to himself that he wouldn't want to, either. "And this is the first I've known of it, at least as far as you're concerned."

"Huh!" they chorus.

"GM tells me the show got put together by one of the club's board members. That's how I got strong-armed, plus I had to tell some players to be there as well. Hope they are—all of us were half asleep there when I gave 'em the news."

"Board member?" Kruse asks. "Don't you mean the club owner? Dude in a garbage truck?" Across the room, from where Lois is rinsing out their empties, the guys hear a sickening moan. Oh Christ, Don thinks, she's freaking out, should have figured she couldn't smooth right over that tits and ass show she gave us. But as Kenny answers his question Lois composes herself and is even coming back to the table with more beer. As she hands him his, Kruse notices the heavy charm bracelet on her slender wrist and feels himself getting aroused.

"What time?" he asks to get his mind off Lois. When he hears "10 a.m." he moans himself.

"Almost five now," Copeland notes. "Let's just party through."

"Fellas," Ken pleads, "I've got a game at three. Then back to the show 'til God knows when."

"And I have my mother and the boys getting here at however long it takes to drive from Chicago," Lois adds, the first real part she's taken in their conversation.

"That would be approximately about four hours," Copeland says, "exactly." Lois gives him a surprised look and he adds, "with Kruser at the rocket controls, that is," and she turns to her husband, who assures her it will take Mrs. Scoggins at least seven hours to make it, especially if she has to go around the city first. "How are the boys," he then asks, and as she answers both Kruse and Copeland get the feeling they're in the middle of somewhere they don't belong.

"Finish my beer, man?" Kruse asks, shoving his full can and half empty glass across the table.

"Always used to be a problem for you," Copeland states, chugging his own as he rises. Then Kruse is saying goodnight and Copeland's trying to apologize through a rapid-fire series of burps while Lois shows them to a room down the hall. "Bunk beds?" Kruse gasps, then she tells them where the extra bath is and closes the door on their mutterings.

For the next half-hour there's soft talk in both the kitchen and the boys' room. Lois tells her husband all about the house and Mr. D while he looks at her fondly, getting excited as he thinks of that little bout of exhibitionism at the door. From the hall there's Kruse's murmurings from the top bunk as Copeland tries to squeeze himself in down below.

"Jeez," the Kruser's saying, "I didn't have any time at all to react, did you?"

"Great tits," Copeland says, too loud for Kruse, who shushes him.

"I mean I didn't really focus that here was this great looking nude woman, you know?"

"Really great tits," Copeland repeats. "I mean approximately the best I've ever seen, at least in months."

Kruse tries to ignore him, but feels compelled to say more about Lois.

"But in the kitchen, you know, with her all dressed—well, I almost got a hard-on there just looking at her."

"At her tits."

"No, when she was dressed. And it wasn't anything about her body. It was that charm bracelet."

"That's all she had on before," Copeland reminds him.

"Maybe that's why," Kruse admits, and decides to drift off with this thought. But his friend has something of his own to say.

"Way she dresses turns me on. Talk about a hard-on: thought everybody'd see mine and I'd get slugged!"

"Huh?" Kruse asks with a start, his happy fantasy ruined.

"The way she dresses, man, you saw it."

"Those baggy jeans? Kenny's old shirt? Are you queer, man?"

"Not that, doofus. Those shoes!"

"Shoes?" Kruse wonders.

"Absolutely," Copeland enthuses. "One white tenny, one pink. And the socks—one green, one blue. I tell you, this lady's one freaky woman!"

At breakfast, to Copeland's disappointment, Lois has her footwear straight, though on his way out the front door he sees the other shoes and socks mixed up in a laundry basket dumped over in the living room. He'd tried to get her talking about her kinkiness, reminding everyone how he's always pitched in mismatched shoes and how Kenny tricked Don Kruse into doing that in the Series. Then the talk shifted to the card show and it was time for the guys to be off.

As their cab pulls up to the Northland Stock Pavilion Copeland gets excited again, but just about the old DeSoto convertible they saw last night and which is now double parked at the curb. In the light of day they can see it's powder blue with a creamy white canvas top, nice looking all around with even its rear plastic window still intact.

"Your players, Ken?" Don Kruse asks and is told yes. The guy struggling to get out is Sal Nistico, left field. Blocking his way is the old Dodge Polara, driven by catcher Stan Sweet and discharging second baseman Billy Harmon. Waiting at the door of the hall is the Latin kid Ken identifies as third baseman Julio Arredondo.

"Hey Kenny," Copeland asks after studying the situation for a while, "why are all your guys in slings?"

"It's my DL, what do you think it is? You think I want to waste the game today? The good bodies are sleeping off the road trip and then go straight to the park."

"What about this guy? He looks like a player." Kruse, who has been glancing around, refers to the tall kid walking in from the parking lot carrying a University of New Hampshire bag.

"Jim Knowlton, first base. Off and on concussion. Banged his head on the luggage rack last night right at the last minute—cost him his sleep this morning," Kenny laughs. Then he gets serious, yelling at Nistico and Sweet that they're parked in a handicapped zone, double parked, at that. Sweet points to Billy's shoulder and Sal, getting the message, nods quickly and indicates his. No dice, their manager says, but lets Sal go in while he takes the convertible's keys to park it in the lot. Copeland makes a note to borrow them himself for a joyride later.

Inside, the three ex–major leaguers and motley group of banged-up bushers walk to the front tables, where they find the club's self-aggrandizing new board member, Mike Jacobs, setting up a display of bats and baseballs. "Mid-Continent League, Constantine Curris, Pres.," Ken can read on the balls, most of which are already rubbed down, but he doesn't say a word. Jacobs is all smiles, pumping everyone's hand and just about sending Nistico and Harmon out of their minds in pain—only Arredondo escapes by slipping behind Mike as if they've already said hello. Then the new board member scurries off and in a moment returns with a short, sallow, and thoroughly serious individual he introduces all around as the show's promoter, this time jerking everyone's arm and catching Julio in the pain.

"Dolf Borman," Mike says to each player as the man offers a curt, single handshake. When they get to Copeland, Dolf pauses to say his offprints just arrived.

Everyone figures these are copies of a *Baseball America* interview or feature he'll be signing for the kids. He, plus Ken and Don, are shown their seats at the big front table while the others are briefed on how to circulate among the exhibitors spread around the big hall. Then Mike Jacobs beats a path to the doors and officiously directs the guards to open up.

Expecting a crowd, everyone's underwhelmed when just one kid walks in, a ten-year-old whose parents must be parking the car. Unintimidated by the draped banners and ranks of tables, he strolls up to see what's offered, stopping in front of Don Kruse.

"Wanna picture, kid?" the former pitcher asks, but is shaken off with a "naah." Copeland, however, fascinates him, and after seeing Jeff's offprint asks if he can have one.

"Sorry, little buddy," Jeff apologizes, "21 or over, only." The kid shrugs and starts to walk away.

"If you've got a big sister," the huge ex-hurler calls after him, "I can bend that a little," but the kid is gone and only Jim Knowlton's left, cruising past to wonder what's in Copeland's stapled folder.

In time others filter in, and after a while a crowd builds up. Around the room kids are fingering their way through boxes spread across the tables while adults, with more cash to spend, flip pages of plastic mounted cards and ask to handle ancient scorebooks from Ebbets Field and Shibe Park. Meanwhile Knowlton has cadged a copy of Jeff's offprint, saying it's for his sister, who's only fifteen but big for her age, and is trying to embarrass Billy Harmon by reading parts of it to him behind the stage. Above it all, Dolf surveys the assembly with a deeply satisfied smile.

In time Ken gets some autograph business as little kids pick out his Reds and Cubs cards from the bargain boxes, and eventually Copeland is able to move some offprints, even though his price range is steep: $2 plain, $3 signed, and $4 for an autograph on the customer's own piece of memorabilia. Kruse is immensely more reasonable, a flat buck for his John Hancock on anything, including his photo as provided, but he's still outdrawn by the spectacle of Copeland's bulk and grizzly looks, the Fu Manchu mustache hacked too high on the left this morning while the rest of his travel stubble's gone unshaved.

Before they notice, it's 1:30. Kruse doesn't care, but Copeland's stomach is growling and Kenny realizes he'd better
get out to the park. With a day game after a road return
there's no BP, but he wants to be sure the guys have stretched and
will be serious about infield, so he tells Mike Jacobs he'll have to
find a ride over to the stadium. No problem, Mike counsels, he's
due there himself to run the extra pop stand out in the bleachers:
it's RC Cola day with fifty-cent pop and a free baseball to everyone twelve and under. The DL guys, of course, will stay here, so
Copeland nabs Knowlton and asks him to watch his stack of offprints. "If you can get the money, go ahead and sign my name,"
he tells the first baseman, who, remembering stories from Spring
Training, is tempted to ask if the autograph starts with "Jeff" or
"Erik" today.

If anyone's been wanting a crowd, they can find it at the ballpark today, as the free baseball has drawn thousands of kids and a
proportionate number of parents. "Looks like capacity," Dave Hunt
smiles, as Mike and Kenny pass through the gates. "In fact, I'm
counting you guys too so we can break a record!" Kenny smiles
himself, knowing this is a classic general manager's trick, padding
the attendance by counting everyone from the players and umps to
the Pepsi guy each time he wheels through with a handtruck. Bet
the show is thinning out now, he thinks, and shares the thought
with Mike, who scowls. Then Mike remembers his plan for today
and grins broadly.

The plan is this: out in the walkway section between the
bleachers, where his RC stand is well out of sight of GM Dave
Hunt, board president Al Swenson, and the others busy in concessions, he's figured a way to amass his own souvenir stock for the
card show's closing hours tonight, hours he hopes will be busy, as
he's having the ushers pass out discount coupons for admission.
But that's just to get some adults at the show. Once there, he
knows they'll want baseballs like the little kids got today, and he
plans on being the one to supply them.

Has he swiped a couple cartons from the sponsor's shipment? No
way—that would be illegal. Instead, he plans to help out these kids
and even give them a lesson in incentive.

It's easy. As dispenser of the pop where most of these kids are sitting, he'll offer to give a free cup of RC to anyone who trades him a souvenir baseball—a nice looking but obvious commercial imitation where the Royals' logo shares space with a big red "RC"—and two free cups to those who chase down and retrieve an actual foul ball. These genuine numbers he'll claim were homers from last year's championship team and sell for five dollars, while the giveaways will go tonight for a buck. He hopes to get a dozen real ones and maybe seventy-five or a hundred freebies, every one of which he knows will move and put a nifty $150 or so in his pocket, all clear profit. The RC's in tanks and there's no cup count, plus with the sponsor's underwriting the pop will hardly be missed.

Back at the exhibition hall Jeff Copeland has been on a foray for food. Inside he's found a caramel corn window and then a cotton candy machine, but these snacks have only made him hungrier. A dealer tells him he can get donuts and coffee at a stand in the parking lot, and so he leaves the stock pavilion to seek it out.

There it is, a brightly painted little trailer with the legend "Tiny Tim Donuts" painted above its service window. Inside, Jeff can see a machine about the size of a movie house popcorn popper twisting and turning the dough, dropping little globs of it into a deep fat fryer, then spitting out silver-dollar-sized donuts the vendor is selling in bags. The price? Fifty cents, seventy-five if you want coffee with 'em.

"Well, I'll be!" Copeland marvels, and a man standing beside him credits his praise.

"You bet," the guy says. "Neatest little contraption I've ever seen. And a wizard at cost efficiency!"

"You don't say," Jeff replies, his interest perked. "Sure not much operator labor there."

"Or material waste. Amortize a baby like this over the ten years the Feds give you and for the last eight you'll double your profits every six or seven quarters."

"Jesus," the big ex-pitcher exclaims, "that's an 18 percent net accrual per annum, half again the food industry standard!"

"A brother of the books if I ever met one!" The guy smiles and puts out his hand. "Newt Olsen. I do Tim's accounting here."

"Jeff Copeland, glad to meet you. Not a brother yet, but I hope to be. We had a problem like this in my class last week."

"Oh, you're studying to be a CPA? Hey, that's great! But you're no kid—what else do you do?"

"Baseball coach at the same school."

"Really?" Newt brightens even more. "One I know?"

"Nope," Jeff shakes his head, "a junior college I'd rather not name, given our record. But I used to be with the Mariners and the Reds."

"Why sure," Newt laughs, "Copeland! But it wasn't 'Jeff' then, was it? You know, we've got an ex-Reds guy with our baseball team right here, Ken Boyenga."

"Yes, I know. That's why I'm here."

"Of course," Newt laughs again, all over himself in mimed apology. "For the card show! I should go in, but I'm just getting Tim's tape here on the way to the ballpark. Big game! We're giving kids one thousand free baseballs, and I have to help in the bar."

"You serve kids beer?" Jeff says in wonder.

"No, no," Newt starts guffawing again. "Kids don't get a ball unless they have a paid adult with them. About half bring Mom *and* Dad, which means . . ."

". . . an automatic 60 percent increase on your gate, having already discounted for the average daily adult crowd and factoring in the kids' admission, right?"

"More like 55," Newt cautions, "but bright boy, bright boy!"

◇ Of the thousand baseballs being given out at the park, Mike Jacobs only wants 10 percent. Fifty will fill a gym bag, so he's brought two. "Sneakin' in your lunch there?" Al Swenson's asked and Mike, offended, has frowned and turned both bags inside out before heading to the auxiliary pop stand. Once there, he finds a line of little kids already pushing each other for position, baseballs in one hand, quarters in the other. He checks the tank pressure, then sets a friendly smile on his face and gets right to work.

"Wanna RC, kiddie?" he leers. "That's seventy-five cents today."

"But Mister," the little girl protests, "you said fifty cents."

"No, I didn't." Mike puts on an affronted look and questions the kid behind her. "Did I ever say that?"

"The ad says fifty cents," he's answered.

"My parents only gave me fifty cents," the younger kid sniffles, and Mike almost feels sorry her folks shorted her.

"So," he croons, "tell you what I'll do. You just give me your baseball and I'll trade you for a free RC!"

The little girl tries to answer but can't, a tear running down each cheek.

"Come on, come on, come on," Mike pushes her—waving off her protest, through sniffles and tears, that she wants this baseball.

"You're really stupid," he finally tells her, " 'cause you got that baseball free and a pop costs fifty cents, I mean seventy-five." But she just stands there crying, so Mike reaches forward, shoves her aside, then leans back to serve the next child.

"Ball or three quarters?" he asks.

"You can have the rotten ball," the boy snarls, but Mike makes the transaction with a broad smile.

"Now you just keep that money, don't give it back to your parents," he cautions, then drops his smile to face the next customer. "Ball or three quarters?" he asks in a quick little bark.

At the card show another line of kids has formed, and though initially happier, the little ones are leaving it puzzled and confused. The crush has started when Jim Knowlton took over Jeff Copeland's table, setting aside the price list and calling out "free autographs and souvenirs here!" In less than ten minutes he's signed upwards of two hundred, and when the kids don't have a baseball, card, or piece of paper he scribbles Jeff's name on one of his offprints and gives it away. A few parents accompanying their youngsters recognize the piece and snatch it away, but more than one little boy or girl has wandered back to find his or her folks and ask "Daddy, isn't that pirate going to get awfully cold with just his boots on?" and "Mommy, how did that

lady get up on top of that sailboat? And why are her pajamas falling off?"

Meanwhile Copeland and Newt Olsen's impromptu meeting
stretches into its third bag of donuts as the pitcher-turned-
romance-writer quizzes the veteran CPA about how far to push his
publisher on serial rights, as the excerpt he sold to a shabby magazine called *Aggressive Females* has earned him almost as much as his
bonus for coming in fifth in the Cy Young voting eleven years ago,
considering what he's made peddling offprints of it.

At the ballpark Newt's being missed, as even an hour before
game time a line has begun snaking from the beer bar all
the way down the concourse and out under the stands to
where Mike's selling RC. Or buying baseballs—there's so much
confusion that the thirsty beer drinkers who've overflowed into his
territory can't really tell which. All they know is that he's been at it
since the gates opened early, half an hour ago, and that what
started with some of the kids either crying or cursing has now gone
the other way entirely, as a jostling chorus of little ones—little rag-
amuffins, to tell the truth, here on courtesy tickets the Lions Club
passed out to the area's underprivileged—crowds around the pop
stand singing out "I gotta baseball, Mister! Gimme an RC" until the
guy's awash in balls and running out of tank mix and cups.

On the field Ken Boyenga's checked everyone's stretching and
told O'Connor and Elliott, still a bit rusty since taking over the
corners, to stay in there for both shifts of infield practice. He
squeezes some additional time to hit each of them an extra dozen
grounders, and is satisfied everything's working all right. But in the
last half-hour before the game, when he likes to get his own head
together back in the privacy of his office, what starts as a request
from T.A. for more baseballs turns into a parade of people knocking
at his door to raid the batting practice bag—and, when that's depleted, begging clean ones from the boxes stacked next to Kenny's
desk.

"What the hell is this?" he's tried asking, but never gets an answer beyond maddening specifics: George Day's not happy with
the seams on those balls T.A. brought out for warmups; Grey and

Alpert lost the one they were tossing on the sidelines; Elliott's goofing off trying to throw a knuckler as he plays catch with Perez. Nothing along the lines of a general explanation, until Pete O'Connor blunders into a tip-off: Mike Blanchard's giving away baseballs as fast as Pete, his warmup partner, can fetch them from the clubhouse.

As Ken emerges from the dugout he sees an empty field. Just about every player is over along the wall. Signing autographs? Everybody, all at once? There's a passel of little kids here today, and a few of them are waving programs. But, far more than autographs, there seems to be some type of trafficking going on.

At first it looks confusing, but by keeping his eyes on a red-haired kid wearing a bright orange Houston Oilers jersey Ken is able to track the action and see what's happening. The little red-head starts out cadging a practice ball from Blanchard, then shoots like a rocket into the gap between grandstand and bleachers. In a moment he returns with a cup of pop, which he takes down the line to the Royals' bullpen. There George Day pauses from his routine of curves and screwballs to accept the drink and drain it in one gulp, at the same time flipping the Oiler kid a fresh white baseball. Then George yells over to T.A.—probably that the seams were too low—and gets a new ball from the pitching coach. By now the child is running back to the stands and emerging with two RCs, one of which goes to Blanchard, the other to Elliott, each of whom trades the boy a practice ball. One of these is handed to an even smaller red-head who puts it in a hamburger sack, while her brother scurries to the pop stand with the other.

And that's just the McNamara or O'Malley kids or whoever these siblings are, thinks Ken. There must be a dozen youngsters working this same routine. And so, uniform, cleats, and all, he follows little Pat or Mike to the source while little Siobhan is left holding the ever-increasing bag.

"Jesus Christ, you little assholes," Mike Jacobs is yelling, "gimme a break!" His pop stand's besieged by scores of youngsters waving and demanding free drinks. Kenny can see two gym bags spilling over with balls—the RC-logoed freebies from today's promotion plus others that are scuffed league balls from the BP sack. Half a dozen clean ones from George Day's bullpen warmups are stacked neatly along the counter. These seem to be the ones Mike is concerned about, for he's shouting, "New baseballs, just real ones— I'm running out of fucking pop!"

As Kenny works his way to the head of the line, Mike becomes more animated, pushing away kids with logoed and dirty practice balls and even throwing quarters back in the face of youngsters who want to buy their pop. Finally he's facing Ken, or at least Ken's uniform top, for things are too busy to take an eye off the growing row of baseballs and the sputtering pop spigot. "Great," says Mike to the manager's chest, "gimme all you got," and looks up into Kenny's withering glare. "Pop, sir?" he asks, quickly shifting gears, but it's too late.

"O'Malley!" Ken says sharply to the little Houston Oiler, who answers "Mahoney?" and is told to take over the stand here—give away the baseballs to any kids who don't have one and pass out the rest of the RC free. "Yes sir!" Mahoney responds and a dozen children around him cheer. Then Kenny grabs Mike by the collar and frog marches him down beneath the grandstand to where the concourse begins. Here, at the beer bar, a crowd of adults starts their own cheering, having seen from a distance Mike's scam and the commotion it's caused.

At the stock pavilion's exhibition hall Jeff Copeland, mustache speckled with sugar grains and donut crumbs, has taken back his autograph and souvenir table, thanking Knowlton for holding down the fort but surprised there's been no money added to the till. He's ready to start making up for lost ground, however, when a short guy, droopy jowled and giving off an iridescent green aura, slides up beside him. He's wearing coveralls, Jeff notes, and sure enough there's a little embroidered patch over his heart reading "Toad." Oh geez, Jeff thinks, another dip collector mired in arrested adolescence, but resolves to be polite.

"I'd be happy to sign an autograph for you, Mr. Toad," he offers, "if you'll just step around to the other side of the table." But instead the fat little amphibian slithers even closer and leans against Copeland's hip.

"You know, I've always fancied being a pirate myself," Toad croaks seductively, and Jeff can see he's holding a copy of the *Buccaneer Accountant* offprint that seems to be stuck to his palms.

As Copeland casts about for help, all he sees are empty tables. Ken Boyenga's gone, of course, but where's Don Kruse? In fact, where's everybody, he asks himself, as he can't even see any of Ken's players bobbing about in their dark blue caps. The whole show seems to be in a lull, as many of the exhibitor tables are covered and even that strange guy who's running things has disappeared, his lofty podium now empty and the spotlight that's been trained on his banners switched off. But some kids are still wandering around the floor, and so, to extricate himself from the pirate business with this odd character, Jeff calls to one of them, the same youngster he'd declined to sell an offprint.

"Hey, little kid," Jeff beckons, "do me a favor, huh, and I'll let you have one of these free."

"Sure, Mister!" the boy chirps eagerly, and Copeland tells him to watch the table while he looks for his friends. "And listen," he cautions in a whisper, "don't let this creep bother you about the Pirates or anything like that."

As Jeff leaves, Toad follows, and for a moment there's a funny bit of broken-field running as the big, lumbering ex-pitcher dodges among the empty tables. With a quick corner step he loses Toad at an exhibit of Brooklyn Dodger regalia, and after that it's out the door and to the donut truck—but that's closed, too, so Kruse and the guys can't be here. Then it's a muddy trip around the building to a back door, where he tries to get in. He pounds, figuring the odds of that fat little green man doubling back inside are infinitesimal.

But nothing. So he pounds again, yells that it's him, Jeff Copeland, and the door is pushed open by a Nazi storm trooper in full battle dress.

Copeland yelps and jumps back, but catches a glimpse of something short and green coming around the building and is faced with an agonizing choice. He takes the SS man and the door, which he dives through and slams behind him. Relieved from one terror, he shudders a bit and tries his best to face this new one. But there beneath the coal scuttle helmet is nothing more menacing than a big, idiotic grin—a grin he's seen as the signature of countless ballpark pranks. It's Don Kruse, now howling with glee at his friend's genuine panic.

As Jeff recovers, Kruse turns to Jim Knowlton, who's back here in this storeroom as well, and says he'd better not march out into the hall like this when the show resumes, if everyone is going to be terrorized like chickenshit Copeland here. Knowlton, however, protests that finding all this stuff back here is too fantastic an opportunity to ignore—and that if this famous major league veteran won't do it, he'll have to make an assault on the exhibition hall himself. This brings an argument from Kruse, which Copeland really can't follow for all the scratchings and pryings at the door, accompanied by soulful pleas of "Come on, you big pirate, let me in."

"*What is the meaning of this!*" Less a question than an imperative shriek, the words freeze everyone and even quiet Toad's murmurings through the door. It's Dolf, who has burst into the storeroom, seen what's transpired, and is flying into a rage. This frightens Copeland even more, but Kruse and Knowlton treat it as one more joke.

"Heil Hitler, Pop," Knowlton shouts, then kicks at Kruse, calling him a swine and rousing him to attention. Kruse complies with a stiff Nazi salute and then collapses with Knowlton into laughter.

"*This is an outrage! This is a disgrace!*" Dolf is screaming in a voice that climbs an octave with each new accusation. But Knowlton can only protest through his laughter that no, it isn't—he and Kruse were only looking for more souvenirs to put out front and blundered into this stuff. As proof, he indicates a carton labeled "1933 Championships" and pulls out a swastika flag enfolding a copy of *Mein Kampf.* Knowlton drapes the flag around Kruse's shoulders and wacks him on his helmet with the book, which sends Dolf right through the ceiling.

"*This is an insult,*" he rages, then draws himself up squarely. "*You are all under arrest!*"

With this Dolf turns on his heel and marches out. Even Kruse and Knowlton are quiet, but as Toad's scratchings have resumed

Don opens the door and the little creature hops in, full of informa-tion, and none of it about pirates.

"Gee, you fellas sure got yourself in trouble with my cousin," he sympathizes. "I never heard him so mad!"

"Your cousin?" Kruse asks.

"Yeah. I set him up in the baseball card business to get him away from all this war stuff."

"He sure has a shitload of it," Knowlton observes.

"You bet," Toad agrees. "Looks like we brought over some of the wrong boxes."

As Dolf strides purposefully across the exhibition hall to find a police officer and put this lawbreaking to an end, Kenny Boyenga continues down the concourse of Mason City Mu-nicipal Stadium on a similar mission. Kruse and Copeland rifling that stockroom and breaking into Dolf's personal treasures; Mike Jacobs ripping off the team's baseballs and ruining the kids' day at the ballpark—in each case something sacred has been violated, and the respective keeper of ritual and myth feels he must act to make it right.

As Tim reopens his donut trailer and the showgoers drift back from their Sunday dinners, they're startled by the spectacle of the local card dealer raging like a dictator in the death throes of his rule, berating a trio of policemen who seem disinclined to act on his call. At the ballpark, fans hear a clatter of spikes competing with the snivelings and moans of what sounds like a trapped and wounded sewer rat, and they turn to make way for a desperate little man being propelled virtually off the ground, his toes dan-gling and occasionally scraping the cement, in the hands of the uniformed manager. Heads pop out from the souvenir stand and concessions windows as Kenny pounds on the office door. But no one's there. Busy as the special promotion day is, everyone from the GM to the ticket manager is out somewhere vending.

"You really want to swear out charges for an arrest?" the ranking cop, a sergeant, is asking Dolf, who's finally persuaded the police to follow him back to the storeroom. The sergeant can't imagine what to arrest Kruse and Knowlton for. Was the room locked? No. Was it posted "keep out"? No. Did these fellows steal anything, or even damage the goods? No to both. So what could be the offense?

As Dolf shrieks about disgrace and dishonor, the younger of the two patrolmen draws his sergeant aside. There is an ordinance dealing with hate crimes—the city's used it to prosecute punks for cross burnings. Hate crimes? The sergeant seems confused, but only until the patrolman points to Don Kruse, decked out head to foot in Nazi regalia. Noticing their attention, Kruse draws himself to attention and gives them a lusty "Sieg heil!"

"You are under arrest," the sergeant begins reciting. "You have the right to remain silent . . ."

"Look what you've done now, you doofus," Jeff Copeland's laughing, when there's another commotion at the storeroom door and two men in suits walk in. Seeing the uniformed police, they address their questions to the sergeant.

"Jerry," the chief detective asks, "you on this Copeland case?"

"No, sir," he's answered. "We're tracking Nazi hate criminals," and indicates Don Kruse, who decides not to salute.

"OK," the plainclothesman says, totally unfazed. "We're looking for a Jeff Copeland, alias Erik Copeland, alias Gaspar the Pirate, whatever the hell that is."

At this Kruse stands up. "There's your man, officer," pointing his SS colonel's baton at Jeff. "Watch out, he's dangerous."

"Is this the guy, ma'am?" the detective now asks, turning to a woman and little boy waiting outside the door.

"Johnny?" the mother asks her son, who says yes.

"All right," Copeland's now told, "you are under arrest. You have the right . . ."

Jeff is flabbergasted, then sees what the other plainclothesman is holding: the cover and stapled pages of his offprint. Knowlton's seen the same and is slipping away. Kruse is leaving, too, hand-cuffed to the younger patrolman, but little Johnny stops him with a request.

"Can't sign an autograph, kid," Don shrugs. "I'm cuffed." But that's not what the little boy wants.

"Hey Mister," he begs, "where did you get all that neat stuff?"

At the ballpark Ken Boyenga's had no luck finding Dave or
Al or anyone responsible for the club. Nor are there any
police officers around. The only uniforms he sees are brown,
those of the rented security men, so that's where the manager
turns.

"I can't make an arrest, sir," the guard tells him. "I only have
powers to detain a suspect 'til the police arrive. And I'm really not
supposed to get involved in things on the field."

"This isn't on-field," Kenny says, but the security guard, staring
at the manager's uniform and cleats, mentions the trouble last
week when his partner wound up slugging an ump. "I was out
of the game by then," Ken reminds him, "and I'm not in the
game now. There *is* no game now," he says, gesturing at the field
where he can see Dave Hunt with a microphone introducing the
sponsor.

"OK," the guard allows, "but what's your problem with this
guy?"

As Kenny sets Mike down, the board member gets his collar
loosened and breath back, and before the manager can say anything more he launches into a violent verbal attack.

"I'm Mr. Jacobs," he announces with a gasp, "and I'm the owner
of this club. I'm your employer, Badge Number 18, and I order you
to arrest this guy here, who robbed my RC stand and gave away
my baseballs and kidnapped me and caused these lesions on my
neck and . . ."

Mike's waving his hands, ripping open his shirt to show off the
scrapes, and is starting to foam at the mouth from all this excitement when he suddenly finds himself wearing handcuffs.

"Eighteen to base," the guard's now saying into his radio, while
keeping an eye on Mike. "Request support from Mason City PD,
please, and send a flash to sixteen to get over here. I'm in Section
W, on the aisle. Got a dangerous nutcase here." He sees Mike struggling with the cuffs and punches his call button again. "Tell the PD
to bring a straitjacket, please. Eighteen out." And now both he and
the manager struggle to restrain a completely hysterical Mike
Jacobs.

Within twenty minutes two police cars and an unmarked detective vehicle are making their way to the station, bearing respectively a handcuffed Nazi, a bound and gagged garbage man gone totally berserk, and a big, goofy-looking guy the desk sergeant will find it hard to believe is a child pornographer.

It makes for quite a day at the Mason City Police Department, but not to the exclusion of routine work, for as the unit with Don Kruse heads into town, the patrolmen notice a rookie friend writing up a ticket at the intersection of Seerley and Fourth. "That's Crownfield," one of them tells his sergeant, who slows to make sure everything's OK. "He can handle it," the younger cop says. "Not like he's trapped a Nazi or something," and they all laugh, even Kruse.

Patrolman Crownfield doesn't see his buddies pass, concerned as he is with the wealth of violations that hardly fit in the space allowed on one ticket: 38 in a 25 zone is what he's pulled the vehicle over for, and while he's at it a broken tail light. But the driver has been unable to produce either a license (it's been forgotten) or registration (it's a son-in-law's car), plus there's no outside mirror and the back seat's piled to the roof with dirty laundry. Those are just the writable violations. There are some questions he has about the driver's story, such as, If she's from West Virginia and her son-in-law lives here but works out of Kansas City, then why does the car have Ohio plates?

"I'm very sorry, ma'am," he apologizes, genuinely pained, because the woman and her little grandsons have been so polite, "but as you're out of state with neither license or vehicle registration I will have to accompany you to the police station so my sergeant can run a check."

"Can't you do that from your police car, sonny?" she asks. "Our troopers in the mountain state do that all the time."

"Again, I'm very sorry, ma'am," Patrolman Crownfield explains, "but our only cruiser with an onboard terminal is on call to the ballpark. That should have been my call, too," he adds, thinking that it's her bad luck he didn't miss her, "but my unit doesn't have a straitjacket, either, which the other does."

"A straitjacket!" the woman exclaims. "I hope there's no trouble. That's where my son-in-law might be!"

"No problem with the ballpark, ma'am," she's assured. "Dispatcher said it was a nutcase having some kind of seizure. Didn't hurt anybody, and he won't hurt himself in that jacket. Supposed to be the owner of the team."

"Oh," she sighs with relief, "that's not Kenny."

"Now if you said he was a Nazi hatemongerer or a kiddie pornographer," the rookie patrolman says to be funny, "we might have something for you."

"Oh no," she laughs, "my Lois would never be involved with anyone like that!"

PITCHERS

Here it is, only the second home game of the season and Ken Boyenga's had to have his pitching coach manage both of them. But at least the umps haven't run him again, a danger, because they're the same crew as before. So Tim Anderson should have no trouble putting this one in the bag.

The game starts routinely, with little for T.A. to do. But in the second inning George Day, who had the worst pregame warmup of his life, falls off the mound with a groin pull. So it takes forever to get a new pitcher ready, and the stands—filled for a soda pop promotion—get restless in the Sunday afternoon sun.

"For crying out loud, what's going on out there?" The complaint, loud enough for half a section to hear even in this packed and noisy park, comes from club president Al Swenson, sitting in his favorite spot three rows above the boxes in the grandstand. Though the game's less than half an hour old he's already had twice the beers he'd normally drink during a full game, for general manager Dave Hunt has asked him to test the new idea of a sixty-ounce pitcher, part of the plan to increase sales while reducing traffic to the bar. Al's been asked to see how long the brew stays cold, but so far there's been no way to tell, as board member Rick Dillon has poured himself two refills and Al has polished off the rest. As a result, the delay on the field has prompted more than a little grousing from the president, who usually saves his opinions for the later stages of the game.

"Oh Christ!" Tim Anderson has sworn at about the same time, dismayed at how poorly Roberto Moreno is warming up out here on the mound as opposed to in the bullpen, as befits his role of reliever. But after ten minutes of awkwardness, he faces his first hitter, gets him out on a weak ground ball, and everyone's happy, including Al Swenson up in the stands. In fact, Al has flagged down Dave Hunt to ask for his own relief pitcher, turning the sixty-ouncer upside down to show it's dry. So on both fronts everything's back under way.

The game proceeds in easy rhythms, punctuated by occasional men on base and great camaraderie in the grandstand. Everyone's happy, especially Al, who has been pouring plenty for friends and is on his seventh draw himself, though he has no way of knowing it. The only evidence of action are some goose eggs up there on the scoreboard and the abstraction of his seemingly bottomless beer pitcher being passed around like a new baby at the family reunion.

Punctuations in the action come when either side misses a play. In the fourth inning, Mark Wiggins comes up with the bases loaded, tries a squeeze, and sees it broken when the runner on third bolts too soon and slides home right into the tag. Up in the stands Al Swenson, accepting a third pitcher from Rick Dillon, hears the commotion and swings around.

"What'd he do?" Al asks, then sees the umpire's right arm pointed up from the dust cloud at the plate and starts bellowing. "For crying out loud," he yells, not knowing if he's more angry at the ump for making the call or at the manager for risking a squeeze. Rick Dillon, trained official that he is, tells Al the tag was made, but that just makes Al change the subject.

"Where'd you get this?" he asks, gesturing with the fresh pitcher, and is told that the bartenders have opened a case of them and are now selling to the crowd, a flurry of inquiries having been made when Dave's trip with the last one drew so much attention. "Hell," Al disagrees, "everybody's just seeing me having a good time for once in my life and they're jealous." Getting a laugh, he hands the pitcher to a VFW friend nearby and asks what the bar's charging. "Five bucks?" he laughs, and pulls out a bill with instructions for Rick: "Hell, go get another!" Meanwhile Dave Alpert, hitting behind Wiggins, lines into a double play, catching Bill Grey off first. "What'd he do?" Al yells, swinging around, nearly capsizing his friend's new pitcher.

Updated on what the inning's strategy has been, Al is anything but calm.

"That damn Boyenga!" he thunders. "Where the hell's his head at?"

"Probably where his body is, boss—and don't end a sentence with a preposition." It's Newt Olsen, up from the beer bar to warn the president that these pitchers are gong faster than prudence would dictate.

"And where the hell is that?" Al demands, indignant but curious.

"Somewhere with the cops," Newt testifies.

"For goddam crying out loud," Al blusters, slamming his hands down and sending the full pitcher next to him splashing across the people in front. "Oh holy Christ," he moans, "folks, I'm sorry," and pulls out his handkerchief to begin mopping up.

At the Mason City Police Department Sergeant Gordy Todorov is getting ready to book the suspects his radio calls say are coming in. It's the ballpark one that bothers him the most—nutcase in a straitjacket, accompanied by the field manager, who's pressing charges. Years ago Gordy used to moonlight as the stadium cop and would pride himself on how nothing ever went wrong. The club's shift to private security still rankles him, especially since the same outfit, Beacon, has a man at the baseball card show, to which two other units have been dispatched. As if this isn't enough, the dispatcher calls him over to read what the crime-check computer is saying about a routine registration and license check.

"Lordy," Sergeant Todorov says when he looks at what's being handed him. "A full page!"

"And still coming," the dispatcher replies, turning back to his printer and surveying all the data being punched out. "Driver says she's on her way here from West Virginia, but all this stuff's about trouble in Ohio and Kentucky."

"Well, I guess she's been leaving quite a trail," Todorov surmises. At least, he thanks God, she's not part of this baseball madness that's spread from the Stock Pavilion to Municipal Stadium and maybe Cooperstown by now.

As the ballpark's growing center of attention, Al Swenson is in no more control of himself than when surrounded by beer cans at the end of an especially vexing board meeting. It's now the bottom of the sixth, the Peoria Rangers are ahead, Mark Wiggins is up again, and his most towering homer in two seasons has just been called foul. For this, Al's run down through the boxes to the screen, where he's pushed past two scouts to start hollering at the plate ump just twenty feet away.

"For crying out loud," he begins, "what're you guys trying to do to us?" This the umpire ignores, or probably doesn't hear at all, trained as he is to disregard individuals. But then Al yells some more and gets folks in the crowd with him, something that has to be noticed. Finally, emboldened by the fans' support and fueled by beer fumes percolating up from his belly, he makes a mistake and gets a little vulgar. Loud as he is, and apparent to anyone who's seen the program photos that he's club president, Al has put the umpire on the spot. There's one more burst of grating insults and then the plate ump calls time, walks over to the screen, and gives Al Swenson a quiet but firm warning.

He sits, but only to complain to the scouts, whom he thinks he knows from previous visits. These guys are as good as umps at zoning out distractions while letting fans seemingly talk their ears off. So for almost an inning Al is distracted and also kept away from the brewskis. Once in a while he'll glance back to make sure his friends are having enough fun without him, all the while presenting his case about how poor this umpiring is. There are, in fact, a few more debatable calls, mostly on low strikes, but with the increasingly boisterous stands in full voice Al sees little need to add his own two-cents' worth.

Then the Rangers get two on, Jim Hiduke comes in to relieve Moreno, can't buy a called strike to save his life, and Al Swenson's on his feet, against the screen, letting loose with his most colorful language of the day.

This time there's no tolerance, as the plate umpire walks right over and speaks his piece. It's said quietly, but gestures make it clear that Al's being shushed and ordered back to his seat. Yet with the crowd egging him on, particularly the tanked-up crew out in the bleachers just around the corner from the beer bar, there's no way he can let himself be shown up. Now, with the umpire waving him back, he has to do something or look even more foolish.

A round of cheers from the bleachers rouses him to action. Seems like a hundred plastic pitchers are being waved out there, saluting him as a hero, so he turns from the screen, climbs back through the scouts, and makes a beeline for the cheap seats and cheering drinkers. Hey, he tells himself as the section sees him coming and bursts into applause, these are my people! In a minute they're opening a space for him in the first row, right in front of the dugout gate, where he now takes his seat like privileged royalty. A moment after that he's flanked with two pitchers and a freshly filled cup he drains in a single tip, eliciting further cheers.

As the beer bar's swamped with yet another rush, Newt Olsen stops to complain more vehemently than ever. "That's keg number twenty," he says to the college kid who's just rolled it out from the cooler to the tap.

"Awesome, man," he's told in response.

"But that's twice the guidelines both the league and the distributor recommend for prudent sales."

"Capacity crowd, man," the kid argues. "Place is jumping!"

"I'm figuring capacity, and not even counting that half the total's little kids. I'm telling you, we gotta shut this off!"

"And start a riot, man? Hey, you're out of touch!"

Actually, the rush is followed by an interval of quiet while the Rangers bat and do nothing to increase their lead. But then the crowd comes alive with the Royals up, and soon T.A.'s guys have two on base with nobody out. And who's up but Mark Wiggins, cheated on both a squeeze play and a homer today. What else can the umpires do to him?

As Wiggins strokes his bat and the pitcher looks in, the crowd starts a rhythmic clapping and stomping that grows until the whole stadium rocks and shivers with excitement. Al Swenson's on his feet, leading his section in cheers that sound terrifyingly primeval, while the opposite bleachers echo them in a staccato effect that must be driving the Rangers' hurler crazy, caught as he is in the middle. Undoubtedly so, for he sends one in medium high and level, a batting practice fastball Wiggins cranks on a line out to deep left-center field.

Barry Gifford, getting a late start from second when the center fielder decoys a catch, is rounding third when the left fielder makes his throw. It comes in perfect, nailing Gifford at the plate. Meanwhile Ray Mungo's raced past second to third and now hesitates as the catcher braces to make a throw. It goes to third. Mungo reverses course, and after three tosses back and forth he's caught in the rundown. But at least Mark Wiggins makes it safely to second, so all is not lost.

But then it is. Heeding a call from the dugout, Peoria's shortstop throws the ball over to first. There the umpire points to the bag and then to Wiggins, signaling him out. A triple play, and on an appeal!

As Mark tries to argue and the Rangers start trotting in from their positions, the crowd erupts. The right field bleacher gang sitting over the bag at first is particularly incensed, for no one saw Wiggins even come close to missing the base, and their anger wells up collectively, like that of a huge beast. There's so much pulsing energy that something has to give, and in a moment it does, as from the seething mass is expelled one individual, who pops through the gate, runs out onto the field, and waves his arms to the heavens: club president and chairman of the board Al Swenson.

There's commotion at the station house as well, where three cruisers, an unmarked car, and the unverified auto being brought in by Patrolman Crownfield all line up outside the door. Sergeant Kutnik calls in for some supervision and assistance for the unloading. Everyone except Sergeant Todorov and the dispatcher come out for the show, even Captain Newby, still sleepy from his Sunday dinner and not quite ready for all this excitement on the normally quiet second shift.

What Newby sees shocks him into wakefulness, for being escorted into the station are a wiry little guy bound in a straitjacket whom he recognizes as one of the area's private garbage haulers, a baseball player in full field dress, a clumsy looking lug stumbling in with the detective squad, looking like a Mexican bandit being rolled out of bed, and—he has to blink his eyes to believe it—a Nazi storm trooper actually trying to goosestep between Kutnik and one of the rookies.

"Lord preserve us," Captain Newby sighs, lifting his eyes to the heavens. But looking up reminds him of the third floor windows across the street, where in the offices of TV-7 a videocam is kept trained on the department's entrance night and day. It's there to give the interns practice with the equipment and to catch the one-in-a-million event that might yield film at 6 and 10 and, if sensational enough, something to feed the network. Newby's eyes, trained to catch the slightest movement, see plenty of it at TV-7, where not just the interns but the evening anchor herself are rushing to check the camera. "Holy hell," the captain now changes his tone, "they've hit the jackpot today!"

Inside at the desk, Sergeant Todorov begins logging each subject and noting who's the complainant: the Mexican bandit's in on a sworn warrant, but the aggrieved are here in person for the Nazi and the nutcase, so he calls a clerk for each to take their depositions. Then, after getting confirmed ID's from each of the three suspects, he has his own clerk show them to the room where a records specialist will mug-shoot and fingerprint them. But first he has words for the arresting officers.

"Is yo-yo here safe to unjacket?" he asks the patrolman who holds him, and is told yes if there's going to be an extra officer at his other side. Then Sergeant Todorov turns his attention to the detail escorting Storm Trooper Kruse.

"Kutnik!" he says sharply. "I could expect it of these rookies, but not you!"

The arresting officer looks confused. "Huh, Gordy?" he stammers, "Whatsa matter?"

"Look at your prisoner."

Kutnik does, then turns back to face the desk.

"Jerry, you moron," Todorov almost rages, "your prisoner's armed!"

"Oh Christamighty!" Kutnik gasps and lunges for the pistol

strapped to Kruse's belt. It's a 7-millimeter Mauser, ugly and frightening as sin once the flustered officer lays it on the desk.

"Where'd you get this, buddy?" Sergeant Todorov asks, fingering the pistol after he's checked its clip and cleared the chamber.

"Where do you think, chief?" Kruse answers, cocky as ever. "Same place I found these glad rags. Man, there were crates of 'em!"

"Of weapons?" Todorov asks with great interest.

"You bet. Looked like some rifle grenades and land mines, too."

Todorov looks down, asks his clerk where's the original complaint, reads it, and calls out the name.

"Dolf Borman!" and Dolf steps forward.

"Is that Adolph?" the desk sergeant asks.

"Yes," Dolf answers, "with an *f*."

"OK," Todorov grunts, making a note on the paper, then looking back to Dolf. "Mr. Adolf with an *f* Borman," he says, "you are under arrest. You have the right to remain silent . . ."

"Kenny!" Puzzling over this scene and wishing he were back at the ballpark managing, Ken Boyenga is startled by the voice, and with even more surprise swings around to see his mother-in-law being led into the station. "Daddy!" come the cries of his sons right behind here, Marty scarcely visible beneath the big blue hat of the policeman bringing them in, a cop who looks (and is) closer in age to seven-year-old Scotty than to Ken.

"Ma!" Ken struggles to say in the confusion, using the term she's always wanted him to call her and which through all these years he's resisted. But now he's caught completely off guard. "What *are* you doing here?" he blurts.

She's about to answer but at the sight of Kruse and Copeland stops.

"I was going to ask you that same question," she replies. "But I think the first thing I want to know is when you started hanging out with these gentlemen you promised my daughter you'd never see again." She gives Kruse a particularly sharp look and adds, while fixing him with a disapproving stare, "I always thought it would turn out something like this."

"And you!" she continues, unable to stop and deciding to pick on

Copeland next. "Haven't you *ever* learned to shave right? And look at those shoes!"

Everyone looks down at Jeff's feet, one of which sports a tenny and the other a wing-tipped Florsheim.

"Just was in the mood, ma'am," he says, glancing down himself and scuffling the shoes from side to side. "Nice to see you."

"Yeah, nice to see you, Mrs. Scoggins," Kruse adds, and boosts Marty, who's been pulling at his Wehrmacht gearbelt, to his hip. "And the boys. Haven't seen the little one here since he was buck naked and crawling."

"Daddy!" Marty now sings with glee. "Where'd you meet this neat guy?"

Scott, meanwhile, is running his fingers down the stocks of the tac squad's shotguns, chained and racked at the door. "Hey Grams," he says to Mrs. Scoggins, "this is the best trip ever!"

◇ Al Swenson's trip out onto the field has landed him at first base, where he pantomimes the ump's call with exaggerated gestures that carry the full weight of crowd hostility. At least the umpires know who he is. Anyone else would have been nabbed by park security, but Dave Hunt has been summoned from where he's running the RC stand, and his first order of business is to locate his guys from Beacon and have them focus on the crowd, not Al. Dave himself stands there at the dugout gate that his president's bolted through, making sure no one tries to follow. Al Swenson remains the umpires' problem, one of the more unique ones they've yet to face in a game.

They start out trying to be respectful. "Would you please return to the stands, sir?" the crew chief asks, but Al doesn't even hear him.

"For crying out loud," he's shouting, and—realizing that even his bellowing won't carry to the noisy, overcrowded grandstand and bleachers—acts everything out in broadly played gestures.

"Sir, would you please sit down?" the second ump requests, but Al can't hear him and wouldn't listen anyway.

"For crying out loud," the president repeats, "can't you dimwits call a game straight? Whadda we have to do, tag each bag twice? Whadda ya want, ha?"

To demonstrate his point and play it up to the crowd Al scampers down the basepath to first, where he stops, stands on the bag, and jumps up and down before proceeding a few steps toward second. Seeing that the umpires haven't followed him but are still waiting where he entered the field, Al retraces his steps, kicks the bag, and readdresses the skeptical men in blue.

"Whadda we have to do," he now asks, "get down and beg when we tag?" Again a demonstration, falling to his knees and beseeching the bases ump with arms upraised. The crowd goes delirious.

This could be trouble, the crew chief tells his partner, eyeing the stands and worrying at the commotion. And so while the second umpire continues trying to reason with Al, the first one walks over to the Royals' dugout.

"Anderson," he calls, and T.A. steps out. "I know that's the club president, but he's inciting the crowd. It's gotta stop, but if my partner and I try to haul him off all hell's gonna break. So listen: get him outta here, OK?"

T.A. would like to help but is at a loss what to do.

"Who's your most popular player or two?" the umpire asks. "Get 'em out here with you, let the fans see some good guys clearing wacko here off the set."

"Popular?" T.A. protests. "This is just our second home game. And it's a promotion, crowd is here for the freebie, they don't know the players from beans."

"Guys from last year?" the ump suggests, getting desperate as he hears the crowd roar and glances back to see Al bent over, miming a kiss to his partner's behind. "Come on—anyone!"

"Alpert, Wiggins," T.A. calls to the bench. "Out here!" In single file the little procession makes its way across the plate and down the line toward first, where the second ump has tried turning to walk away, only to have Al scoot after him like a tin can tied to a dog's tail.

By the time the rest of them catch up Al is down on all fours, nose to the ground and tracking the ump like a bloodhound. The fans are cheering, some of their howls sounding like a pack of hunting dogs at bay, when the action stops and there's a momentary quiet. Al's now standing up and wondering what to do, when the plate ump approaches from behind and taps him on the shoulder.

"Whazzis?" Al sputters as he swings around, and—suddenly confronted by what looks like a hostile gang—punches out wildly. Too wildly to hit anything, really, except the ump, who ducks right into it and is felled by an uppercut to the jaw.

"Sergeant Todorov!" the dispatcher is calling excitedly. "Call for assistance from the ballpark: an assault. And my last free squad is at an accident, personal injury, I can't take 'em off that!"

"Kutnik!" Sergeant Todorov calls in turn to the processing room. "Finish with the bunker crowd later. Take your cubs and get out to Municipal Stadium, lights and siren." In a flash Sergeant Kutnik and his squad are out the door, running past the little Boyenga boys, who chorus, "Neat-o!"

Kenny himself is now at the desk asking what's happened at the park, but Sergeant Todorov regards him with suspicion. This Ken doesn't catch, but when he says it's time to be getting back there himself the sergeant tells him he's not going anywhere. Instead he's asked the spelling of his name and his local address.

"Christ, why?" Ken protests. "My wife just rented, I don't even know the street name. I only saw the place last night at something like four in morning."

"All right," Todorov grunts, and checks a box on his form reading "no known address" but crossing out letters and adding others to say "does not know address." Then he looks up to Kenny, says he's under arrest, and begins reading him his rights.

"What's this?" Kenny chokes.

"All right, hold that," Todorov says as he stops reading. "You're right. I should ask you this first: are you the owner of a yellow Oldsmobile Cutlass, vehicle number AH7024D1893? Registered to Kenneth L. Boyenga, 4612 Usinger Drive, Willow Springs, Ohio?" Ken says yes, and the sergeant begins reading a long list of unpaid tickets and traffic citations, some of them from across the upper Midwest yesterday and today, others dating back to Covington, Kentucky, four or five years ago. The Kentucky offenses are the worst, and these Ken immediately questions.

"Unpaid bar bill and subsequent sexual assault," the sergeant repeats. "That last is the arrestable one. Charge got buried in the traffic warrant, that's why Kentucky never came after you."

"Huh?" Kenny asks, deeply confused.

"Commonwealth of Kentucky doesn't reciprocate traffic with the State of Ohio," Todorov advises, then smiles. "But they do with us!"

"Sexual assault?" Ken now questions, getting to the serious part.

"Says here you parked your car in a handicapped zone, had an expired license tag, dodged a bar bill, and sat on a waitress. Also stole one of her shoes."

"Copeland!" Kenny shouts. "That moron borrowed my car . . ."

"Doesn't have a name here," the sergeant confides. "All they got was the license number. 'Fraid you're the one who has to answer, buddy. Now let me continue. You have the right to remain silent . . ."

Sergeant Kutnik and his rookies highball it to Municipal Stadium but once there find everything in order. All that remains, in fact, is paperwork: taking down a complaint of assault and battery from one Roger Hardman, umpire, Mid-Continent League, as aggrieved by one Albert Swenson, electrician and owner, Swenson & Son Electric, acting in the capacity of president, Mason City Minor League Baseball, Inc. Injuries sustained: none. So why are charges being pressed?

"We're going to call this game a forfeit," the ump explains to the officers, "and we need an escort to get us out of here alive."

"Yeah," his partner agrees. "I think we'd all feel safer down at the police station."

FLYING HOME

As Sergeant Kutnik brings his people in, another person makes her way to the Mason City Police Department— Mary Rohrberger, city attorney, who, because of the backup in processing and the department's inability to hold this motherlode of suspects, has been asked to stop by. Sunday or not, she can review the charges and make at least a preliminary decision on those she might want to prosecute, so that some can be held for arraignment and the others released.

Rohrberger's work is quick business, a reckoning based on how supportable any of these charges could be if brought before a judge. Nearly all of it takes place in the privacy of Captain Ted Newby's office, though there is one moment when she asks to take a peek at Storm Trooper Kruse. In half an hour she has the day's work of the Mason City Police Department reviewed, and Captain Newby is not about to argue with her thinking. For the convenience of Sergeant Todorov and his paperwork she disposes of things alphabetically.

Adolf Borman—no firing pin in the pistol, no catalogued evidence of other firearms or weapons, no suspicion of illegal sales: no basis for prosecution.

Kenneth Boyenga—outstanding vehicular violations referred to traffic division, warrants to be issued if fines unpaid after five working days; nonvehicular charges referred back to Commonwealth of Kentucky in lieu of positive identification.

Jeffrey Copeland—materials distributed do not meet local guidelines for obscenity: no basis for prosecution.

Michael Jacobs—purportedly stolen items (baseballs) not removed from premises, charges of theft not filed by property owner (Mason City Minor League Baseball, Inc.): no basis for prosecution.

Donald Kruse—no public statements made that would enflame hate: no basis for prosecution.

Albert Swenson—alleged assault took place on an athletic playing field involving professional personnel: not jurisdiction of Mason City legal authority.

"Thank you," Captain Newby tells Ms. Rohrberger, who asks for a copy of the photo of Don Kruse in his get-up as filed with the mug-shots—"for my nephew, who's a World War II nut."

"Fun's over," Sergeant Todorov tells the roomful of former suspects who've been waiting at the fingerprinting apparatus for processing.

"What Nazi?" asks Sergeant Kutnik, on his way back out to his patrol car when excitedly approached by TV-7's Dan McCool, the blow-dried pretty-boy reporter who's come over with a camera crew, lights, and a battery of microphones. The network, thrilled with the tape from the police department steps, has told him to make his interview look like a big press conference. There are some folks McCool recognizes coming out the door—Ken Boyenga, Al Swenson, and a goofy-looking guy he thinks he remembers as Jeff Copeland, or was it Erik Copeland, from the old Cincinnati Reds. But no Nazis, just as the sergeant says, so he gets some film of the baseball figures he knows. Kruse, meanwhile, is being hustled out the back door with Dolf Borman, who's carrying the 7-millimeter Mauser himself and urging Don to be careful with—and respectful of—the uniform.

Sergeant Kutnik's patrol car takes the first group back to the ballpark, while a detective hurries Dolf and Kruse to an unmarked vehicle for the trip back to their card show. Both places turn out to be ominously empty, the baseball game having been forfeited and the card show swept of kids by angry parents shocked by the proliferation of Jeff's offprint. But Don's clothes are still in the storeroom, and he pleases Dolf by not only packing away the uniform so carefully but giving it a formal Nazi salute before closing the box. "You know," the card and memorabilia dealer confesses to him, "you would have made a very good German soldier." When

Kruse raises an eyebrow at this Dolf continues: "Yes, if there had been just a few more like you . . ."

At the ballpark there's not much said. The only person still around is Dave Hunt, and Al Swenson stays well out of his way. But the forfeit, already faxed to Boston and from there sent on to both the league and Kansas City, has elicited some electronic responses from the Royals' farm director. Dave's read them already, wondering at the repeated phrase "horsefeathers," and hands them silently to Ken. It's not a pretty story, consisting as it does of questions Ken would rather not have to answer.

Why was the game declared a forfeit? Why were theft charges made against a Mason City board member for their own equipment? Why was Ken involved in a commercial promotion on the day of a game without obtaining permission from the farm director's office? And—here's where "horsefeathers" keeps appearing— why is ABC News calling with questions about their minor league manager's association with the Nazi party?

Concluding the message are some instructions Ken doesn't like any better: to reply in writing by return fax, then await instructions on an impending meeting at Royals Stadium, Kansas City. It's signed "Tom O'Reilly, farm director."

"Can I use your typewriter?" Kenny asks and Dave says sure, leaving him to face the music alone. And music is all it is, a little "ding" as the message is sent out and then, an agonizing half-hour later, a loud "ding-dong" as the machine signals O'Reilly's reply. Dave's heard the bell as well and has stepped back into the office to check the news, which is the least pretty of all.

"Can you book me a flight for sometime tomorrow?" Ken asks and Dave says sure, asking what's up. "O'Reilly wants me in his office by four. T.A.'s in charge of the team for now; you might give him a call."

"No problem." The GM steps aside for Ken to leave the office, but Al Swenson's standing in the doorway, blocking the way. Flustered, the president steps to his right just as Kenny moves left. Then a moment later both go to the opposite direction, blocking each other's way again. Finally Al blusters, "For crying out loud," grabs Kenny by the arm, and pulls him into the stadium concourse, now deserted except for some empty popcorn boxes and program inserts blowing in the wind.

"Listen," Al begins, uncomfortable now that the two are alone. "I made a real horse's rear end out of myself today. And if that adds to your trouble in Kansas City, I'm terribly sorry for it. Listen," he says while shuffling a bit. "Lefty Dunsmoor is willing to talk to old Tom—O'Reilly, our boss—about my end of it, at least. But not if you don't want us butting in."

"Well," Ken says, pausing to consider this board president he scarcely knows, "why don't you let me see how things go down there, and if I need Mr. D's help . . ."

"Mr. D?" Al says to himself—something must have been going on here, no wonder Lefty spoke up. But he shrugs it off with an "OK," gives the manager a little punch on the shoulder, and then leaves.

Kenny's wondering how he'll get home when an answer materializes: Mike Jacobs, lurking in the shadows like the cat who ate the canary. Now, like a grade school pageant actor getting ready to speak his lines, he draws himself up to face the worry-worn manager.

"Quite a day, huh?" Mike says for openers.

"Oh, nothing unbearable," Kenny replies.

"'Course not," Mike now beams, "you big league guys are tough!"

Kenny thinks for a moment of the fellow ex-major leaguers he's dealt with today, then lets the thought pass.

"Listen," Mike says, all seriousness. "Between the trouble with the show and that misunderstanding about my baseballs I guess you could say I caused a lot of your trouble today." Mike waits for a response, but Kenny just stares. "So I want you to accept my humble apology for contributing to your possible demise with the Kansas City Royals farm system."

Contrite as Mike's now looking, Kenny just can't let him bear this weight alone. And so he brushes away the lingerings of rage at all the new board member's done today and takes his outstretched hand.

"Forget it," Kenny says. "It really wasn't your fault."

"I didn't think so!" Mike chirps gleefully. "But Al said I'd be kicked off the board if I didn't say it."

"For crying out loud," Ken mutters under his breath, but Mike responds as if it's been spoken aloud, so perhaps it has.

"Hey, that's just what Al says. You know, you're a lot like him. Just like Newt on our board's an accountant like your friend Copeland wants to be. Never know, becoming an electrician might be in your future!"

"Who knows," Kenny rues, "maybe that's next."

In her dream home off Cedar Bend Drive, Lois Boyenga's vigil for her husband's return has been interrupted by Don Kruse and Jeff Copeland coming back for their bags, then making a hasty exit in a waiting cab. She's called out, "Where's Kenny," but heard nothing from the guys except a quick "Bye" and what she thinks may have been Don's mumbled "nice to see you with your clothes on." Then, tired of waiting any longer, she's turned her thoughts to a TV dinner when the sound of their family automobile draws her to her window, and for the next hour it's a happy reunion with her mother and the boys.

The trip has surely agitated Mama, so much so that Scott and Marty have become party to her fantasies. Jeff Copeland a pirate? Don Kruse an industrial-strength Nazi? She tries to follow their simultaneous, overlapping stories, but soon decides a deaf ear and patronizing smile are best until their travel momentum dies down.

Finally there's a deeper rumble out at the curb, a sound that at once makes her stomach churn grotesquely. She takes a look and it's the big blue garbage truck, disgorging her husband and what seems to be the full set of luggage he left with for Spring Training over a month ago. Thankfully the truck pulls away as Kenny heads up the walk, and she throws the door open happily, her big smile as much for Mike Jacobs' departure as for her husband's arrival.

"Board member," he says, and she replies "I know."

"Trying to be a nice guy," Kenny adds. "Wanted to take us out to dinner—Country Kitchen, Salisbury steak. I said no," and Lois grabs him in a bear hug and smothers him with kisses.

Their evening goes quietly—what is there to say? The boys shower him with questions, but not ones he can answer. Not about his ball team, not if they can be batboys, not even if they can be in the dugout during games. He does his best at brief answers to the ones about the neat Nazi and the big funny guy with the crooked mustache that Scotty says he remembers from when Dad played with the Reds and not the Royals.

After this first hour the kids are back in their own worlds, Scott retreating to a show he likes on TV and Marty asking for some domino games with his mother. Ken and Lydia Scoggins have a little talk about traffic tickets, hers and his, while Lois jumps up from dominoes every thirty-five minutes to run another load through the washer. Kenny's pleased to find the house has a utility room on the main floor; the dryer's swish and warmth seem as comforting as a fireplace fire. When the clothes basket returns he lets himself be buried in the warm flannels of his boys' freshly laundered shirts and in a world of static electricity and fuzz balls. He slips into a nap as his wife and mother-in-law talk about the week's events in Huntington. When Ken wakes, he thinks for a moment they're home.

Across Mason City Kenny's players face the boredom of a Sunday night. The bars are closed, and so is the mall. Of the seven movies in town, six have been seen in Florida or on the road—and no one's up for the re-release of *Bambi*, not even Billy Harmon.

Bad enough if they'd have hit the streets at seven. But with the forfeit they're free at a quarter to five, and vexed with uncertainty to boot. Most of them have no sooner reached home than their phones ring with a message from T.A.: Ken's suspended, T.A.'s now the acting manager, report to the ballpark tomorrow at ten for a re-organizational meeting.

Up above the meat market Derrick Stevens takes it stoically, but cringes when he has to pass the word to Sal Nistico, who seems startled close to tears. "Later for the phony agony, man," Derrick wants to say, until he sees that Sal is genuinely bothered. So he manufactures a sympathetic line instead—"Advil time, friend, your shoulder is hurting, I can see"—and Sal seems grateful for the excuse to break down almost completely.

No such drama at Picadilly Trace. "Fuckin' Boyenga's history, gang," Jim Knowlton turns to tell Webster, Arredondo, and Perez. Marius is the only one to react, and it's just with a shrug.

But over at the four-plex Billy Harmon has no one with whom to share the news. Knowlton and Arredondo have dropped him off after the card show closed, and his roommates are nowhere to be seen. T.A's call is utterly perplexing until the forfeit is explained, but then Billy's left with just four walls to talk this out with. This strategy he actually tries, but after a few minutes it's obvious he needs a friend.

Of the three Dunsmoors in the book, Billy guesses that the one he wants is LeRoy, and Lefty answers on the first ring.

"Well, I'll be darned," the young man hears, and gets treated to a nonstop account of Mike's behavior at the pop stand, Ken's run-in with the law that almost got him tossed in the slammer, and president Al Swenson's disastrous affair with the umps.

Billy finds it hard to believe, and asks for a recap of how his manager could in any way be involved with neofascism.

"I know you can't believe it," Lefty counsels, "and I really don't, either. But my old friend Tom O'Reilly sure has it in his head, and if you'll excuse me, I'll keep trying him on the phone as Swenson asked me to."

"Yes, sir," Billy says with obvious disappointment.

"Sorry to cut you off," Lefty apologizes, "but I got to keep trying to get past that screecher on his phone down there."

"Screecher?" Billy asks.

"You bet. Every time I dial that number I get this screeching whine. You'd think they'd have a busy signal that's easier on your ears—"

"That's his fax machine, sir," the young second baseman interrupts.

"Well, that's what I'm calling him with," Lefty protests, and Billy can visualize his head cocked back in suspicion of what's going on. "Why do they need a machine for those?"

"Not facts, sir—fax. It only talks with other machines, like the one out at the ballpark."

"And you know how to operate it?" Lefty asks warily.

"Yes, sir."

"I'll be right over," Lefty says in a hurry. "You listen for my honk, OK?"

In short order the old man and youngster are making the turn off Stadium Drive and trailing dust across the parking lot. Lefty unlocks the gate, Billy pulls it open, and the two walk past the closed souvenir stand to a reinforced metal door that secures the office.

"Don't look at what I'm doing," Lefty cautions, and as Billy turns around to stare along the concourse the veteran board member wrenches up on the handle and then tugs it to the right while at the same time wedging his foot against the bottom. "Quicker than finding the right key," he says, "but you didn't see me do this," and Billy agrees that he hasn't.

"Now where's this machine," Lefty asks, "and what buttons do I push?" Billy explains how it's a device that sends printed messages, so Lefty asks if he can write one out.

Thirty seconds later a bell rings in the Kansas City farm director's office, where an exasperated Tom O'Reilly barks out "horse-feathers" as he reaches for the message: "Call me pronto, 232-2130—Dunsmoor."

For twenty minutes Billy Harmon sits and listens to a conversation that, except for the technology of the club's speaker phone, could be taking place thirty years ago. It begins with Tom and Lefty kidding each other about being stuck in the office on a Sunday night, then moves along to some talk about a favorite Mason City hangout, the Hickory House, and whether even Trotter's in KC can touch it for ribs. There are a few jokes about people on the board, followed by some solemn words on those who've passed. Or at least Billy guesses so, for they're names he never heard last year or this.

Finally the two get down to business, Lefty mentioning that he hears Tom's put off by the reports he's gotten out of Mason City, Tom changing moods entirely to begin a surprisingly stern lecture on what the Royals expect from their affiliates. For what seems an eternity Billy and Lefty sit there, glances meeting now and then in mutual embarrassment, as Tom O'Reilly preaches to the choir about responsible behavior and the seriousness of minor league ball.

In time O'Reilly begins listening to himself and halts in flustered discomfort, remembering who's on the other end of the line. "Dunsmoor," he mumbles, "don't let my excitement bother you." Lefty just shrugs while Billy blushes, and from the speaker phone these two can imagine Tom O'Reilly's eyes darting nervously around his own office. "Oh, horsefeathers," the voice comes through in renewed bluster, "at least you haven't run me through a boodle of excuses."

"No excuses, Tom," Lefty says into the receiver. "Just wanted you to know I'm keeping an eye on things up here." O'Reilly thanks him and the conversation ends.

As Lefty fumbles to hang up the phone and Billy reaches over to switch off the fax machine, the quiet of the empty stadium surrounding them begins to feel oppressive. They both know O'Reilly will demand a scapegoat and that rookie manager Ken Boyenga is finished. But without any words they close the office and walk out to the concourse.

Billy's halfway to the gate when Lefty calls him back. "Gimme a hand here, son," he beckons, unable to get a proper grip on the bolt he's just unlocked that spans the concessions door. Billy slides it to the left as indicated, and stands back while Lefty reaches in to grab a boxful of Snickers bars from the rear counter.

"What do you got there," his mentor asks, "a dozen room-mates?" As Billy protests, he's handed a thirty-six-count carton, minus just one the old man takes for himself, dropping a ten-dollar bill in the empty till as he leaves.

Monday morning Lois Boyenga drives her husband to the ballpark where Dave Hunt has his ticket, then it's back home to pick up Mama, who's also flying out today. Her flight's first, an 11 a.m. Mississippi Valley Airlines shot to Chicago connecting with the Charleston-bound Delta flight at four. "That's quite a layover, Ma," Ken worries, but is told his friend the Nazi slipped her some complimentary coupons for the Seven Continents Restaurant, which she hears is quite nice.

Lunch for Ken and Lois fills the time until his TW Express commuter to Kansas City is called at 1:15. A nineteen-passenger puddle jumper, it's boarding only five people here but will pick up more at Waterloo. For now it's just Ken and four salesmen, and his departure scene with Lois looks ridiculously out of place. But they've been together only two days out of the last forty, plus the frank truth is that his future with the farm system is in question, if not deeply in doubt. So they do their hugs and kisses and once more Kenny's boarding an airplane as he's done scores of times each year since making it to Triple-A, where baseball teams fly.

He has no impressions from Mason City to Waterloo, and there'd be none after that were it not for a young boy and mother who've boarded for this longer leg of the flight. They're seated right behind him, and as it's the boy's first time up, there's a nonstop monologue from the moment the plane leaves Waterloo's ramp.

That's OK with Kenny, and for the first half-hour he calmly tunes it out. But then the kid's tapping him on the shoulder and pointing out the great adventure coming into view below.

"Mister, hey Mister," the kid is urging despite his mother's cautions to leave the man alone, "that's Des Moines coming up."

Biggest town the kid has ever seen, Ken figures. But all these years in baseball, the last of them spent trying to compensate for unacceptable behavior from some of his friends, have schooled Ken Boyenga in the art of public relations, of remembering at all times that he represents not just the national pasttime but an American ideal. So it's no problem to be polite and feed the kid's tiny ego by pretending to be pleased with what he sees out the window.

"See that?" the kid asks.

"What?"

"The capitol. Wow, it looks like my train set."

"Yeah," Kenny laughs, "it really does." They're at about six thousand feet, he guesses, from which everything's just about to Lionel scale. There's even a train track he can see, and so he gives the kid this little gift in return.

And what a payback: as the capitol disappears beneath the wing, something else comes into view—a patch of green surrounded by the bleachers and grandstand Ken recognizes as Sec Taylor Stadium, home of the Iowa Cubs.

Better than his view of Fenway, Tiger Stadium, or Comiskey Park eight months ago, it hangs there in suspension, the plane high enough to make the image last yet sufficiently low that the basepaths are distinct.

"Hey Mister," yells Kenny's little friend, "that's where the Cubs play"—Ken allows that for this child these Cubs might as well be *the* Cubs—"and there's a game today."

Sure kid, Kenny wants to say: a businessman's special, afternoon start for the Des Moines yuppies who want to pretend they're in Harry Caray's league. In his own time here the club tried it, too, and he wonders if it's working any better now. He guesses he could judge the crowd even from a mile up, then decides not to—decides he doesn't want to see another ballpark just now. But the monologue continues.

"Mister, I can see the bases! Hey, the Cubs got two men on—look, they're running! Hey, look!"

Kenny doesn't turn. He's staring straight ahead, down the aisle and through the open cockpit door over the pilot's shoulder and along the flightpath to Kansas City.

Which disturbs the child even more, since Kenny's missing everything. Doesn't he realize these are real baseball players: pros, guys who are just a phone call from Chicago? Geez, Kenny thinks, the kid's sophisticated beyond his years. Probably could tell him some of these phone calls might be for just a cup of coffee, he'd know that term as well. Amazing how the business of baseball reaches all the way to kids even his own kids' age.

"Come on, Mister, look," the little boy begs. "This is real baseball!"

"Sure kid," Ken tells him, pretending to turn back to the window. "Been there," he says, "done that." He doesn't look down.

Jerry Klinkowitz has spent the past seventeen years as a minor league baseball owner, operator, and consultant. His *Short Season and Other Stories,* published by Johns Hopkins in 1988, was selected by *Sport* magazine as the best baseball fiction of the year. During the off-season he teaches at the University of Northern Iowa, where he has published thirty books on literature, art, history, philosophy, air combat, baseball, and jazz.

Fiction Titles in the Series:

Library of Congress Cataloging-in-Publication Data

Klinkowitz, Jerome.
    Basepaths / Jerry Klinkowitz.
        p.   cm. — (Johns Hopkins, poetry and fiction)
    ISBN 0-8018-5092-4 (hc)
    I. Title.   II. Series.
PS3561.L515B3 1995
813'.54—dc20   94-40448